He was close enough to lean into.

Near enough to touch.

She should back away. She should stop staring at the inviting vee of skin where the base of his throat met the sturdy ridge of his collarbone. She should stop wishing she could bury her nose there and have his strong arms wrap her up and keep the terrors of the world at bay.

Maddie lifted her gaze to his. "Why are you here? You said you wanted nothing to do with me or my family."

Edged with shadows she didn't understand, those gray-green eyes looked deep into hers. "Some fights a man can't walk away from. No matter how much he wants to."

SEARCH AND SEIZURE

JULIE MILLER

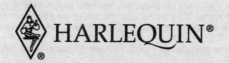

HARLEQUIN®

TORONTO • NEW YORK • LONDON
AMSTERDAM • PARIS • SYDNEY • HAMBURG
STOCKHOLM • ATHENS • TOKYO • MILAN • MADRID
PRAGUE • WARSAW • BUDAPEST • AUCKLAND

Thanks to Kimberly McKane and Scott E. Miller for answering all my DFS questions.

For two bright, talented young people who are near and dear to my heart—Emily and Darin Binger. Thanks for being a part of puzzles and poker, Easter egg hunts and dinosaurs, family reunions and cool movies. The bond you share as brother and sister is an amazing thing to see, and reminds me of the bond I share with my brothers. Work hard, use your brains, listen to your heart and make a difference. The world is waiting for you.

ISBN 0-373-22898-8

SEARCH AND SEIZURE

Copyright © 2006 by Julie Miller

This edition published by arrangement with Harlequin Books S.A.

® and TM are trademarks of the publisher. Trademarks indicated with ® are registered in the United States Patent and Trademark Office, the Canadian Trade Marks Office and in other countries.

www.eHarlequin.com

Printed in U.S.A.

ABOUT THE AUTHOR

Julie Miller attributes her passion for writing romance to all those fairy tales she read growing up, and shyness. Encouragement from her family to write down all those feelings she couldn't express became a love for the written word. She gets continued support from her fellow members of the Prairieland Romance Writers, where she serves as the resident "grammar goddess." This award-winning author believes the only thing better than a good mystery is a good romance.

Born and raised in Missouri, she now lives in Nebraska with her husband, son and smiling guard dog, Maxie. Write to Julie at P.O. Box 5162, Grand Island, NE 68802-5162.

Books by Julie Miller

HARLEQUIN INTRIGUE
588—ONE GOOD MAN*
619—SUDDEN ENGAGEMENT*
642—SECRET AGENT HEIRESS
651—IN THE BLINK OF AN EYE*
666—THE DUKE'S COVERT MISSION
699—THE ROOKIE*
719—KANSAS CITY'S BRAVEST*
748—UNSANCTIONED MEMORIES*
779—LAST MAN STANDING*
819—PARTNER-PROTECTOR†
841—POLICE BUSINESS†
880—FORBIDDEN CAPTOR
898—SEARCH AND SEIZURE*

*The Taylor Clan
†The Precinct

CAST OF CHARACTERS

Dwight Powers—Justice's staunchest ally. This tough-as-nails prosecutor has a reputation for winning inside the courtroom. The last thing he wants is a woman and child around to remind him of everything he's lost outside of court.

Maddie McCallister—A child's truest friend. This full-figured teacher will risk her life to protect the niece and grandnephew placed in her care. But does she dare risk her heart on a man with nothing but law and order flowing through his veins?

Katie Rinaldi—She made a deal with the devil to help a friend. Reneging on the bargain could get her killed.

Joe Rinaldi—Katie's father. Dwight put him away in prison.

Roberta Hays—The family services case worker only wanted to help.

The Hulkster and Stinky Pete—Who are they working for?

Cooper Bellamy—The Fourth Precinct cop assigned to the case. Not your typical babysitter.

Roddy—Talent scout from New York City.

Tyler—Only a few weeks old, he can bring down an entire criminal network.

Alicia and Braden Powers—Will the memories of one lost family haunt Dwight forever?

Prologue

"Excuse me, have you seen this girl?"

Madeline McCallister swallowed her fear and approached the tall, dark-skinned woman standing beneath the street lamp. She averted her eyes from the amount of skin revealed by the woman's tight shorts and sequined halter top and concentrated on the dark eyes framed by sparkly lashes.

The black woman looked right past her, straight through to the cars that were cruising by on Tenth. The slow parade of headlights briefly illuminated the shadowed alleyways and door stoops, exposing the dangerous, sick, sad and soulless creatures of the urban night before driving past and giving them back to the darkness.

No-Man's-Land was a foreign world to Maddie. But she had no intention of leaving until she had answers to her questions.

Holding up the worn photograph she carried like a shield, Maddie took a deep breath and made herself taller. "Excuse me, could you take a look? Her name is Katie."

The black woman, who wore a rhinestone pendant in her cleavage that said Cleopatra, blinked once, sparing a glance at the photo. "Move along, sugar. You're bad for business."

No doubt. Of all the women Maddie had seen thus far, walking the streets of the neighborhood that the KCPD had dubbed No-Man's-Land, none of them had been of the plain and sturdy variety. Certainly none of them was wearing anything resembling the loose denim jumper and tailored blouse she had on. And not one of them seemed to be affected by the August heat and humidity the way she was.

Cleopatra turned her back on Maddie and struck a pose with one hand on a very round, very revealing hip. "Sugar, go away. You're not a cop, you're not the competition, but you don't belong here."

"Neither does my niece." Maddie darted around the other woman to stop her from walking away. "She ran away from home a couple of weeks ago. She's pregnant. I need to find her."

Cleopatra twirled around on her white patent leather boots with an annoyed huff. "Your girl's pregnant? Find her boyfriend."

Maddie fell into step beside her. "He hasn't seen her. He's already signed away his parental rights. They haven't been together for months."

"Typical man."

Maddie wouldn't know. Her experiences with men ran from the extreme nightmare to nonexistent. "I'm sorry to bother you while you're…working, but I'm asking everyone."

Cleopatra finally stopped. She glanced at Maddie, glanced at the photo. "I ain't seen her."

"Look harder. Please."

The taller woman waved and winked at a car that slowed down as it passed by. "I'm trying to work here."

"*Please.*"

"Sugar, do you know how many kids come walkin' down this street? Runnin' away from a beating or trying to find their next fix?"

"Katie's not like that."

"Sure. They're all good kids. They're just lost in a world that doesn't want them." Maybe Cleopatra was speaking from experience.

But that wasn't Katie's story. "Please, ma'am—"

"Now, sugar, don't you go ma'amin' me—"

"I'm looking for one girl. One child. I have to find her."

"Ain't the cops lookin' for her?"

"Yes. But they're not having any success. She's due to give birth this month. I can't let her go through that on her own."

"That's rough." Cleopatra lifted her gaze over the top of Maddie's head and scanned up and down the sidewalks on both sides of the street. Then she held out her hand. "Give me some money."

"What?"

"Give me somethin'. I can't stand here talkin' to you when I'm supposed to be workin'."

"Oh, I see." Maddie fished into the pocket of her jumper. One of the homeless men she'd talked to earlier had asked for money before sending her to Tenth Street to talk to the 'ladies,' as he'd called them. Maddie pulled out all she had left: a twenty.

Cleopatra snatched it from her hand and stuffed it inside the top of her boot. "Now give me the picture."

Sparkly lashes fluttered against her dark cheeks as she studied Katie's junior yearbook picture. Maddie prayed for a glimmer of recognition.

"I ain't seen her." Cleopatra pressed the photo back into Maddie's hand. "She ain't workin' this street, at any rate.

And the mission's been closed for over a year now, so I haven't seen her hangin' around for a handout, either."

Twenty dollars for another no.

Maddie lovingly straightened a bent corner of the photo before returning it to her pocket. She tried to focus on the reassuring notion that Katie hadn't resorted to prostitution to support herself. Two weeks ago, Maddie never would have suspected a teenager who was eight months pregnant would be in demand on the streets. But she'd seen some disturbing things since she'd begun her search.

Still, the crushing disappointment of hitting yet another dead end kept her from feeling hopeful. "Thanks."

It also kept her from sensing the large black man who'd walked up behind her.

"Zero!"

Cleopatra's shout masked Maddie's own startled yelp as two big hands closed around her upper arms. The first thing she saw was all the bling on each finger and wrist. The second thing she noticed was the stale smell of rum-soaked breath as the man's lips brushed against her ear.

"I don't know whether to cut you or kiss you."

Cleopatra shoved at the man's shoulder. "Back off, Zero. She's just lookin' for somebody."

"Yeah, well, look somewhere else, sweetmeat." He grabbed the hand Cleopatra had shoved him with and tugged and twisted. Even Maddie winced at the angle at which he bent the woman's arm behind her back. "You. Get back to work. I don't look out for you so's you can shoot the breeze with no lady." He pushed Cleopatra away. "Find a customer."

With a proud tip of her chin, the black woman straightened what clothes she had on and sauntered across the street, leaving Maddie alone with the pimp.

Zero wrapped his arm around Maddie's shoulders, pulling her tight against his side. When he forced her into step beside him, she knew a stark moment of wondering if she'd ever get back to her car, much less see her home again.

Still, the violence sickened her. How many times had her sister shown up at the house with a sprained wrist or black eye? "I was just asking her some questions. I paid her for her time. You didn't have to hurt her."

He squeezed her tighter, steering her toward a secluded archway beneath a concrete stoop. "Cleo's been hurt worse than that. Now you tell me exactly what kinds of questions you were askin'."

As she had so many times over the past two weeks, Maddie ignored her own terror and pulled out the photo to show him. "I'm looking for my niece."

Zero snatched the photo from her hand. "Now she's a fine girl."

"Have you seen her?"

"You paid Cleo for an answer. You have to pay me."

"I'm out of money."

Zero stopped, laughed, crumpled the photo in his fist and spun Maddie around so that he could back her into a brick wall and press his thighs and hips and other vile things against her. "You gotta pay me somehow. That's how things work around here."

Maddie's blood chilled in her veins, despite the humidity that lingered so long after sunset. She stared at the thick gold chain around Zero's neck. "I can't do that."

He slipped one hand behind her to squeeze her butt and tangled the rest of his fingers in her hair. "You need a serious makeover, darlin'. But I like some meat on my women. And hair this color of red could be good for business."

"Let me go."

Her flare of panic only made him laugh. He pulled the hair from her ponytail and draped it over her shoulder, dragging his palm over her breast. "Uh-huh. Lots of meat."

Maddie swallowed her gag reflex and batted his hand away. "My niece is pregnant. Don't you have any heart in you to help her?"

Zero rubbed her reddish gold hair against his nose and sniffed. "Word's out about a clinic in town that helps young girls who get knocked up. They'll take the girl in until she delivers. Then, in exchange for the baby, they'll pay a nice price. I thought about letting one of my girls go off the pill just to see how much money we could get off that scam."

Revulsion aside, Maddie lifted her gaze to Zero's hooded eyes. "They buy the girl's baby?" She shook her head in disbelief. "Katie wouldn't do that."

"I'm just tellin' you what I heard."

"Does this clinic have a name?"

"Sweetmeat, you don't pay me or flash a badge, you don't get an answer."

In a surprisingly quick move, he grabbed her arm and slung her toward the street. Maddie stumbled off the curb and smacked into the fender of a parked car. But she ignored the pain radiating through her hip and elbow. Katie could be suffering something far worse. Maddie had no right to complain.

"Please," she begged, throwing pride and safety to the wind. "Tell me what you know."

Zero laughed and tossed the crumpled photograph at her. "You ain' worth it, sweetmeat. Now get off my street and go home where you belong."

Chapter One

Assistant district attorney Dwight Powers loosened the knot on his paisley silk tie and unhooked the top button of his wilted broadcloth shirt as he rode the elevator up to his eighth-floor office.

Night should have cooled the air and tempered his mood. But the midnight humidity had captured the day's heat radiating off the concrete and asphalt of downtown Kansas City. It steamed through his pores and into his blood, melting into a suspicious tension he couldn't quite shake.

The three-hour drive from the state penitentiary in Jefferson City had given him plenty of time to think about the parole hearing he'd attended. Plenty of time to consider the crocodile tears in Arnie Sanchez's eyes as he apologized to Dwight for the death of his family—without ever admitting any responsibility or connection to Alicia's and Braden's murders.

He'd had plenty of time to replay the high-priced words that Sanchez's lawyer had used to claim that his client was being cruelly and unusually punished by a prolonged sentence. The KCPD and the Kansas City district attorney's office had a personal beef with his client. Sanchez's business had suffered. His wife had divorced him. His grown sons were feuding over property entitlements, and his grandchildren were growing up without ever knowing him.

Sanchez had paid his back taxes and court costs, the lawyer claimed. He had a spotless record of good conduct during his incarceration. The State of Missouri had no right to punish a man for crimes that had only been attributed to him—crimes that the KCPD and other law-enforcement agencies had never proven. They claimed locking him up under maximum security for another five years was harsh and unfair.

Dwight scraped his palm across the blond stubble that peppered his jaw and rolled his neck to ease the weary kinks from his body.

It had taken him all of five minutes to present himself to the parole board and outline in succinct terms the crimes Sanchez *had* been convicted of. He'd explained in remarkably cool, detached logic that Sanchez's ex-wife and grandchildren could visit him in prison any time they so desired. Even if parole was never granted, after twenty years he'd be free to spend as much time as he wanted with his family.

Dwight had neither option. His family was gone.

Permanently.

Courtesy of Arnie Sanchez.

The light for the seventh floor lit up and the elevator began to slow its ascent.

The parole board had voted quickly, without debate. They thanked Dwight for his time, denied Sanchez's petition and moved on to the next hearing.

On the drive back to Kansas City, Dwight had had plenty of time to recall the cold, black fury in Sanchez's eyes and wonder why that unspoken threat hadn't fazed him. Maybe he was hoping that Sanchez would blow any chance for an early release by giving voice to that threat in front of witnesses.

Or maybe it was because a threat was useless against a man with nothing left to lose.

The number eight lit up, the elevator dinged and Dwight switched the briefcase to his right hand to dig the keys out of his left pocket as the doors slid open.

As soon as the elevator closed behind him, Dwight sensed trouble. Not the Arnie-Sanchez-is-beating-the-system kind of trouble. But something was off-kilter, out of place.

He peered into the long, deserted tunnel of marbled walls and shadows, letting his eyes adjust to the dim glow of the security lights illuminating the hallway. His soft-soled oxfords made no noise on the marble tiles as he headed toward his office.

The emptiness was no surprise. By this time of night, even the die-hard workaholics like himself would have gone home. And he'd passed most of the cleaning crew outside at the utility entrance, taking their first break of the night.

He listened to the cranking, whooshing sounds of the air conditioner regulating the building's temperature against the August heat. Perfectly normal.

And yet…

Dwight crinkled up his nose. Maybe it was the whisper of cigarette smoke. Someone had broken the rules of the smoke-free building. But that wasn't what nagged at him. Beneath the tobacco pungency that lingered in the air, he detected something fresher, sweeter—definitely out of place in an environment that typically smelled of leather attaché cases and disinfectant.

He wasn't alone.

But he didn't for one moment think that a friend had dropped by to pay a surprise visit. The people he called friends knew he didn't do surprises anymore.

A slice of light cutting across the hallway diverted his attention to the emergency stairwell, where the door stood ajar. He paused in front of the inch-wide gap to listen but heard nothing beyond the usual creaks and moans of the old steel-and-limestone building that had adorned the skyline of downtown Kansas City since the Truman era.

Dwight pulled off his tie and stuffed it inside his suit jacket pocket. He'd never considered himself any kind of paranoid alarmist. But he'd learned a thing or two about survival over the years. Not just in the courtroom, but in life. He took note of details, no matter how small or insignificant they might seem. Then he processed them until they made sense.

This didn't make sense.

Did the open door mean someone had escaped? Or snuck inside?

The roar of the air conditioner fans shut off as the thermostat leveled off. But instead of the eerie silence Dwight had expected, he heard a low, mewling noise somewhere in the dark interior of one of the offices down the hall. Had a stray cat gotten trapped inside the building? But how could a streetwise feline account for that sweet, oily scent?

His gaze dropped to a fleck of crimson, almost unnoticeable on the mottled gray-and-black pattern on the marble floor. How did he account for that?

Crouching down on his haunches, Dwight touched the dot of color. The floor was icy cold beneath the tip of his finger. But the spot was wet, sticky and definitely fresh.

Blood.

Suffused with a wary energy that heightened his senses

and put him on guard, Dwight stood, balancing himself on the balls of his feet and prepping for whatever adversary lurked in the shadows.

A muted howl turned his attention back toward the hallway. The glow from the stairwell spotlighted another drop of blood. And another. The irregular pattern of droplets zigzagged across the floor, as if whoever was bleeding had staggered from side to side. Had the wounded creature struggled to get into the building? Or to reach the exit?

Dwight overruled his instinct to close the stairwell door behind him to protect his back. If the eighth floor had become a crime scene, the CSI team would want everything left just the way he'd found it.

But if it was just a stupid cat—maybe one who'd gotten into an alley fight—he wasn't waiting for the police to find out and make the ADA their joke of the week.

Dwight followed the trail to his office and cursed. He could hear music now, something instrumental and indistinct. Had a maid left a radio on? Cut herself on a sharp object and run downstairs for help? Why not take the elevator? Why not use the crew's walkie-talkies and call for assistance?

An image of Arnie Sanchez's cold, black eyes popped into Dwight's head. Just because the bastard was locked away in Jefferson City didn't mean he couldn't make a phone call, didn't mean he couldn't make arrangements to add to Dwight's misery.

Dwight slipped his key into the outer door, but, already unlocked, it drifted open. This wouldn't be the first time someone had broken into his office. But he had a feeling that what awaited him on the other side of the door was far more dangerous to him than any burglar or maid or injured stray.

Dwight crept through the set of cubicles that served his secretary and department clerks. The music was louder here—he could make out the wordless melody from a children's movie now. The tune was punctuated by discordant wails from… Please, God, be that damned cat.

Clenching his jaw with a tightness that shook through him, he narrowed his gaze to the trail of crimson dots along the gray carpeting. There was a smear on the wall beside the door to his inner office, as if someone had tried to wipe it clean.

Dwight hurried to the thick walnut door that separated his work space from the others. He didn't even bother with his keys. He pulled out his handkerchief and, as he suspected, the doorknob turned without protest and he stepped inside.

The full force of that soft, powdery scent, tinged with the odor of something slightly more pungent, caught him off guard and sucker punched him in the gut. He gripped the knob tightly, just short of snapping it off in his fist. This was a bad dream. Another one of those damn nightmares.

Only he was helplessly awake. "Son of a bitch."

In four strides, he'd dropped his briefcase, circled his desk and taken note of the bloody palm prints on his telephone receiver and on the note tucked beneath the music box that played beside it. "No way. No friggin' way."

But the blood didn't scare him half as much as the bundle sitting squarely on the middle of his desk, bawling through toothless gums and batting at the air with helpless fists.

Dwight's jaw hurt with everything it took to keep himself from crying or cursing in front of the tiny, abandoned baby.

With shaky fingers, he unfolded the blood-stained

blanket, unhooked the straps on the carrier and checked the infant. He was small, fragile and clean. Dwight's hands were big and out of practice—and afraid. He quickly re-buckled the straps. Thank God. No visible signs of injury. The blood had another source.

"You're okay, kid. You're not..." His breath stuttered and caught in the tightness of his chest. The baby wailed in earnest now, and the sound shivered along Dwight's nerves, chilling him and awakening dark things inside him.

The kid was stinky. Hungry, no doubt. Alone.

And Dwight couldn't do a damn thing to help him.

He curled his fingers into his palms and pulled away as his vision blurred behind a sheen of tears. The tiny, blue knit cap and appled cheeks were too similar, too much of a reminder of his own son's sweet, angelic face. A face that had been bruised and pale and still the last time he'd seen it.

"Stop that." Dwight turned away, not sure if he was talking to the infant or the nightmare. He smashed the knob on the music box with his fist, silencing the repetitive tune. Then he picked up the folded note, scrawled on a sheet of his office stationery.

Depositing a baby in his office was too cruel to consider any type of joke. And if this was some kind of sick message to remind him about his own son... If this was the manifestation of that unspoken threat from Sanchez...

Dwight opened the note and read the short message scribbled inside. "Son of a bitch."

He turned his back on the baby, embarrassed to have cursed in front of the kid. "This can't happen." He almost crushed the paper in his fist but, at the last moment, remembered the whole concept of untainted evidence. He tossed the paper back on top of the desk. "I won't let it happen."

More at home taking action than dealing with emotions, Dwight pulled the cellphone from his belt and strode out of the office, leaving the smells and softness and memories behind him. He was out in the hallway, pacing the length of the cool, dark corridor before the number he'd punched in answered.

"Rodriguez."

"A.J." Dwight hadn't even considered the time, but the sleepy sound of a woman's voice in the background reminded him. "Damn." Dwight planted his feet and filled his deep barrel chest with a cleansing breath as he gathered his wits about him. "Sorry to call so late. I didn't mean to wake you or your wife, but I need a detective's expertise."

A subtle rustle of movement told Dwight that A.J. was moving out of bed.

"The ADA doesn't call at twelve-thirty in the morning unless there's a problem. What's up?"

"I'm at the office."

"You work too much, amigo."

"I wish this was about work. It might be. I came in to check messages and… Hell, I don't know. I've probably already compromised the crime scene."

"Crime scene?" The sudden gravity of A.J.'s voice was drowned out by the renewed fussing of the infant two rooms away. "Is that a baby? *Madre dios.* What's going on?"

Dwight turned and walked away again. "You once said that you owed me one after helping you and Claire take care of that incident at Winthrop Enterprises last year."

"I meant that. Most of KCPD owes you a favor, counselor." A.J.'s hushed voice was insistent now. "Tell me what you need."

"I need to call in that favor."

"YOU WENT DOWN to No-Man's-Land on your own?"

Maddie glared across the desk at the bald man who sounded more like one of her high-school students than a badge-wearing, gun-toting detective. How many times was he going to ask that same question? "Yes."

"At night?"

"Yes. I was there last night."

"Are you crazy?"

The detective, who looked almost ten years younger than her thirty-six, wasn't bald so much as he'd shaved his head. And he wasn't impressed by the temerity of her forays in the night so much as he seemed to think she was totally bonkers for taking it upon herself to help the only family she had left.

"I'm desperate, Detective Bellamy. Katie's only seventeen. I'm supposed to be raising her and protecting her."

"From what?"

From monsters like the man who killed Katie's mother. From users like Zero. From a world that overlooked a woman who was shy and sensible and took advantage of a girl who was vulnerable and afraid.

"I need to protect her from whatever made her run away in the first place."

Cooper Bellamy nodded and thumbed through the papers in his file. It was pitifully thin, considering she'd first reported Katie's disappearance a month ago. "Let's see. You said there was no inciting incident that prompted her to run away—no breakup, no family squabble, no change in location?"

"No. None of that." For four years now, Maddie had done everything she could think of to provide Katie with a stable, secure home life. "She's a normal, healthy teenager."

"Except for the pregnancy?"

Maddie kneaded her purse in her lap, feeling the stir-rings of the temper she worked so hard to keep in check. "Katie was fine with the baby. I was fine. She and the father amicably parted—he didn't want any responsibilities to ruin his opportunity to attend Stanford, and she didn't want a father who wasn't interested in the baby."

He flipped another page in the file. "Do you think she could be trying to reach her own father?"

Joe Rinaldi. The sickness that infected Maddie's and Katie's lives—shadowing every memory, coloring every decision.

Trust me, sweetheart. The only time I'll send you flow-ers is for your funeral. He'd sent a dozen roses to the house just after Maddie's sister, Karen, and Katie had moved in. The roses had arrived the day before Karen had disappeared from work. Two days before Maddie had been called to the morgue to claim her sister's mu-tilated body.

But that was four years ago. Karen had been his obses-sion, his daughter little more than an afterthought. Katie had been an innocent bystander trapped in the nightmare.

But that nightmare had nothing to do with this one, right?

Maddie steeled her voice against the inevitable guilt, fear and loathing she associated with mention of her ex-brother-in-law's name. "Joe's in prison, serving a life sentence. He's not a part of Katie's life anymore. He's not a part of *our* life," she enunciated, as if saying it could make her believe it. "Joe Rinaldi couldn't have had any-thing to do with Katie's disappearance."

"You'd be surprised what a man can accomplish from inside a prison cell if he's determined enough."

Hadn't Joe made a similar promise to her on that last

day of sentencing in the courtroom? A private little aside for her ears alone before the bailiff led him away?

I'll find a way to get to you, bitch. Tellin' those lies about me. You're just jealous I married Karen instead of you. You turned her against me. Don't think no jail cell is gonna keep me from giving you what you deserve.

But someone else had heard the threat that day. The prosecuting attorney, Dwight Powers. A cold, unflappable man who'd done the one thing no other man had ever done before or since in Maddie's life—he'd saved the day. Defended her honor. Got in Joe's face and told him, in no uncertain terms, that he would be watching every move Joe made. And if he did one little thing to challenge the verdict or violate the sentencing he'd worked so hard to obtain…

"Ms. McCallister?"

There were no heroes in Maddie's life to save the day now. She pressed her back into the vinyl chair, sitting up as straight and tall as five feet five inches would allow. She had to fight her own battles. She had to be the hero Katie could count on.

Weary from a night without sleep, Maddie wished she'd taken the time to do more than shower and throw on some lipstick and jeans. Maybe a power suit. She should have at least put her hair up in one of those sensible buns that made grown men and the high-school students in her English class take her more seriously.

She tucked one brash-colored strand of hair behind her ear and put on her best schoolteacher voice. "I don't think Joe has anything to do with Katie's disappearance. I'm more interested in what that man named Zero told me last night."

The detective stopped shuffling his papers. "Zero? Hefty black guy? Lots of jewelry?"

Maddie nodded. "I'm sure he's a pimp. I was talking to one of his girls first, a woman named—"

"KCPD is well aware of who Zero Chambers is. You don't have any business messing with him."

"Yes, well—" she breathed deeply to ignore the memory of his hands and body rubbing against hers "—he mentioned something about a clinic. One where pregnant women go to sell their babies. I guess it's more profitable than giving the child up for adoption."

"Wait a minute. Go back." Cooper touched his fingers to the back of Maddie's hand, where she still clutched her purse in her lap. "Zero knows about a clinic where they're buying babies?"

Isn't that what she'd just said? "Is Zero—this Mr. Chambers—reliable? He talked as if it were something he'd considered investing in." Maddie pulled her hand away, embarrassed that she wasn't a better judge of men. "Maybe he just made it up. I'm sure he was trying to shock me."

Instead of another lecture on the foolhardiness of conducting her own private investigation, Cooper Bellamy was suddenly, intensely interested in everything she had to say. "If there's word on the street, Zero would know about it." He pulled out his pen and notepad and turned to a fresh page. "Now tell me again exactly what he said about this clinic."

Hoping that she'd finally provided a lead in the search for Katie while praying that a place that bought and sold babies couldn't really exist, Maddie carefully related the details of her encounter with Zero—minus the touchy-feely, groping part. "I can't imagine anyone doing something so awful—taking advantage of the most vulnerable people in our society—and not hearing about it on the news."

Detective Bellamy raised his dark eyes from his notes

and looked at her as if he thought she was simpleminded. "It's not something they want to advertise, Ms. McCallister. Those babies are for sale. They want to keep their operation way under the radar so that it *doesn't* generate any press. They have to be sidestepping a bunch of legalities— medical licenses, government inspections, forged documentation, taxes."

"Who'd want to buy a baby?"

"Wanna-be parents who can't or don't want to conceive themselves. Couples who've gotten stuck for years in the legal-adoption process or who don't qualify for some reason. If they can meet the asking price, Junior can be theirs." He pulled up something on his computer and scrolled down the screen.

"KCPD suspected something like this was going on." He spared her a glance from his furtive work. "Six months ago, we had an eighteen-year-old show up in rehab. The girl's parents claimed she'd been pregnant before disappearing on a meth binge. The girl wasn't pregnant when she surfaced again, and she had no recollection of the baby's whereabouts or even having been pregnant."

"Katie isn't a drug addict. If that girl you mentioned was a meth user, then her baby might have—" it was tragic to even suggest the possibility "—died. Katie wouldn't take drugs, drink or smoke anything that could harm a fetus."

Bellamy nodded, but Maddie had a feeling the detective's interest in her search had moved way beyond Katie. "We had another vic, unidentified, show up two months back who, according to the medical examiner, had recently gone through a healthy delivery. The mother was dead, but there was no sign of the baby—alive or dead. It matches a case in St. Louis. We haven't had any leads—"

"Dead? The mother was dead?"

The idea that anyone would treat an innocent baby like a commodity didn't stun her as much as the expression on the detective's face that said Zero's story could be true.

Maddie felt the blood draining to her toes, leaving her light-headed and sick to her stomach. "Katie doesn't want to give up her baby. She picked out names. We decorated the nursery together. We're not rich, but we're not hurting for money, either. She wouldn't get involved in something like that. Not if she had a choice."

But Cooper wasn't listening now. He was on his feet, glancing through the deserted rows of paired-off desks and cubicle walls that filled the Fourth Precinct's Detectives Division.

Katie wouldn't sell her baby. Where would she meet such people? Why?

For the first time in twenty-nine days, Maddie hoped that Katie *was* just another teenage runaway.

The blood of determination started pumping through her veins again. Maddie braced her hand against the desk and rose to her feet. "Katie's in more trouble than I thought, isn't she? She might already be dead."

Cooper's own color blanched, as if he just now realized how many gruesome details he'd shared. "I'm sorry, ma'am. I was just thinking out loud. I'm sure your niece will turn up perfectly fine. The baby, too. The possibility of that clinic is just something we were briefed on. Something to watch for. If it happened in another town, it could be happening here. But we don't have any proof of that yet."

Maddie didn't want his apologies and reassurances; she wanted cold, hard facts. "You think it's a possibility, though, don't you? That this baby-selling clinic exists. That Katie's a part of it."

"I don't know, ma'am."

"She's important to you now because she could be a lead on a major case."

"Just sit tight for a sec. Please." He waved toward the chair beside his desk and urged her to take a seat. "Let me run this story by someone else. Make sure I'm not crazy for even considering it."

Maddie hesitated. Was this a brush-off or a reason to hope? "What about Katie?"

"Ms. McCallister, if your niece is involved in an illegal-adoption ring—whether by choice or against her will—then I can guarantee you that every resource KCPD has will be put into finding her. This could be a huge case."

"And if this adoption ring doesn't exist?"

"We'll still find her."

He asked her to sit one more time before zipping toward a door marked Captain. But Maddie hugged her arms around her middle and chose to pace instead.

Whether Katie was involved in a major criminal operation or just a seventeen-year-old girl, confused and alone on the streets, Maddie was beginning to fear that she'd never see her again.

Chapter Two

"What am I supposed to do with it?"

The Fourth Precinct's briefing room was generally empty on a Saturday morning. But drawn like bees to a dewy flower, a surprising number of plainclothes and uniformed officers alike had gathered around the front table. Some of them weren't even on duty. Grown men spouted nonsense words; professional women cooed. Stories about kids and grandkids and kids some hoped to have one day filled the air like a party.

Dwight hovered near the back of the room, staying well away from the happy throng. His all-night marathon of answering questions about the baby's mother and what the blood in his office and on the note might mean made him testier than usual. "There's no way I'm taking it home with me."

"He's not an *it,* Dwight," A. J. Rodriguez insisted. "His name is Tyler, and even though he's only been around a couple of weeks, he's still a living, breathing human being. You have to deal with him."

"No, I don't," Dwight enunciated, in case there was someone on the planet who didn't yet know just how little he wanted to be responsible for the welfare of a child. "I bought him a bag of diapers and some formula. I gave you my report and turned over all the case files you requested. The Department of Family Services is on the way to take care of the kid from here on so he's not in any danger. If they can't locate any family, they'll find someone else. I've done my part."

"Nice speech. But I don't think you really believe that you can write off that kid."

Dwight didn't even blink. "Believe it."

The Latino detective wore his guns, his badge and his usual cool-under-fire expression. Dwight hadn't rattled him one bit. "If what the note says is true, that baby is the grandson of a man who murdered his wife and terrorized his family. Maybe he *is* in some kind of danger."

"Then it's a good thing I turned him over to you."

"What happened to the bulldog prosecutor who goes to the mat for victims who don't have the right kinds of allies? Where's the man who had the *cajones* to back me up when the DA said my wife had only imagined that bastard hit man who was after her? People count on you, counselor. That baby's counting on you."

"That baby doesn't know me from Adam."

"His mother knows you." A.J. held up the handwritten letter that had been sealed in plastic and labeled as potential evidence.

Dwight already had the desperate adolescent words memorized.

Dear Mr. Powers,

I wanted to talk to you in person, but I can't stay any longer. It's probably better this way. I always bawl at goodbyes.

Let me introduce you to Tyler. He was born

August 2nd. I have something important to take care of, so I can't be a mom right now. But I need to know that my son will be okay.

I don't know how to say this so a judge will believe it, but I'm giving him to you. I remember my aunt reading an article in the newspaper a long time ago that said you had lost your son, so I figured there'd be room at your house. Please take care of him. You can change his name if you want, though I think Tyler Powers sounds pretty cool. Don't forget to tell him how much I love him.

You saved me from Daddy when no one else could. Now I'm asking you to save my son, too.

Someday, I hope

The last sentence had been scratched out without being completed. Then the letter was simply signed

    Thanks!
    Your friend,
    Katie Rinaldi

Dwight pulled back his jacket and splayed his fingers on his hips. He breathed deeply, trying to ease the tension that corded his shoulders and arms. Troubled as he was by the letter, the blood and the abandoned baby, he was hardly equipped to play the role of savior. "According to my files, Katie can't be more than seventeen years old. She probably just contacted me because I'm the only attorney she knows."

A.J. didn't buy the argument. "She doesn't want an attorney. She thinks you're some kind of superhero who's gonna save the day."

Dwight edged toward the door when the kid began to

fuss and the buzz of conversation turned to who wanted to hold the baby next. A superhero he wasn't, not if an infant's needy cries could turn him inside out like this.

"Hell, A.J., I barely know this girl. I prosecuted her father four years ago. Outside of my office and a few minutes in the courtroom, I've never even had contact with her. It doesn't make any sense to leave the kid with me."

A.J. pulled out his notepad and glanced at a notation. "When I ran Rinaldi's name through the system, I found out that MODOC moved him to its mental-health facility in Fulton, Missouri, for psychiatric testing. His sentencing said he's not to have any contact with his daughter, right? Maybe some paperwork got mixed up in the transfer or there was a glitch in supervision and he found a way to get a message to her."

A chill of suspicion temporarily cooled Dwight's pulse. "I just saw Warden Vaughn yesterday at a parole hearing. He would have mentioned if the Department of Corrections had had any trouble with Rinaldi."

Unless he'd been so focused on keeping the man who'd ordered the murder of Dwight's wife and son in prison that Ralph Vaughn hadn't wanted to bother him with details on another prisoner. Dwight swiped a hand across his scratchy jaw. He needed a shave, a shower and a few hours of guilt-free sleep.

Yeah, right. Like that was gonna happen.

But he sucked it up, voided his own needs and gave A.J. the relevant feedback he was seeking. "It's worth looking into, I guess. Rinaldi tried to pass himself off as some kind of Ichabod Crane in the courtroom. He tried to convince the jury that a skinny guy with glasses couldn't possibly have committed murder. But there was something missing when you looked him in the eye. Like a conscience. It wasn't any mild-mannered accountant who cut up his wife like that."

A.J. dotted an I and closed his notebook. "So if this potentially crazy, definitely violent dad did somehow contact his daughter, that could spook her. Make her fear for her own life or her son's. Make her turn to someone she trusts for protection—namely you—whether that threat was real or perceived."

Dwight worried about the possibility of Katie Rinaldi being in danger, even as he shook off the notion that he could serve as her protector. "I've got issues of my own right now, A.J. I need to be out of the picture."

"We can handle the investigation and keep tabs on Rinaldi's activities. The mom's already on our missing-persons list. But until we hear differently from family services, this document states that you're the baby's guardian."

"That letter would never stand up in court."

"Forget the legalities for two seconds." A.J. thumped him in the chest. "What's it telling you, right in here?"

Dwight absorbed the flick against his skin like a heavyweight punch. Sure, with Joe Rinaldi as a father, Katie had been given a bum deal. Her abandoned son wasn't getting such a hot start in life, either. But Dwight couldn't fix those kinds of problems.

"You're killing me, A.J. Give me murderers, rapists and drug runners to deal with any day. But not that kid." He searched for logical reasons to back up his emotional claim. "I'm forty-three. Old enough to be his grandfather. I'm single. I work hellish hours. I have enemies. He needs…" Dwight fisted his hand in a frustrated plea. But he had to say the words. "The kid needs somebody who can be a father to him. That isn't me."

Damn the man. A.J. never even batted an eye. "When are you gonna let go and move on, *amigo*?"

A vein ticked along Dwight's jaw, the only betrayal of the emotions he held in check. "Maybe when I find something to move on to."

"I think you just did."

The baby cried, right on cue. And while half a dozen police officers surged forward to help, Dwight slipped out the door into the hallway. There were consequences to caring that he wanted no part of ever again.

He squeezed his eyes shut against a gruesome image that was half memory, half imagination. Had Braden cried out like that, lying in his car seat on the edge of that deserted road next to his murdered mother? Had Dwight's son suffered any pain that fateful night? Or, like Alicia's, had Braden's death been mercifully quick?

"Counselor." A.J.'s low, emphatic voice cut through the haze of guilt and grief.

He should have known his friend wouldn't give it a rest.

"I know. Live in the present, not the past. Fill your life with meaningful work, acknowledge your fears and all that other crap." With a little embellishment, Dwight could recite the advice he and his trauma-recovery therapist had been discussing on and off for over five years.

But *recovering* from grief and guilt was a hell of a long way from *being recovered.*

Katie Rinaldi and A.J. were asking too much of him. "Tell you what, if that kid needs legal help, I'm your man. Pro bono, no questions asked. If I can't handle the case personally, I'll hook him up with the best attorneys in the business. I'll pay for his care—hell, I'll pay for his college—if I have to." Dwight leaned in, using his size, strength and crisp, deep voice to make his point. "But I am not letting some panicked teenage girl turn me into a daddy again. I'm not responsible for that kid—period. End of discussion."

The screech of a metal-chair leg sliding across the floor punctuated Dwight's closing argument and diverted his attention down the hall into the main room. Normally a bustle of activity, the baby in the conference room and the weekend hours had left the detectives' desks practically deserted.

Except for one young, exasperated officer. "Ma'am—"

And one shapely, compelling woman who'd shoved her chair aside to pace a circle around his desk. "That's it? He's going to look into it?"

The detective scratched the back of his shaved head. "Captain Taylor said he's taking it to the commissioner herself. You just have to be patient."

The woman spun around, the fires of anger and frustration coloring her cheeks. "No, I don't *have* to be patient. I've been patient for twenty-nine days."

"Ma'am—"

She raked her fingers through her hair, scattering the shoulder-length waves. "I've been *patient* all my life. And where has it gotten me? Waiting here, twiddling my thumbs, while you get permission to launch an investigation. I've seen for myself what's lurking out there on the streets. And a lot of it isn't pretty. I don't know that *waiting* is an option my niece has, so don't ask me to be patient!"

Dwight wasn't sure if it was the woman's distress that caught his attention or the color of her hair. It was a memorable shade, like a shiny copper penny, and it fanned against her shoulders and neck. He knew that hair. The last time he'd seen it, though, it had been twisted up, under control—prim, even—not free and flowing and bouncing with every shake of her head as it was now.

Dwight rarely forgot a name, and he never forgot a face. Though the packaging was different, there was something familiar enough about the thirtysomething female that he instantly started sorting through remembered details until he could place her.

"She's an underage girl," the sturdy redhead went on, articulating her words in a precise, passionate voice, "out there on her own."

"Ma'am—"

"What if she's hurt? Or worse? You have to do something now."

"Ma'am, I—"

"Quit *ma'aming* me!" Red stopped her pacing, took a deep, steadying breath, and squeezed her palms to her temples. "Oh, God, I sound like that hooker now."

Hooker?

A.J. nudged Dwight's elbow. "Looks like Bellamy's got his hands full."

Dwight was still processing the details.

"I know you're upset—" Bellamy tried again.

"You think?" The woman braced her hands against a rounded set of hips and prepped for round two of the battle she was fighting. "What does it take to get you people off your butts? What if you're already too late to help Katie and her baby?"

Katie. Bingo.

Baby. Salvation.

The band of tension squeezing Dwight's chest eased with the satisfaction of details finally falling into place. At the same time, a layer of guilt lifted from his conscience and he almost—almost—smiled with relief.

Though he'd never have suspected she had a mouth like that, he remembered the woman now. Four years ago, she'd worn a bland, shapeless dress instead of curve-hugging jeans and a sheer-sleeved peasant blouse. She'd been so soft-spoken and stoic on the witness stand that he'd had to ask her to speak up.

There was a fire in her now he hadn't noticed four years ago. Or maybe it hadn't been there. Maybe that tight clench of desperation lining her full mouth had ignited the flame inside her.

Dwight didn't believe in coincidence, but he knew enough about how lives interconnected and twisted around on themselves to know that the Joe Rinaldi case, the baby in the conference room and this woman were all connected. Something was up. Something big. He just had to figure it all out.

And Red was going to help.

"Excuse me a minute, A.J." Dwight was already moving toward the argument in the main room.

Some men might see a woman in need of a gallant rescue. Others might walk on by, thinking her size and attitude meant she could take care of herself. Dwight saw his chance to do right by Tyler Rinaldi without exposing himself to the emotional risk of caring for the child.

Dwight smoothed his lapels and straightened his collar as he went, donning an air of authority he wore as easily as his tailored suit. Shading his voice with a pinch of arrogance, he addressed the detective while the redhead paced away from the desk. "Is there a problem, Detective?"

Cooper Bellamy was a good three inches taller and more than a decade younger than Dwight. But the bald detective seemed relieved that backup of any sort had arrived. He offered a deferring nod. "Sir."

"Yes, there's a problem. I'm—" Red spun around but halted mid-charge, swallowing her words on a quick, stuttered breath "—oh, um, you."

Though Dwight tried to see her as nothing more than a means to an end, he got caught up in the darkening tint of her deep blue eyes. Two seconds ago, she'd been circling Bellamy's desk like a lioness in her cage. Now the energy seemed to drain from her like a popped balloon.

Her breasts heaved and a blush of color started beneath the drawstring at her cleavage and crept all the way up her neck. Her hand and Dwight's gaze went to that same stretch of creamy, rosy skin. Despite his ill-timed fascination with the generous dimensions of her figure, he was more intrigued to see her backbone sliding into place as she overcame whatever had temporarily sidelined her and extended her hand. "Mr. Powers. You probably don't remember me. I'm Maddie—"

"I know who you are, Mrs. McCallister." Dwight wrapped his bigger hand around hers, liking the firmness of her grip. "You sat with Katie Rinaldi at her father's murder trial. Offered key testimony. You stood up to his threats and helped me put him away."

With her pale, alabaster skin, she couldn't hide the remnants of her temper. Or was that embarrassment staining her cheeks now?

"Wow, you do remember me." Her grip trembled before she pulled away. She tucked her hair behind her ears and offered him a wry smile. "*Mrs.* McCallister was my mother, though. I'm just *Ms.* I'm Katie's legal guardian now."

"Even better."

Those blue eyes narrowed. "Better than what?"

Instead of giving her the satisfaction of a straight answer, Dwight took her by the elbow and gestured toward the conference room. "Ms. McCallister? I have someone I'd like you to meet."

WITH A NOD TO A.J., Dwight cleared the conference room and closed the door. He hung back, leaning against the door frame to watch Maddie and Roberta Hays, the DFS caseworker, verbally duke it out. Mrs. Hays—a skinny sixtyish woman who seemed to have gotten up on the wrong side of the bed that morning—had arrived twenty minutes ago. She flashed an ID from family services and announced that she was here to take the baby.

Dwight might have been content to allow the authorities to handle the kid's placement if he hadn't already gone to the trouble of introducing Tyler to his great-aunt. But guilt made a mean conscience. And while he wanted nothing to do with that baby, leaving Red to fend for herself against the State of Missouri felt like abandoning a client in the middle of a case.

Aunt Maddie, as she'd called herself when picking up the boy, was a natural talent in the maternal department. She'd cried when he first told her Tyler was Katie's son. Tears of overwhelming emotions that couldn't be contained. Tears that turned her eyes a deep shade of midnight-blue and made him squirm with the urge to say or do something to make her pain go away.

When she'd finally smiled, caught up in her grandnephew's bright gaze, that tight fist of discomfort inside him released its grip. Then she'd cried some more before wiping her tears and getting down to the business of tending to the infant. She'd fed him a bottle, changed his diaper and soothed the little one to sleep with a gentle, husky tune that had pricked Dwight's nerves into an uneasy state of awareness.

Sturdy was not, perhaps, the kindest—or most apt—word Dwight could have used to describe Maddie McCallister. This more mature, more vibrant version of the plain, quiet woman he remembered filled out the curves of her jeans and gauzy blouse. Yet she wasn't poured into them, trying to pretend she was something she wasn't. His eyes lingered longer than they should have on the plump breast where she cradled the infant as she answered the caseworker's questions and asked a few succinct queries of her own.

"Who else would he be?" Maddie argued. "I don't understand why I can't take him home with me."

Roberta Hays tucked her spiky salt-and-pepper hair behind her ears and shrugged an apology. "It's a matter of proper identification. DFS needs irrefutable proof that this baby is Katie Rinaldi's son before we can turn him over to a family member."

Maddie adjusted Tyler onto her shoulder and patted his bottom. "What kind of proof?"

"Blood tests. DNA. A birth certificate would be nice." Mrs. Hays packed the items Dwight had purchased into the diaper bag she'd brought with her. "You'd be surprised at how desperate some people are to have a child, Ms. McCallister."

"So I've heard."

"They'll bypass legal-adoption channels and claim abandoned babies as their own." She continued on when Maddie would have protested the veiled accusation. "Ever since that Baby Jane Doe's body was found in the city dump last year, the demand for babies in the Kansas City area has skyrocketed. Everybody wants to save a child."

"Baby Jane Doe was murdered," Maddie pointed out through clenched teeth. Was she afraid that would be Tyler's fate, too, if she let him out of her arms? "I would think you'd be glad that people are stepping forward to accept responsibility to keep our children safe."

"Not if it means separating a child from his real family."

"I *am* Tyler's real family."

Roberta shrugged. "Your last name's different, your niece isn't here to verify—"

"Because she's in trouble."

"You have to admit, dear. You look suspicious."

"What?"

Roberta shook her head, then grimaced as if even that small movement made her weary. "You're an unmarried professional woman. Childless. A little past your prime, if you'll pardon the expression. Your biological clock must be ticking off the wall."

"Excuse me?" Shock and frustration colored Maddie's skin and Dwight shifted squarely onto his feet, half obeying the urge to join the fight.

"I'm just saying you fit the profile of someone who raises a red flag when it comes to custody and adoption. It's not a flat-out no, but our policy is to do some extra research into the prospective caregiver in a situation like this. We don't want the legal parents to show up and have to tell them their child is gone." Raising her hands in a placating manner did nothing to soothe Maddie's defensive expression.

"If Katie could be here, I'd give her Tyler in a heartbeat. In the meantime, I would hope that she'd be a little less worried about whatever she's going through if she knew her son was safe with me."

"I'm sorry, ma'am, but my hands are tied. You might get a judge to rule in your favor but not until the courts open on Monday. And then you have to get scheduled on the docket and get tests done and paperwork filed. In the meantime, Tyler's in the custody of DFS. I have to place him in temporary foster care."

"He's already lost his mother—for the time being,"

Maddie emphasized. "He shouldn't lose the only other family he has."

Maddie McCallister was a fighter. But she was losing an uphill battle.

Dwight stepped forward and interrupted the debate. If his conscience dictated that he be here, he might as well be doing something useful.

"Mrs. Hays." The older woman faced him, her hangdog expression and fatalistic tone indicating a need for lunch, sleep or, perhaps, early retirement. Dwight offered her an easy way out of having to maintain her tough stance. "As Katie's legal guardian, Ms. McCallister has the credentials to be a qualified foster parent."

"Of course." Maddie's blue eyes perked up. "I was Katie's foster mom before the court awarded me full custody after the trial."

Roberta was slower to catch on to his logic. "That's all well and good, Mr. Powers, but that doesn't prove she's family."

"You have to place Tyler in temporary foster care—for the rest of the weekend, at least." He tilted his head toward Maddie. "She's your temporary solution."

"Well, I suppose I could call my supervisor to check Ms. McCallister's license. If her name's already in the system—"

"It is," Maddie chimed in. "My foster-care license should still be valid."

"And I'll vouch for her personally," Dwight stated in a deep dare-you-to-contradict-me voice that had swayed juries and now prompted a pair of deep blue eyes to gape at him in surprise.

Roberta's skinny frame seemed to gain strength at the prospect of someone else shouldering her responsibilities while she got the rest of her Saturday off. "I suppose." She turned to include Maddie. "The boy seems to like you, at any rate. But just until Monday. Then I will have to insist that we do everything by the book as far as any long-term placement goes."

"Sounds like a fair compromise." Dwight nodded his agreement.

"Yes." Maddie's hopeful energy eclipsed the taller woman standing beside her. "I'll contact a judge on Monday, do blood tests, whatever you need. Thank you. I promise I'll take good care of him."

"You'd better." The hint of a smile subtracted years from Roberta's face. She glanced from Maddie to the baby, then back to Dwight before grabbing the cellphone and a pack of cigarettes from her purse. "Just let me make a couple of calls. My supervisor, Mr. Fairfax, will be out on the golf course today. It'll take me a few minutes to track him down."

Dwight watched the older woman scuttle past him out the door, wondering how long it would take her to place the calls and get her nicotine fix before she returned. Wondering how long it would be before he could clear this crisis from his life and get down to some serious, solitary paperwork.

"Thank *you*, Mr. Powers."

Dwight dragged his attention back to Maddie. She was smiling again. Not that weary expression of relief that had marked Roberta Hays's features but a bold, full-lipped curve of unabashed gratitude. Her azure gaze boldly held on to his from across the room, and her wide smile transformed her plain features into something remarkable. A chink in Dwight's defensive armor scraped open, exposing the strangest desire to smile back.

But, no, that would only encourage conversations and

connections. And she was too into her momness for him to be able to handle anything other than this brief, business-like transaction.

Dwight cleared his throat, breaking the expectant silence and flattening her unanswered smile. "Well, if that's all you need, I'm out of here. It's been a long night." He thumbed over his shoulder to the door. "The detectives or Mrs. Hays will answer any other questions you have. Good luck with everything."

Chapter Three

Good luck?

The man who'd come to her rescue four years ago after Joe's trial didn't seem willing to play hero a second time.

But what kind of professional dismissed a frightened woman, an innocent baby and an unsolved mystery that had literally landed on the middle of his desk with a *good luck?* Maddie had been ignored by men more than once in her life. But she'd never had one so openly eager to escape her company.

She shifted Tyler into one arm, already falling in love with the precious weight of him and soft smells she inhaled with every breath. Dwight Powers's broad, unyielding back triggered a different, more volatile reaction inside her as she followed him out into the hallway. She braced her hand to catch the door before he accidentally closed it in her face.

"Hey."

A storm brewed in Dwight's gray-green eyes as he turned to face her, despite his politely calm voice. "Was there something else?"

"We're not finished here," she insisted, tilting her chin and pretending there was nothing intimidating about the height and breadth and dour countenance of the man blocking the exit. "Aren't you concerned at all about Katie? I was hoping you could tell me something more."

He propped a forearm on the frame beside her head, bringing those turbulent eyes and that unrelenting jaw even closer. "Trust me, I know very little about how the mind of a teenage girl works."

Maddie fought her body's urge to retreat a step as Dwight's shoulders filled her peripheral vision. Tyler stirred against her as if he'd absorbed her tension, even in his sleep. She slowly rubbed his soft, warm back, for her own comfort as much as his. "You're the one she entrusted her son to. You must have some idea why."

"Actually, I don't." He glanced down at Tyler, his nostrils flaring as if something about the baby's sweet talcum-powder smell offended him. But his expression shuttered so quickly that Maddie wondered if she'd imagined his reaction. "I'm sure it was just an impulsive mistake. She'd want you to have him."

"Mr. Powers." In a bold move fueled by fear, frustration and way too little sleep, Maddie grabbed a fistful of Dwight's lapel and tugged him back into the conference room. He was startled enough to let the door close, giving them privacy once more. When her thighs bumped into the table behind her, Maddie loosened her grip and brushed at the wrinkles she'd put in the summer-weight wool.

But just as the warmth and hardness of the body beneath that suit jacket registered through her fingertips, Dwight stopped her hand, pushed it away and retreated a step. "What do you want from me? Legal advice? Money?"

That warmth must only be skin-deep. "I want answers. I want my niece back. I need to know why she turned to you."

"I wish I knew."

He turned away and circled the end of the long, narrow table. Without missing a beat, Maddie mirrored his path, pacing along the opposite side. "I'm very grateful to you for convincing Mrs. Hays to let me keep Tyler. I didn't even know he'd arrived. Believe me, I'm relieved to know that he's all right. But now I'm really worried about Katie. Did she have a healthy delivery? Is someone taking care of her? What if..." Maddie paused. She didn't know where all these words were coming from or when she'd developed the nerve to say them, but she refused to give voice to the possibility that Katie hadn't survived Tyler's birth. "She's like a daughter to me. I won't rest until she's home safe, too."

"Detectives Rodriguez and Bellamy can answer your questions better than I can." He spared her an annoyed glance before pivoting back toward the door. "Now if you'll excuse me—"

"No."

He slowly turned and glared at her. "No?"

"No."

As they faced off across the table, Maddie could see it. She finally understood why Katie had left Tyler with Dwight Powers.

The evidence was in Dwight's massive shoulders and blunt, unsmiling features. It was there in the flecks of silver camouflaged in his trim, wheat-colored hair. The brawny lawyer radiated strength—not just the physical kind, but strength of will and character and life experience. It was there in the square set of his jaw, the succinct articulation of his voice, the keen intelligence and inexplicable shadows in his storm-cloud eyes.

The resentment Maddie felt, knowing Katie had more faith in Dwight Powers than in her own flesh and blood, ebbed, even as her pulse tripped into overtime under his intense scrutiny. It still hurt that Katie hadn't trusted her enough to share whatever troubled her, that her niece thought it was smarter to run away than to rely on her. It broke Maddie's heart to know that, despite her best efforts to be there for her, Katie had chosen to go through child-birth on her own.

Dwight Powers might be a grouchy old bear who needed a few lessons in PR and patience. His bold, in-triguing face might need a shave and a smile to make it handsome. But an enemy would think twice about going after anything he held dear.

Katie would feel safe with Dwight Powers standing between her and whatever threat pursued her. He'd stand like a rock between the world and her baby.

If he was so inclined to take such a stand.

This hard-edged attorney had little in common with the hero who'd stood for a few moments between her and the monster who'd killed her sister. So far, Maddie had seen little evidence of this older Dwight caring enough about anything, except a speedy departure, to believe he would fight for her niece.

But Katie had faith in the ADA. Though Maddie was less willing to put her trust in such a hard, heartless man, she prayed that the teenager was right. "Detective Bellamy said Katie left you a note. Can you, at least, tell me what she said?"

Lines furrowed beside his gray-green eyes. "Ask Detec-tive Rodriguez. He took possession of the letter."

"I'm asking *you*."

"You wouldn't like what she had to say."

"Tell me, anyway."

His chest heaved in a mighty sigh. He splayed his hands

on his hips and shook his head. "She wants me to call the baby Tyler Powers and tell him she loves him. She didn't say a damn thing that would give us a clue as to where she is or what's got her so spooked."

Tyler *Powers?* Maddie fought to ignore the fateful implication that changing Tyler's name meant Katie didn't think she'd be back to claim her son. "So, you agree—Katie's running from something."

"If she shares any of your stubbornness, Ms. McCallister, I imagine that handing her baby over to me was a last resort. So, yeah, she's scared of something. Of course," he paused, but his gaze never flinched from hers, "the blood we found in my office might have something to do with that."

"Blood?" Maddie's own veins seemed to stop up. Then the blood rushed to her feet and her breath got stuck in her chest. Dwight's face blurred in front of her eyes. Katie wasn't coming back. "Katie's hurt?"

Dwight reached straight across the table and gripped her shoulder. He grabbed the chair beside her and shoved her down onto it. "Easy, Red."

Red? Maddie pressed a hand to her clammy forehead. She felt so dizzy that nothing made sense. "Of course, the blood would be red. What…what happened?"

The table groaned as it took Dwight's weight. And then she felt something warm press against her arm, pushing Tyler closer to her chest. The warmth stayed, radiated across her chilled skin and woke her from her stupor.

She'd nearly dropped the baby!

Maddie blinked Dwight back into focus. She hugged Tyler tight with her own strength and apologized. "Sorry. I didn't sleep last night and I skipped breakfast this morning—it's hard to tell, I know. Katie's been gone for a month and I'm just tired of being scared for her."

"It's okay." He waved aside her rambling excuses. "Stuff happens. You're tough."

She glanced down at the large, battle-scarred hand still braced against her forearm. What Dwight Powers lacked in charm and subtlety he made up for in solid, steady strength.

"That's what I keep telling myself." Maddie's self-deprecating laugh never quite left her throat. With a last wishful look at Dwight's blunt, masculine fingers resting against her sleeve, Maddie rose. It was nothing new to realize she had to stand on her own two feet. "I suppose I'd better put Tyler down before I get distracted again. Do you mind holding him for a minute while I get his carrier ready?"

Dwight jerked his hand away and shot to his feet when she lifted the baby toward him. His face creased with something like pain—shock, perhaps—as if she'd just asked him to strip naked to see if his chest and biceps were really as big as they looked under that jacket.

"I'm sorry. I…"

With a deep noise she could only describe as a wordless curse, he plucked the carrier off the table and tossed aside the blanket. He loosened the strap buckles, adjusted the stand and locked it into place with an efficiency that indicated he'd done the task before. He set the carrier on the table between them and folded the yellow blanket into a neat square before pausing for an audible breath. Maddie felt her own held breath seeping out along with his as the burst of physical activity ended.

"*I'm* the one who should apologize." Now she could see that he was looking at the smeared drops of crimson that could be nothing other than blood on the corner of the blanket. He tossed the material aside and pulled out a clean cover from the bag Roberta Hays had brought. "I should have dropped that bombshell with a little more tact. We don't know for a fact yet that it was Katie's blood. The crime lab is going to do some checking. At any rate, they didn't seem to think there was enough of it to indicate a serious injury. It could be related to childbirth—if it's even hers."

Maddie pressed a kiss to the crown of Tyler's head, still trying to make sense of Dwight's reaction—make that overreaction—to her request for a helping hand. "And that's supposed to reassure me?"

"You wanted the facts. There aren't many to share."

Maddie nodded, corralling her fear the way she had for the past month. The way she had for so many years when she'd known Karen had been in danger and that every effort to help her had ultimately proved futile. She laid Tyler in the carrier and strapped him in place. Then she covered him with the blanket Dwight had set out. "I appreciate hearing at least that much information. It's more than the police could tell me."

"I'm sure they're doing their best to find Katie."

Maddie tried not to scoff. "They're more interested in locating that illegal-adoption clinic that may or may not exist. If she's not mixed up with that, then I'm afraid they'll never find her."

Dwight angled his head toward the door, shifting his whole body in that direction. But when she thought the conversation between them had ended, he shoved his hands into his trouser pockets and turned back to face her. "When was the last time you heard from Joe Rinaldi?"

She imagined that abrupt change of topic was a useful tactic to use in the courtroom to catch a witness off guard. But any mention of the ex-brother-in-law who had butchered her sister put Maddie on alert.

"I haven't. We have an unlisted number, and the Department of Corrections keeps him locked up pretty tight." But Dwight's hesitation only upped her suspicions. "Why?"

He pulled his wallet from his pocket. "Joe Rinaldi is being transferred to a new prison for a psychiatric evaluation. Could he have contacted Katie without you knowing it?"

"He's not allowed to call or write her. And if he had, surely Katie would have told me." *You'd be surprised what a man can accomplish from inside a prison cell if he's determined enough.* No. She couldn't go there. "Is Joe getting out?"

"He's getting transferred. There's a difference."

"But for you to mention it, you must be concerned—"

"You wanted me to tell you everything I know. Now I have. Here." As he slipped his wallet back into his pocket, he held out a business card. "I'll report to KCPD if I hear from your niece again. Detective Bellamy's young and ambitious, but I'll make sure he keeps you informed and that Katie doesn't get lost in the shuffle of pursuing a bigger case. You can call me if you don't hear from him soon."

Maddie took the card, trying not to make too much of how quickly he pulled his hand away from hers. "What about Joe?"

"I'll keep you posted on anything I hear from that end, as well. Let's hope he's proved perfectly sane and MODOC puts him right back where he belongs."

"Let's hope." Maddie summoned a smile. Whether it was his intention or not, Dwight Powers had given her the best comfort she'd known in a month. Maybe not in a tender here's-a-hug-and-some-reassuring-words kind of way. But his straightforward taking-care-of-business bluntness went a long way toward easing her fears and making her feel as though she wasn't in this battle all on her own. "Thanks."

"KCPD will find out what Katie's running from and bring her home." The tight set of his jaw told her this last point wasn't open for negotiation. "But I'm not an investigator. I'm not in the protection business. You and I are done here. Understood?"

So much for allies and support.

"And you can get me a list of all state-sanctioned adoptions in the past twelve months?" Cooper Bellamy pushed open the conference-room door, ushering in Roberta Hays ahead of him.

"If they're public record," Roberta huffed. "Not all of them are."

Cooper seemed unfazed by her halfhearted answer and unaware of the tension that filled the room. He was grinning as big as a boy at an amusement park. "Ms. McCallister?" He nodded to Dwight. "Excuse me for interrupting, sir, but I've got some photos I'd like her to look at."

"You're a go," Roberta stated. Maddie barely minded the odor of cigarette smoke stinging her nose as the social worker gave her a thumbs-up sign. "I just need to know where to reach you in case…"

Detective Bellamy opened a folder on the table in front of Maddie and dealt out five pictures. "Do you recognize any of these girls? Would your niece have contact with any of them?"

An auburn-haired teenager with a heart-shaped face jumped to her attention. "That's Whitney Chiles. A friend of Katie's. They sing together in the show choir."

"And what about…"

While Maddie's multi-tasking brain answered the pertinent questions and filtered out the rhetorical ones, her thoughts were focused on the man who gave her one last, hard look before striding from the room without a good-bye. A man of immeasurable strength who had an aversion to smiling. A man who would do only his job and nothing more.

Dwight Powers had made it clear that he wanted nothing to do with Katie. Or the baby.

Or with her.

So why did she feel as if her best hope had just walked out the door?

OH, MAN. THERE must be an elephant sitting on her head.

Katie Rinaldi tried to roll over to a more comfortable position. But a bombardment of fireworks and clashing swords exploded inside her brain.

She groaned. At least, she thought that was her voice. Her tongue felt swollen, her throat was scratchy. She was so thirsty.

Her breasts were tender and her joints ached from being twisted up like a pretzel while she slept. Or had she passed out? And why the hell wouldn't that elephant get off her head?

"She's movin'."

"Make the call."

"We call when she's awake, not before."

"You gave her too much juice. It's been twenty-four hours."

"You finally got some shut-eye, didn't you? I told you this one was trouble from day one, when she came lookin' for us, instead of the other way around. You should be thankin' me instead of complainin'."

"The boss is the one who'll be complaining if she doesn't come out of it soon."

Who was arguing? Where was she? Was it morning or night? And what was that foul, rancid smell? Somebody seriously needed a breath mint.

"C'mon, darlin'." Rough hands shook her. She curled up into a ball and tried to escape back into the comfort of oblivion.

"No." There was something very important she needed to do today. But she couldn't get her brain around the concept of opening her eyes, much less remembering that...thing...she needed to do. Her mind was floating. Funny, since her head felt so heavy. "Just a little longer. Please."

"Wake up! Where's the kid? Katie!" The little one smacked her hard across the face.

Her eyes popped open. "Tyler!" The cry grated through her dry throat. She grabbed her empty belly and squinted her surroundings into focus. "Where's my baby?"

"That's what we want *you* to tell us."

Katie's thoughts grew more coherent as the blow carved a path through her muddled brain. *Not them again. No, no, not this place.* She crawled into a sitting position. *How the hell did she get back here? Had they recaptured Whit, too?*

"Oh, my God," she rasped. Tears filled her eyes. She'd really screwed up.

She was back in the hospital bed. Neat white sheets. IV stands. Antiseptic smells. Even a call button beside her on the blanket. But this wasn't really a hospital.

And neither the tall porker on her right nor the garlic-chewing shrimp on her left was a doctor. Or a male nurse. Or even an orderly.

Katie lifted her hand up to her aching cheek and winced at the sharp pinch of pain around her wrists. She looked down. A thick plastic band, as secure as handcuffs, was bound around her wrists.

Next time, escape wouldn't be so easy.

If she had a next time.

"She's with us now. Make the call, Fitz. Welcome home, darlin'."

While the big man pulled out his cellphone and punched in a number, Stinky Pete sat on the edge of her bed and mocked her with a smile. She'd seen that same sort of leer before—on her father's face when he looked at her mother.

As a little girl, Katie had never wanted to leave the room when she saw that particular smile because she knew that the minute she was gone that smile would vanish. And her mother would bear the full brunt of the savagery beneath that smile.

Katie lowered her eyes and sank into the pillow, trying to make herself as small and insignificant as possible. She didn't feel like the brave crusader anymore, out to save the world one friend at a time. She didn't even feel seventeen. With those dark eyes laughing at her, gloating over her, she felt like a scared little girl again. She wanted to go home. Aunt Maddie would keep her safe. Aunt Maddie would love her baby.

"Tyler?" she whispered.

"Not here, darlin'." Stinky Pete pinched her chin between his thumb and finger and forced her to look at him. "We thought maybe you could clue us in. He's bought and paid for and we want him back. What'd you do with him?"

Her plan had failed. Maybe she hadn't helped anyone, after all. Just because she was in a private room now didn't mean Whitney had escaped. They might have recaptured her friend, as well. She could be tied up and drugged somewhere else in the building. Or Whit could be dead. And it would be Katie's fault. Instead of helping her friend, she'd gotten her killed.

Katie had made a critical mistake in calling for help. She'd trusted the wrong person and given away their location. Now she was back with Stinky Pete and his big buddy, the hulkster.

But if she was here—and they were asking these questions—that meant they didn't have Tyler. A perverse sense of hope tried to take root. Thank God. Mr. Powers would take care of him. Even if she didn't survive this, her baby would be safe.

Her mother had made the same sacrifice for her. Katie felt through the thin cotton of her gown for the chain she wore and closed her hand around her mother's ring.

The big man named Fitz held out the phone. "The boss wants to talk to you."

The boss? There was someone else these two goons answered to? Other than the grandmotherly midwife who'd help deliver Tyler, Katie hadn't seen anyone else but the other girls. Katie held up her battered wrists. "I can't hold the phone."

The little man with the scary eyes and false smile grabbed the cellphone and pushed it against her ear. "Talk."

Katie caught a startled breath and obeyed the command. "Hello?"

The voice on the phone was sickeningly familiar. "I'm very disappointed in you, Katie. I went out of my way to help you and this is how you repay me?"

By the time the call had ended, Katie was numb with fear.

But Tyler was still safe. Please, God, let him stay out of harm's way.

She heard the big man speak. "The boss wants us to take

out some insurance. Something to improve the new mama's cooperation."

Stinky Pete grinned. "Now *that* should be interesting."

Insurance? There was nothing these men could do to make her tell them what she'd done with her baby. Nothing. She'd die first.

Katie had resigned herself to doing just that by the time the needle pricked her arm, filling her head with the weight of that elephant and sending her back into oblivion.

MADDIE ROCKED BACK and forth slowly, softly singing her own version of an old movie song about fish swimming and birds flying and loving dat boy of mine.

Tyler had finished his bottle, burped like a pro and drifted off to sleep. But Maddie was in no hurry to put him in his bassinet. She loved the warm, gentle weight of him nestled against her and found his contented slumber a balm to her own fractured sense of peace.

Katie had done a wonderful job taking care of herself during her pregnancy. The vitamins, exercise and careful diet had produced a healthy boy.

But Maddie was no closer to understanding why Katie had run away. What had changed in the girl's life? As Dwight Powers had suggested yesterday morning, something pretty drastic must have occurred for Katie to risk Tyler's health and her own during the last month of her pregnancy.

How could she not have seen it? She and Katie talked every night over dinner. Had she not been listening?

Maddie replayed those last few evenings together in her mind. Maddie had talked about the summer class she'd been teaching; Katie about the classes she'd be taking in the fall. With tutoring from her favorite aunt to compensate for the first few weeks of school she'd miss, Katie had been thrilled that she'd still be able to finish high school and graduate with her own class. She'd be forced to give up most of her extracurricular activities, but a couple of her best friends had promised to still come to the house to hang out, keep the gossip fresh and help with the baby.

Katie had been a little despondent about not having her mother around to see Tyler. But more than once, she assured Maddie that she'd fill in just fine as a grandma.

Joe Rinaldi's name hadn't come up.

The baby's father hadn't come up.

One evening, Maddie and Katie were commiserating over swollen ankles and the summer heat; the next, Maddie was alone with a note in her kitchen.

> Dear Aunt Maddie,
>
> You know I love you more than anything in the world, right? Well, maybe just a nanobit less than I'm gonna love Tyler or Amanda. But don't be frightened if I'm gone for a while.
>
> I need to take care of something. Something I know you'd understand if I could tell you about it. But I promised to keep it secret.
>
> I'll always remember how you tried to help Mom. How you've always helped me. It's my turn to pay it forward now.
>
> I'll be home as soon as I can.
>
> Love ya,
> Katie

What did she mean? What sort of debt did a seventeen-year-old have to pay that would be shrouded in such secrecy?

Tyler cooed in his sleep and Maddie smiled for his benefit. "Where's your mommy, sweetie? What's so important that she can't be with you right now?"

Even if the baby couldn't understand, Maddie refused to mention the possibility that someone else might be keeping mother and son apart.

Not for the first time, Maddie considered the neatly cut stump of Tyler's umbilical cord and the tiny little ring ready to fall off his circumcision. Wherever Katie had been, whatever she had done, Tyler had received medical care.

Had Katie? Maddie still hadn't shaken the memory of the blood on Tyler's blanket or Dwight Powers's blunt words about the blood in his office. "Please don't let it be your mama's," she whispered into the darkness.

Was Katie in good hands, recovering from the delivery? Was she in a hospital far away or close by? Had she been in an accident and lost her memory and forgotten her way home? Was she, God forbid, in that secretive baby clinic that Cooper Bellamy and the KCPD were so anxious to investigate?

One phone call. That's all Maddie needed. One call from Katie to tell her where she was and Maddie would move heaven and earth to bring her home.

"She'll be here soon." Maddie made the foolish promise to herself and the boy. "And then your mommy can rock you to sleep. That's how it should be. That's how it will be."

Tyler dozed as Maddie rocked in the old walnut chair handed down from her grandmother. It was one of the few surviving family treasures. If it had gone to her sister, Karen, it would have been destroyed. Busted up with an ax and burned in the fireplace. Thrown across a room.

Backed over with Joe Rinaldi's pickup truck in one of his sick, controlling rages.

A silent tear ran down Maddie's cheek and soaked into the bodice of her white cotton nightgown.

Karen had once confided that it was the not knowing that scared her most during her marriage to Joe. Would Joe be in a good mood when he came home from work? What would set him off this time? Was he asking a question to make conversation? Or putting her through a test she was bound to fail?

Karen had described a scary place inside her head where she'd lived 24/7.

And while Maddie had witnessed the external effects of Joe Rinaldi's abuse, she hadn't truly understood the internal fears her sister had lived with until now. Not knowing Katie's fate—imagining the worst, trying to plan a way to make things right, praying it wasn't foolish to hope—had to be the truest hell Maddie had ever gone through.

Sometime later, after the twilight shadows had muted the primary colors of Tyler's nursery to shades of gray that matched Maddie's mood, she got up from the rocking chair and put Tyler in his bassinet. She bent down and kissed his cheek. "Good night, sweetie. See you in another four or five hours."

She would have stayed there even longer, just standing in the shadows and watching him sleep, if the flash of headlights hadn't streamed through the window and swept across the room. It was enough of a visual alarm to wake her from her wistful yearnings and remind her that she needed to get some sleep, too, if she was going to do Tyler any good tomorrow morning.

Maddie padded on bare feet to the window and adjusted

the curtain. She paused a moment to rest her head against the bright yellow frame and look out across the familiar northern Kansas City neighborhood that had been her home all her life.

She saw the familiar one- and two-story houses set close together with deep, narrow yards. She saw the familiar cars and trucks parked in the driveways, lining the street. She saw the familiar trees and gardens, the street lamp at the corner.

But tonight, the homes felt less friendly, less familiar. The shadows seemed darker, the sleeping windows like spiteful, spying eyes. It had to be her imagination, fueled by fear and fatigue. "Where are you, Katie?"

As if to answer, a sixth sense led her gaze to an unfamiliar car—gray or dirty black—parked across the street, just beyond the fringe of light cast by the street lamp. There was nothing extraordinary about the car, nothing alarming or sinister about the metal or rubber or glass. It just felt…wrong. It didn't belong in her familiar world.

Maddie sighed, shook her head and let the curtain close. She had enough to worry about. She didn't need to imagine enemies or curious eyes where none existed. The Dixons, who lived catty-corner across the street, had two teenage boys. One of them had probably bought a new car or had a friend over for the night. Or maybe Cooper Bellamy had made good on his promise to step up the KCPD's efforts to find Katie. Chances were that was just an unmarked police car with an unseen protector inside.

But before Maddie climbed into bed, she checked the window from her room. The car was still there. Dark. Out of place.

And she couldn't shake the feeling that someone in the darkness was watching.

Chapter Four

Dwight went after the heavy bag as if finally landing a good punch could blank his mind of all the unnecessary details from the past weekend it kept trying to process.

Work hadn't helped.

Sleep hadn't helped.

A cold shower hadn't done a damn thing.

That left going a couple of rounds with his guilt at midnight down in his basement gym.

"You did—" he hit the bag with a left-right-left combination, then danced back on the balls of his feet "—what you had—" he leaned in for a right-left "—to do."

A final cut left the body-sized bag shaking on its suspension mounts. Dwight tipped his head back and closed his eyes, relishing the blood pounding in his veins and the stretch of muscle through his chest and shoulders as he breathed in deeply.

But as he inhaled the smells of vinyl mats and exercise, a softer scent crept into his thoughts. Baby powder. He squinted his eyes open and stared at the ceiling's steel beams, cursing as familiar ghosts refused to die.

He'd been right to walk away from the Tyler Rinaldi case. A. J. Rodriguez had briefed him on the latest developments. The special-victims unit had launched an investigation, looking for some sort of illegal-adoption ring. The police department had set up regular patrols around Maddie McCallister's house and tapped her phones. The KCPD was on top of things. They'd protect Tyler. They'd locate his mother.

There were too many similarities to Braden's death for Dwight to be effective in any role. He was a grown man with a law degree and a Golden Gloves trophy from his stint in the Army. If he couldn't save his own son, what good could he possibly do for someone else's kid?

He shouldn't be involved.

So why the hell was it still nagging at him?

Dwight punched the bag one more time for good measure.

Walk away, Powers, he warned himself, as personal history warred with his conscience. *You'd be doing everyone a favor if you just walked away.*

Intending to do just that, Dwight peeled off his gloves and hugged the bag to stop its wobbling. But as his arms absorbed the vibrations, another buried detail surfaced. His fingertips clutched the vinyl-coated mesh, but he was remembering smooth, telegraphic skin and a delicate heat that bloomed beneath his palm.

He rested his forehead against the cool surface and closed his eyes, recalling another scent, as well. One as subtle as the baby smells that haunted him but much more alluring. Ginger. Mixed with orange. A warm and spicy fragrance that reminded him of copper-colored hair. Framing a warm smile that seemed to light up from the inside out and cut through even his cold shield of armor.

Dwight's temperature continued to rise, even though the workout had ended. He remembered curves aplenty, too.

Enough to fill a man's hands if he dared touch them. Curves and smiles and copper and spice….

His cellphone rang before a complete image of Maddie McCallister could really screw with his head. Dwight rubbed at the back of his neck, wishing he could ease the kinks from his entire body.

It was just as well. He was fantasizing about the wrong woman. His wife had had dark hair. And she always wore that… "Damn." He couldn't name the perfume Alicia had worn.

Dwight mopped his face and chest with a towel, snatched up the phone and ground out his frustrations through the tight rumble of his voice. "Powers."

"My turn to wake you, counselor."

"A.J." Dwight recognized the smooth Latin accent immediately. His detective friend knew him better than that. "You know I'm awake. What's up?"

"Have you turned on your TV, amigo? There's news from Jeff City."

Dwight had a sick feeling in his stomach that he was about to land on the front line of a battle he was in no shape to fight.

Walking away from Maddie McCallister and her piece-meal family had never really been an option.

He was already involved.

"Tell me."

Maddie tucked the blanket around Tyler and set his carrier on the kitchen table so she could keep an eye on him while she cleaned up. Under Roberta Hays's recommendation, the DFS had granted her an extended foster placement until her court hearing on Thursday. And though the three books on child rearing she'd checked out from the library that afternoon all recommended getting some sleep whenever the newborn napped, her odd hours with Tyler and restless worries over Katie were quickly turning her into a night person.

As a result, after Tyler's midnight feeding, Maddie was still wide-awake, puttering about the house in her nightgown.

Maddie started the dishwasher, then wound her hair back into a ponytail and slipped on some rubber gloves to wash the baby bottles and plastic nipples in the sink. After setting them on a towel to dry, she tackled the iron skillet from dinner.

She was barefoot and humming and as happy as a woman who'd had little to be optimistic about over the past month could be. Now she had a tap on her phone and cell, and a police technician on the street outside, listening and watching for any word from Katie. Detective Bellamy had ordered periodic checks of the house and neighborhood, either by himself, his partner, Charlotte Quinn, or a black-and-white cruiser.

If Katie called or physically approached the house, the police would be there. And if anyone else was scouting out the house or showing any undue interest in Tyler, they'd know that, too. If Cooper Bellamy's theory was true, Tyler was a commodity Katie had stolen from the mysterious baby clinic. Someone would want him back.

Well, they could damn well try. Maddie finally had a tangible role to play, caring for the baby. It was one thing she could do to help her niece. She didn't intend to let Katie down.

The sudsy water was sucking noisily down the drain when the telephone rang. 12:31 a.m., according to the clock. An instinctive moment of panic was quickly replaced by a flare of hope.

Katie.

Let it ring at least twice, Cooper had instructed, giving the recording device he'd installed a chance to kick in. Once. Her hand hovered beside the phone. Twice. The detectives' technical assistance team should have their tracers and recorders activated by now. Three times for good measure.

Maddie released her white-knuckled grip around the dish towel and grabbed the cordless receiver. This could be it. "Hello?"

A beat of silence ended with a low, biting laugh. "Hey, Madeline. How's my favorite sister-in-law tonight?"

Her knees turned to jelly at the horrid voice from her past. *Hang up! Hang up!*

But the need to stand up to the ex-brother-in-law who'd already destroyed so many lives beat strongly inside her. Bracing her hand against the counter, Maddie trimmed the fear and loathing from her voice. "What do you want, Joe?"

"How's Katie? How's my little girl?"

Grown-up. Missing. Alone. Maddie told him none of those things. She gazed over at the tiny infant, snoozing peacefully, blessedly oblivious to the hell this man had put his mother and grandmother through. "Tell me what you want or I'll hang up."

"No, you won't. Karen might have been the pretty sister. But you're the smart one. You'll listen to me." Joe Rinaldi had always had a twisted way with words that cut to the bone. "You know, if you'd been even half as fine as she was, I might have chosen you instead."

Was that a threat or an insult? Knowing Joe, it was both. "Is that all you wanted to say?"

A tremor in her voice betrayed her growing discomfort.

She could imagine Joe on the other end, adjusting his thick, black-framed glasses on his nose and smiling because he'd gotten a rise out of her. "Oh, I'm just getting started, sweetheart."

The phone line beeped, indicating another incoming call. Maddie slipped her thumb to the disconnect button. It might be Katie. She should clear the line.

"And I'm finishing it." Whatever request he had in mind, she wasn't having any part of it. "I'm not driving to Jefferson City. I'm not sending you anything. Now I have another call coming in. Good-bye."

"Hang up on me and I'll just keep calling. I'll tie up the line until I get what I want."

Maddie released a pent-up breath. She hated giving him control of anything, but she knew he'd do what he promised. Better to give him a moment longer and then get rid of him. "I have nothing you want."

Joe laughed at his own private joke. But then, he'd always laughed at her. "Let me talk to Katie."

Absolutely not. Even if she was home. The phone beeped again. "You know you can't have contact with her."

"I'm her daddy."

You're the murdering son of a bitch who killed her mother. "The court said you can't have access to her until she turns eighteen. Then it will be her choice as to whether she wants to have anything to do with you, and I wouldn't hold my breath. Besides—" she could levy a little threat of her own "—I don't know who you paid off, but once I report you, they'll put you in solitary for making an illegal call after lights-out."

"They can try." *They can try?* The line beeped like an ominous death knell. "Put my daughter on the phone."

Where were the prison guards? How did a convicted

murderer get access to a telephone in the middle of the night?

Maddie's bravado quickly evaporated, and a bone-chilling dread took its place. Her gaze drifted to the front door. Where were *her* cops?

What had Dwight Powers said about Joe being transferred to a psychiatric hospital?

"Madeline?"

She slipped through the darkened foyer to the porch window and pushed aside the sheer curtain. In the shadows beyond the street lamp, she could just make out the unmarked utility van parked on the opposite side of the street. A small flare of orange diverted her gaze to the uniformed officer standing in the shadows beside the van, smoking a cigarette. Weren't they hearing this? Didn't they know who Joe Rinaldi was? What he had done? Weren't they concerned?

The same dark car that had spooked her last night turned the corner and cruised by at a steady, leisurely speed. But even the wash of light from the street lamp couldn't illuminate the dark blob of a driver inside. It turned the next corner and disappeared from sight.

No. Surely not. Panic surged through her veins. Maddie checked the dead bolt. "Where are you?"

"Where's Katie?"

"She isn't home right now."

"You don't have any idea where she is, do you?"

Do *you?* But she bit her tongue. Tires ground into the asphalt as a car spun around the same corner and rushed up the street. Not the same black car as before, but this one moved with a definite purpose. Maddie dropped the curtain and retreated into the darkness. "I'm hanging up."

"I'm coming to see you."

Beep. The speeding car braked and squealed to a halt

in front of her house. She curled her toes into the rag rug beneath her feet. "You can't."

"I'm coming for Katie."

"No."

A man climbed out of the car. His broad, faceless silhouette raced up the front sidewalk.

The van doors swung open. In the pool of lamplight, she saw the uniformed officer crushing his cigarette beneath his shoe. He was pulling his gun, chasing after the man.

The beep repeated itself like an alarm, waking her from a stupor of fear. Maddie ran into the kitchen and reached out to lay a protective hand on Tyler's tiny chest. "Where are you?"

"Closer than you think. You turned Karen against me. Told all those lies in court. But you won't keep me from my little girl."

The shadowy figure reached the porch.

No. It couldn't be. Maddie dashed to the sink and grabbed the iron skillet.

"Maddie!" A fist pounded on her door.

She jumped inside her skin and the skillet and phone clattered to the floor. She danced out of the way to save her toes but was on her knees, scrambling to retrieve the makeshift weapon when she heard Joe's final taunt.

"You won't keep me from my grandson, either."

"What?" She snatched up the phone as she crawled to her feet, positioning herself between Tyler and the front door. "How do you know about…"

A dial tone was her only answer.

"Joe!"

Tyler whimpered in his sleep, stirring at her scream.

"I'm sorry, sweetie." Maddie tossed the phone onto the counter and curled both hands around the skillet.

The fist pounded again. The door rattled in its frame. She swung the iron pan up like a baseball bat. "You won't hurt us this time."

"Maddie! It's Dwight Powers. Open up!"

Dwight? What was he... A ragged sigh of relief tore through Maddie's chest as she unfolded her arms. "Dwight?"

"Police! On the ground. Now!"

"I'm with the DA's office. I'm reaching for my ID."

"Hands where I can..." Beams of light flashed through the sheer curtains. Someone swore. "Sir, I'm—"

"Dwight!" Maddie dashed to the front door, switching on every light along the way.

"Get him up."

A flurry of curses and shouts became the bark of orders. "Secure the house. Check every parked car and open window on this block."

"Yes, sir."

She flipped on the porch light in time to see two uniformed officers scurrying away into the night with their flashlights. Maddie unlatched the dead bolt and reached for the knob. Help was here. She and Tyler were safe.

"Dwight? Thank God, you're..."

Or not.

A blast of humid summer air swished beneath her cotton gown as the door swung open. She skipped backward, shielding her chest with the skillet as Dwight barged inside. He slammed the door behind him and locked it. Then, in the same decisive motion, he pried the skillet from her grasp, closed one big hand around her shoulder and pushed her farther into the interior of the house, away from the porch and windows. "The next time I call, you answer the damn phone."

"I…" The beeping. "That was you?"

"Yes, it was me. How the hell is anybody supposed to warn you?"

"Warn me about what?" She twisted out of his grasp and darted into the kitchen. He followed, right on her heels, forcing her to back into the counter when she spun around and shook the phone at him. "This creep?"

"That was Joe Rinaldi?"

He knew. Damn him, he knew. She inhaled the musky heat of him on her next feverish breath and shoved the phone into the center of his chest. "Yes, but thanks for nothing. You scared the bejeebers out of me by banging on the door like that. God, it took me back to those nights when…with Karen… I didn't realize he could still rattle me like that."

A steely calm tempered the emotion that had lined his face. He closed his fingers around the phone and her hand, short-circuiting her panic. He moved even closer when he reached around her to set the skillet on the counter. "No wonder you were ready to bash my head in."

"I don't know if I really could hurt someone like that."

"I've seen you in action, Red. If you had to do it to protect your family, you could."

It was an odd compliment. But she found Dwight's words a better boost to her ego than any false platitudes about her looks or talents.

Maddie's gaze zeroed in on the size and contours of his hand, so big and warm and masculine in contrast to her smaller, paler fingers. His was a very business-like hand, sure of itself, more firm than gentle. It was a scarred, calloused hand that seemed at odds with a man who wore suits and ties and relied on mental abilities rather than physical skills in his work. Curious. Comforting. Commanding.

A hand that released her, just as the intimacy of the contact they shared registered. For a few short moments, they'd stood nearly thigh to thigh within the cozy confines of her kitchen, while the hushed velvet of the night shut out the rest of the world.

But Dwight had stepped away, allowing the air-conditioning to cool the space between them and denying her the physical contact she foolishly craved. He set the phone down beside the skillet and moved to the archway connecting the kitchen to the dining room and hallway beyond.

A guarded watchfulness had replaced Dwight's anger, filling the room with a different sort of tension. Maddie curled her arms around her middle, wishing she could hug away the chill that suddenly consumed her. She crossed over to the table and fiddled with Tyler's blanket, confirming that he'd settled into a deeper sleep. "Joe knows about Tyler. He said I couldn't keep him from his grandson. And he knew that Katie was gone. He said he was coming to see me."

"You thought *I* was him?" Dwight's voice dropped a note in pitch and angled in her direction. "At your front door?"

Maddie rubbed her fingers up and down her bare arms, feeling like one giant goosebump. "I couldn't see very well, and fear is playing games with my imagination. And, dammit, you do come on like gangbusters. But I should've…"

Speech evaporated in a puff of air when she turned around and got an eyeful of chest. Right there. Close enough to lean into. Near enough to touch. A whiff of dampness clung to Dwight's clothes and the heat of his skin as if he'd jumped straight from the shower into a pressed shirt and suit.

"You should have *what?*" His deep voice, bold and direct, stroked across her eardrums.

"I should have known better. You're bigger than Joe is." She should back away. "You're older. Not as tall." She should stop staring at that inviting vee of skin where the base of his throat met the sturdy ridge of his collarbone. She should stop wishing she could bury her nose there and have his strong arms wrap her up and keep the terrors of her world at bay. "Besides, he's locked up, two hundred miles away."

In an oblique turn of thought, Maddie lifted her gaze to his without really answering his question. "Why *are* you here? You said you wanted nothing to do with me or my family."

Edged with shadows she didn't understand, those gray-green eyes looked deeply into hers. "Some fights a man can't walk away from—no matter how much he wants to."

So he was here out of duty, not choice.

Despite the fact that she couldn't stop shivering, a self-conscious heat crept across her skin, "How did we become your fight?"

Dwight shrugged out of his jacket. With an efficiency of motion she was quickly getting used to, he draped the light-gray gabardine jacket around her shoulders, surrounding her in a bear-sized hug of earthy smells and warmth. "Sit."

Obeying the brusque invitation, Maddie gripped the lapels of his coat together and sank into the closest chair. Any sense of caring was fleeting. His unexpected consideration frightened her more than his gruff bouts of temper had.

He said nothing to soften the shock. He simply pulled out the chair beside her, leaned forward and spelled out a nightmare in that matter-of-fact way of his. "Joe Rinaldi stabbed his escort detail while he was being transferred back to lockup in Jefferson City earlier this evening. One guard is dead, the second in critical condition. His escape was planned and executed with outside help. He drove off with two men—one large, one small is all the description we have. The highway patrol, FBI and local precincts from the capital to Kansas City are looking for him."

"Joe has escaped?" Maddie snuggled down inside the jacket, clinging to the only warmth she could find. "He's here? In Kansas City?"

"We don't know that yet." A sharp rap at her front door told her the uniformed officers had returned. Dwight rose and headed for the door. "But the car he left the hospital in had Kansas City plates."

Maddie stood and followed, needing the answers only he seemed able to provide. "So you think he's on his way here?"

"Most likely. That's why I tried to call. I remember threats he made at the trial—to both of us. And if he knows about the kid…" He left the ominous possibilities hanging in the air as he unlocked the door. Dwight blocked the opening while the young officer reported in.

"Everything's clear, sir." The twenty-something man deferred to Dwight's air of authority as if Dwight were a ranking officer at KCPD. "The TAC team in the van says Ms. McCallister kept Rinaldi on the line long enough to trace the call's origin to a truck stop about sixty miles west of here. Chances are, the perp's moved on, but they've already notified the highway patrol."

Only sixty miles away?

"Good work, officer." The young man shuffled on his feet. Dwight picked up on the same nervous hesitation Maddie did. "What else?"

"Sorry about the mix-up before—with the guns and everything. Next time you drop by to visit, sir, give us a heads-up. I didn't realize you two were friends."

Friends? His tone even indicated the officer thought she and Dwight were something more. Probably because of the worn cotton gown she'd been parading around in, or the late hour, or the suit coat now draped over her shoulders.

But before she could correct the shorter man on his erroneous assumption, Dwight spoke. "You were doing your job. Until you hear otherwise, I expect you to be as vigilant with anyone who comes to this house."

"Yes, sir. You can count on me." The officer peeked around Dwight's shoulder and tipped the brim of his hat. "Ma'am."

Maddie nodded her thanks and Dwight closed and locked the door. "What am I supposed to do now? Wait until Joe shows up? Pray he doesn't find Katie first?"

"Does Rinaldi know where you live?"

"Of course."

"Then put some clothes on and pack a bag." Dwight gestured toward the kitchen. "One for the kid, too. We're getting out of here."

"MAYBE THIS ISN'T such a good idea. That cop thought we were a couple. Throw in a baby and people will talk."

Dwight halted beneath the chandelier of his front hall and bit back a curse. Carrying two suitcases and a ton of misgivings, he wondered what the hell had possessed him to make such an impulsive invitation. And why the redhead who'd planted herself in his open doorway had such a hard time accepting.

He turned to face Maddie. "We talked about this in the car."

She stood with the baby carrier hooked over one arm

and a purse and diaper bag draped over the other. "You said we were going someplace Joe couldn't find us. I didn't think you meant you wanted us to move in with you. We barely know each other. I won't put you out like this."

"Now's hardly the time to worry about decorum or convenience. I promise to keep my hands to myself if you'll do the same."

Rosy dots spotted her cheeks. The woman broadcast every emotion on that pale, milky skin—embarrassment, fear, joy, desire. She sent other nonverbal signals, too. Ones he doubted she was even aware of. Like the tight press of her lips and the determined angle of her chin— both good indicators that she had more to say. "If school was in session, I'd have to be careful about being seen shacking up with a guy. Half of KCPD already has the mistaken impression that you and I are old friends."

"Shacking up?" He hadn't heard that term for a while. What exactly did Ms. Spinster McCallister think he'd invited her to do?

"On second thought, DFS might not think too highly of us living together. We can't stay."

Dwight dropped the suitcases at his feet and searched for a logical argument. "Katie left Tyler to me in the first place. I don't think DFS would care if we shared guardianship for a few nights. I'll square it with the judge at your hearing if she has a problem with it."

Maddie's lips curled into a kissable pout and his weary body leaped to attention. Crazy. Thus far, he'd been the only one with grabby hands and a roving eye. But each time he'd touched her or studied her, it had been for a practical purpose. To save his skull, to keep her calm, to erase the goosebumps on her skin, to keep his eyes from staring at the dusky tips of her full, round breasts he'd been able to see through the translucent cotton of that plain, white, incredibly sexy nightgown. But his dysfunctional hormones couldn't seem to grasp the idea that Maddie McCallister wasn't sending out any intentionally seductive signals.

Nah, right now those lips just meant she was thinking of more ways to make his life difficult. "Doesn't Joe know where you live, too?" she asked.

"He could look it up in the phone book and find out."

"So we're not really safe here, either."

"At the moment, he's looking for you and Tyler, not me."

"But you're the man who sent him to prison."

"I can take care of myself."

"Not if you're busy looking out for us."

There were a hundred hotels in the Kansas City area where he could have put his guests up for the night. There were women's shelters. Safe houses. Halfway houses.

But no, he'd driven straight south through downtown and headed for his residence off Ward Parkway. Practicality said it was smart to be on home turf—he knew the neighborhood and would immediately recognize anything or anyone out of place. The remodeled 1920s Tudor home had fifteen rooms, making it easy for him to still maintain the solitude he needed. And one of the perks of being an assistant district attorney was the necessity of the state-of-the-art security system he'd installed.

If he was going to protect anyone from Joe Rinaldi, this was the place to be.

Now if he could only get Maddie McCallister to revert to that shy mouse he once knew, get her pretty little butt inside and start cooperating. He opted for a completely different tactic. "You're letting the air-conditioning out. Close the door."

"Oh, sorry." Maddie set the carrier down on the black-and-white tiled floor and finally shut the door behind her. But she didn't move any closer.

Interesting. Dwight scratched at the grizzly stubble of his jaw. He didn't give one wit about the utility bill at this late hour of the night, but appealing to her overdeveloped sense of responsibility had done the trick. He'd have to remember that.

With the hope of a few hours of slightly less-guilt-ridden sleep still in hand, Dwight crossed the room. She moved farther into the foyer to avoid contact as he reached behind her to lock the dead bolt and set the security system on the keypad beside the door.

She looked around, taking in the austere tidiness of a house that was just a house. "Wow. This is…big."

He wasn't looking for compliments. "If I take your suit-cases upstairs, will you come with them?"

"I can't stay."

Well, by damn, at least her bags were spending the night. He picked them up and headed for the stairs. "This way."

He heard the crunch of plastic rubbing against plastic and knew that she'd picked up the baby carrier to follow—to continue the debate if nothing else.

"What if Katie calls?"

"She can still reach you on your cell."

"What if she doesn't have enough change to make more than one call?"

"Maddie."

"What if Katie shows up at the house looking for me?"

"The cops will be there."

"But—"

Dwight turned with a huff on the step above her

and looked down at her startled face. "What if Joe Rinaldi shows up?"

He watched that reality blanch the color from her cheeks.

There. He'd finally ended the debate.

So why didn't it feel like much of a victory?

It probably had something to do with that blue gaze blurring in focus and dropping to the middle of his chest. Without the adrenaline of battle to warm her skin, the shadows of fatigue and worry deepened beneath her eyes.

If the load she carried would have allowed it, she'd have curled her arms up into that same self-preserving hug that had prompted him to give her his jacket earlier that night. The same jacket he wanted to strip off and wrap around her again, since hugging her himself was out of the question.

For his own peace of mind, he needed to get her settled out of harm's way and put some distance between them. "Look, I'm sorry. I can be blunt."

"I noticed." Her eyes were bluer, deeper and focused when she tipped her chin to him again. "But you're right. I can't let Joe get to his grandson."

He turned away from her soft, brave smile before he tried to buck her up with some useless platitude. "Up here."

"It's just that I've felt helpless since Katie first disappeared."

Dwight shook his head. He should have known better than to think the discussion was over.

"Now that there's finally something I can do to help find her—to wait for her to call or come for Tyler—I don't want to run away and hide."

He turned to the right and nudged open the first door past the landing. "There's a difference between running away and making a smart move. If Rinaldi gets to you, Katie loses her strongest ally. If he gets to Tyler—"

"She loses her best reason to come home." Maddie flipped the light switch on behind him and set her bags and the baby on the bed. She unswaddled the blanket and cooed some silly words about her "good boy" before lifting each tiny fist and kissing it. "I won't let Joe hurt anyone else in this family."

Neither would he.

Dwight set the suitcases beside the dresser. "KCPD will continue a watch on your house. If either Katie or her father makes an appearance, they'll call us. I have to be in court tomorrow at ten, but I'll make sure there's an officer here before I leave."

He could see that Tyler was awake and that his tiny blue eyes seemed to follow the sound of his voice. Right. Time to go. "The bathroom's next door. The linen closet's on the other side of that." Braden had been three months old before he slept through the night, but Dwight wasn't volunteering for any feedings. "If you need the kitchen to heat a bottle, it's on the first floor, back of the house. Help yourself to whatever you need."

Dwight would have made a quick exit and called it a night, but Maddie stopped him at the door with a gentle hand on his arm. "If there's a smarter way to handle this, we'll think of it tomorrow. Okay?"

He looked into her earnest expression and saw a spark of the fire that had both captivated and confounded him. "Fine. In the meantime, give my conscience a rest. Accept my hospitality and go to bed. Rinaldi won't find you here tonight."

Pulling away, Dwight strode toward his own bedroom at the far end of the hall.

He almost grinned when he heard her follow him out the door to get the last word. Almost.

"Do you always get your way, Mr. Powers?"

Wry laughter echoed inside his head but found no outlet. Yeah, right. He always got what he wanted. That's why he had this hardheaded woman with the ingenuous eyes and die-hard loyalty to her family staying in his house tonight. Invading his sanctuary with her questions and curves—and baby.

Yeah, he always got what he wanted. That's why he was all alone in this oversized house with nothing but his nightmares and guilt to keep him company.

Dwight turned at the door to his room. "Good night, Ms. McCallister."

"You didn't answer my question."

He didn't intend to.

"Good night, Mr. Powers." She smiled and closed the door.

Dwight waited there a moment, in the silence and shadows of the landing. That woman needed to stop smiling at him. Didn't she understand it was a wasted effort?

Chapter Five

Dwight leaned inside the driver's side window and gave his wife a kiss.

Oh, God, no. He didn't want to dream this again. He rolled over in his sleep but couldn't wake himself. The beauty of it all was just a cruel trick. A reminder of all he had lost and would never risk having again.

But he couldn't wake up. He was forced to remember.

Alicia's chocolate-brown eyes warmed with the love they'd shared since their first year of law school together at Mizzou. "Are you sure you don't want to change your mind and skip town with us? We could leave Braden with Mom and Dad and stay at a bed-and-breakfast all by ourselves." She reached up and twirled her fingers through his tie. "I'd love to get a little us-time, wouldn't you?"

Dwight let his gaze slip to his son in the backseat. The little guy was babbling his first coherent sounds and pounding his stuffed tiger against the side of the car seat. Way to go, champ. Braden was going to grow up with a mean left hook, just like his daddy.

"Don't tempt me, sweetheart." He willingly dragged his gaze back to the slender brunette beauty in the front seat. "You know duty calls."

His chest swelled with the arrogance of a man about to embark on a mission in which he knew his enemy would be begging for mercy. He was young, moving up the ladder at the DA's office, damn good at his job and about to prove it to the world. "Today's the grand jury hearing on Arnie Sanchez. I intend to nail him to the wall and make good on every indictment."

Alicia tugged on his tie. "That's my hero. Slaving away to make Kansas City safe from the bad guys."

"Sanchez is one of the worst. But I've got him on rack-eteering, narcotics distribution, witness intimidation, tax evasion, conspiracy to commit—"

"I love when you talk shop, counselor." She pulled him in for another kiss, wished him luck and said goodbye.

While she started the engine, Dwight circled around and opened the back door to give Braden one more kiss.

"Da, da, da, da, da."

"That's right, champ. I'm your daddy." He beamed, at-tributing each and every gurgle of sound to his nine-month-old's enormous intelligence. "Take care of Mommy for me."

Dwight glanced at his watch. He needed to be down-town at the courthouse in an hour. Today was the day he made a name for himself. Nothing would stop him from making the charges stick on Sanchez and putting himself on the fast track to becoming K.C.'s future district attorney. "Gotta run. Drive safely."

Braden's tiger fell to the floor and he opened his mouth and wailed at the loss. Dwight quickly grabbed the toy, tossed it back into his son's arms and shut the door. He stepped away as the car backed out of the driveway. Alicia's "Love you" and Braden's cries were the last sounds…

Dwight thrashed in the bed, fighting to wake himself. "No," he groaned. "No."

He knew what was coming, but the nightmare wouldn't let him escape.

"Mr. Powers? Mr. Powers?"

Dwight turned and glared at the young security guard. No one but no one interrupted him before he gave his opening statement. "Later, Smitty."

"But, sir, I think you need to read this now."

The guard's ashen skin gave Dwight his first ripple of unease. Sanchez's interest in this private conversation from his spot at the defense table provided the second. Dwight snatched the pink telephone message from Smitty's hand.

"I'm sorry, sir."

Braden was crying. He needed his daddy. But Daddy couldn't help. Daddy didn't mean for it to happen.

Dwight rolled over in the tangle of covers that had twisted around his legs and buried his head under a pillow.

"Da, da, da, da, da."

"Braden. No." He crushed the pillow in his fists the same way he'd crushed that pink slip of paper. "I'm sorry. I'm so sorry." The baby's cries echoed in his ears and ping-ponged inside his head. "Stop it."

"Da, da, da, da, da."

"Love you."

Crying. Louder and louder. His tears. Braden's.

"Da, da, da—"

"Stop it!" Dwight sat up in bed and hurled the pillow across the room. It knocked something off the dresser that crashed into the darkness. The loud sound grated across his raw nerves. "Stop it."

Kicking off the covers, he swung his feet over the edge of the bed, burying his head in his hands.

His face was wet, his chest and back slick with sweat

that gathered in the waistband of his pajama pants. He couldn't catch his breath or shake the graphic images that burned inside his brain.

Ah, nuts. He was really losing it. He couldn't tell his waking nightmares from the ones that haunted his sleep anymore.

He could still hear Braden crying.

His fault. His guilt.

"Mr. Powers, we regret to inform you that...gunshot wound to the head...suspect a professional hit... Your son died in the resulting crash... So sorry."

"Stop it!" He pounded his fist into the second pillow and slung it after the first. He heard quiet footsteps in the hallway, a woman's soft tread. Like that ME down at the morgue who'd needed him to ID Braden's body. "Damn it, when will you get out of my head?"

His own gut-deep wail was swallowed up by the darkness of his empty bedroom. He shot to his feet and stalked into the bathroom. Without turning on the light, he ran cold water in the sink and splashed it on his face and chest. When that wasn't enough to completely wake him, he dunked his head beneath the faucet and let the icy spray cool the fever inside him.

After toweling off his face and torso and slicking back his hair, Dwight could still hear the cries. He splayed his fingers on his hips and let his shoulders sag as waking reality finally gave him a break. "Idiot."

He *was* nuts. He had company in the house.

He was torturing himself over nothing.

Not Braden. Tyler Rinaldi was crying at five in the morning.

But understanding didn't necessarily bring relief. Why wasn't Maddie taking care of him?

That's what he'd heard a few moments ago, no doubt. Maddie tiptoeing down to the kitchen to fix a bottle for the kid's late-night snack. The baby was just fussing until she returned with the good stuff.

Identifying the sounds and probable scenario calmed him a bit. He breathed in deeply and let the knowledge of his surroundings soothe his frustrations.

Maddie. Of the red hair and soft skin and surprising stubbornness. Armed with a skillet and a sharp tongue, ready to take on the world to protect her family.

Protect them from Joe Rinaldi.

Joe Rinaldi escaped from prison.

"Ah, hell." Footsteps in the hall?

"Maddie?" Dwight slung open the door and stormed across the landing. The alarm hadn't sounded. The security lights hadn't come on. Except for the moonlight streaming through the foyer windows at the base of the stairs, the house was utterly still and dark. But that didn't mean it was empty.

He hadn't protected Alicia. Hadn't kept Braden safe. Joe Rinaldi was here.

Tyler cried out.

"Maddie!"

"Wait…"

Dwight shoved open the door and plowed into a soft, warm, nearly naked woman.

He snaked his arms around her to keep her from crashing to the floor. "Dammit, why didn't you answer me?"

Maddie shrugged, lifting her breasts against his chest with nothing but the thin barrier of that damned nightgown between them. "I was changing the baby. I couldn't leave him uncovered."

"I thought…" Dwight swallowed hard. Muscles, skin

and nerves leaped to life with a sudden pricking of heat wherever their bodies touched, temporarily distracting him from his fears. He squeezed his eyes shut and focused harder. Firm thighs. Round hips. Full, luscious breasts. *No!* "I called out…"

Her fingers dug into his biceps, clinging for balance.

"Dwight?" Her soft voice was a drowsy balm against nerves that couldn't seem to relax. Softer fingertips brushed against his jaw. "Is something wrong?"

Yeah. This. You. Me.

He opened his eyes to look down into a sea of deep blue concern. *Is something wrong?* Hell, he had her bent halfway back across one arm with her toes barely touching the floor. He was the one who should be asking that.

"Sorry." He eased the death grip he had on her and retreated a step. "You weren't answering. I thought maybe… I thought you were in trouble." He'd feared the worst. And he knew damn well he couldn't deal with the worst again. He rubbed his palms across the red marks he'd left on the pale skin near her shoulders. God, he wasn't any better than Rinaldi. "Did I hurt you?"

"You startled the pooey out of me, but I'm all right."

"The pooey, huh?" He almost smiled at the silly word. But the frissons of fear and guilt and unexpected lust still firing through his system wouldn't allow it.

One glimpse over her shoulder to the center of the rumpled bed reminded Dwight of the sound that had awakened him in the first place. Tyler lay inside a fort made of pillows, wearing a diaper, a blanket and nothing more.

Dwight's mouth seemed to have a hard time getting around his next question. "What about the kid. Is he all right?"

"Tyler's fine. He generally gets hungry about this time.

I'm sorry if we woke you. I was trying to keep him quiet."
Even in the darkness, he could see the blush rising from
the neckline of her gown. Her fingertips drummed against
his arms in a nervous rhythm. "I heard you cry out. You
must have been having a nightmare. I was going to knock,
but then Tyler—"

"It's probably best if you stay out of my bedroom." The
irony of his husky request sounded teasing and intimate,
standing in the middle of *her* bedchamber.

The blush reached her cheeks as she dropped her gaze
to the center of his chest. "Of course. I mean, I wouldn't
intrude."

"You know, we really have to work on this communication thing. If I say something, you need to respond."
Before he got all worked up and started imagining the
worst. "I don't know if you're being shy or you think I'm
going to snap your head off. I know I can be demanding."
Her lips pressed together in that seductive pout. Was that
a giggle in her throat? Amusement or nerves? He needed
her to understand the kind of grief she'd put him through.
"But it's always for a good reason. Raising my voice
doesn't mean I'm going to hurt you."

"I know." But did she believe it?

"I expect answers."

"I know." Her gaze stayed riveted on his chest, where
her fingers tapped against his skin, teasing him into a state
of hyperawareness. What was she doing? Counting gray
hairs? "I guess I'm just not used to having anyone around
to answer to."

"I'm not used to having anyone around, either."

She cocked an eyebrow and nodded. "I can tell. Messing with your regular routine makes you grumpy."

What? Didn't mouthy Ms. Spinster Pants have any idea

what it cost him to get close to anyone? To get involved? To care? And she wanted to make a joke?

But any argument died on his lips when she tilted her chin to face him. There was nothing plain about the way the moonlight and shadows deepened her eyes to a rich midnight-blue. Nothing spinsterish about the hint of amusement that warmed her cheeks. Nothing he minded at all about the timid smile she directed his way.

"I'll try to do better."

"Yeah." Now there was a snappy closer. He wouldn't win any arguments with that one. "Me, too."

Why was it so damn hot in here? He had the air conditioner running at full blast. And why was she standing so close? Or was he the one who couldn't seem to move away? Her skin glowed in the moonlight? It looked so soft….

It *was* soft. Dwight realized he'd been running his palms up and down her arms this whole time.

The sultry promise of the August heat outside had worked its way between them. The fever from his nightmare still simmered in his veins. And something else— something long dormant and unexpectedly potent—flared to life deep inside him.

Dwight slid his hand up Maddie's neck beneath her hair. Her skin was cool to the touch until that responsive blush caught up to the stroke of his hand. Her hair was such a warm color, her eyes so beautiful, her lips more inviting than a starving man's next meal.

He inched half a step closer, letting his arm fall down behind her shoulder. With just another tug, the soft curves of her body flattened against his harder planes. He loved that nightgown she wore. It was modest in design, from the square neckline to the ruffle at her knees. But it was worn and soft and thin enough to reveal just enough to drive his imagination crazy with what he couldn't see. Spicy ginger teased his nose, and his body leaped to life, wanting what he'd denied himself for far too long.

Dipping his head, they exchanged breaths and heat. He hadn't wanted a woman for so long, but he wanted this one. Right here. Right now. If he could lose himself in just one kiss…

"Dwight."

Maddie's husky voice danced across his skin. Her cool palms braced against his chest, scorching his skin. Color flooded her cheeks. Her chest expanded in a stuttered breath and her taut, pearled nipples thrust against him.

Dwight moaned at the sweet rush of heat that went straight to his groin, canceling the pain and penance of re-membering. Oh, yeah.

"What are you doing?" she whispered. Her fingertips clutched at his shoulders in an unintended caress.

"Making the nightmares go away." Oh, yeah. One kiss. Lose himself in her fire. Get this crazy lust out of his system. "Just once, Red." He licked the rim of his suddenly parched mouth and touched his lips to hers. "Just one."

Tyler's high-pitched cry twisted through Dwight's gut and jerked him back to reality.

Dwight closed his hands around Maddie's shoulders and pushed temptation firmly away from him. Then he held his hands up, as if his abrupt withdrawal and foul mood weren't already enough of a deterrent to keep any woman at a distance.

The color drained from Maddie's skin and she hugged her arms around her middle and turned toward the bed. The kid was bawling in earnest now, his eyes squinched shut and his tiny limbs thrashing in distress.

"Make him stop." Dwight ground the plea between his teeth.

Maddie's back stiffened at the taut request and he felt even lower than the scumbags he prosecuted. Without a word of protest or censure, she removed the yellow baby blanket and finished dressing Tyler.

She picked up the baby—rocked him, paced, soothed him with a gentle melody—and ignored Dwight.

He clenched his fists at his sides, squeezing hard until the muscles in his chest and arms shook with the effort. But he couldn't form his words around an apology. He couldn't get past the needy, helpless sounds that tore through his conscience. He couldn't ease the fever that still burned through every pore of his body. "Maddie—"

"Get out of my room." She picked up the bottle on the nightstand, speaking over her shoulder in his general direction without ever making eye contact. Tyler latched on to the nipple and sucked with a greedy satisfaction Dwight envied. "Sorry to be such a bother to you. I promise, next family crisis, we'll leave you alone."

"It's not that. It's me. I'm—"

"Rude? A tease?" She was looking at him now, glaring, advancing. "I don't have that much experience with men, Mr. Powers. For obvious reasons." Obvious? How? And what happened to *Dwight?* Not the point. "I'd appreciate it if you'd just stick to business, since that seems to be what you're so good at. I hate to admit it, but until Joe's caught, until Katie comes home, I need your help. I don't need to be confused by…whatever that was that didn't just happen between us." She nudged the door shut, forcing him out into the hallway. "Good night."

With the closed door staring him in the face, Dwight felt strangely, bitterly alone. *She* was confused? For years, his detachment from people had been his solace. He'd done without sex, without cuddling or bantering, without closeness—without company—and he'd survived. Barely.

Suddenly, he was craving every one of those things. But he shouldn't.

He didn't want to feel anything for Maddie McCallister. Not respect for her courage. Not this burning drive to argue his point until she understood him or he conceded to her. Not this unexpected hunger for her softness and fire and sweet, sweet smiles.

Kissing her would have been a mistake. Giving into that sort of physical need would have plunged him over a precipice he couldn't climb out of. Maddie came with a baby. She came with a family. She came with a threat that echoed all he had lost six years ago.

He couldn't deal with losing like that again.

Joe Rinaldi wasn't in the house. Dwight had overreacted because of his irrational fears and guilt. He'd hurt Maddie and frustrated himself in the process.

Still, he checked every window and door on his way down to the basement gym, where he pulled on his boxing gloves and took out his crazy, mixed-up cravings on the heavy bag. He could sweat the physical desire out of his system if he worked out long and hard enough.

He didn't even want to consider how he was going to get rid of these decidedly unbusiness-like emotions that wouldn't leave him alone.

THE PHONE WAS RINGING.

Not Dwight's line. Her phone. In her purse. Upstairs.

"Katie?"

Maddie dropped the stack of towels from the laundry onto the curving newel post at the bottom of the stairs and took off running.

"Katie!"

Pushing her legs up the stairs, two at a time, Maddie quickly turned the corner and dashed into her room. She grabbed her purse and headed into the hallway so she wouldn't wake Tyler.

"Don't hang up," she begged, digging through her purse. When she had the cell in her hand, she dropped her purse, verified the Out of Range source of the call and punched the talk button. "Hello?"

A beat of silence gave her a moment to replay the questions Detective Bellamy had instructed her to ask—condition, location, names, descriptions, time line…

"Where are you, Madeline?"

Maddie's breath stopped up in her throat. "Joe."

"I'm at the house and you're not here. Your bed doesn't even look like it's been slept in."

"You—you're inside my house?"

He paused long enough to let her imagine the things he was touching, violating. "I'm in your girly little bedroom. Too much lace and too many old things for my taste, but your bed's mighty comfy. You still sleeping alone in it?"

"That's none of your business."

"I'll take that as a yes."

Maddie paced before a defensive retort slipped out. She had to stay calm. Should she notify Detective Bellamy, who was parked in front of Dwight's house? Was the listening van picking up this call? The officer last night said it was important to keep him on the line for as long as possible in order to get a trace. "How did you get in?"

"A lock has never stopped me before." It hadn't kept

him away from Karen that last night. "I used the back door off the driveway. That's where all the family comes in, isn't it?"

All the family who was welcome there.

"What do you want?"

"I told you I was coming to see you."

Where were the cops who were watching her house? Why hadn't they tackled Joe and forced him to the ground the way they had Dwight?

Dwight.

Something lurched inside Maddie's chest. She wished he was here.

Last night's would-be savior seemed miles away at the courthouse in downtown Kansas City. An apparently compulsive need for punctuality had brought him downstairs early, shaved and polished and ready for a courtroom killing in his charcoal-gray suit and burgundy tie. Their conversation had consisted of "Thanks for the coffee" and a rundown of how the security system in his house worked.

Any mention of that almost-kiss last night had been conveniently ignored.

Or forgotten.

Maybe she was the only one still reeling from that close encounter of the awkward kind. She believed everything Dwight had ever said to her—about Katie, Tyler, Joe—but she couldn't trust that the desire she'd read in his eyes or the need she'd felt in his body had been for her.

Joe Rinaldi had once claimed a fascination with the size of her breasts and the extra contours of her figure. That had been a lie, pure and simple. She'd been a means to get to her sister.

Now he was using her to get to Tyler and Katie. She wouldn't allow it.

"The police are looking for you, Joe. The highway patrol. My house is one of the first places they'll look for you."

"You talking about that cop in the van outside?" His laugh grated across Maddie's nerves, leaving dread in its wake. "He won't be bothering you, me or anyone else for a while."

Oh, God. "What have you done?"

He didn't answer the question. Maybe she didn't want to know. She found herself standing outside Dwight's door the way she had last night, when she'd heard him cry out in his sleep.

Last night, she'd felt too unsure of herself to offer the comfort she'd longed to give him. He'd been in such pain. Then something crashed to the floor and she'd jumped back, remembering the violence Joe had brought into her life. Tyler had cried and her decision was made. She'd retreated to her room, suspecting she might not be what Dwight needed in the middle of the night but knowing she was everything Tyler needed.

This morning, however, she put aside any shy hesitation and opened Dwight's door. There. On the table beside the bed. A telephone. She could dial Cooper Bellamy's number and let him know she was on the phone with Joe right now. That he was in her house. And that the cop outside was... *Please don't let him be dead.*

"I didn't know you kept a picture of Karen on your dresser." The affection in Joe's voice sickened her more than his obvious threats. Maddie startled at the sound of glass smashing against wood. "You don't mind if I keep it as a souvenir, do you? I didn't get to attend her funeral, you know. As I recall, you filed a complaint that got me arrested that very same day. That's pretty heartless, don't you think?"

More heartless than stabbing your own wife dozens of times to keep her from leaving you?

Maddie perched on the edge of Dwight's bed, feeling weak at the sounds of Joe trashing his way through her house. She experienced an odd sense of comfort at the firmness of the mattress and the way it refused to give beneath her weight. Not too unlike the man who slept here. Solid. Unyielding. She needed to summon that kind of strength.

"I'm in my grandson's room now. I'm sure he's a fine boy. He needs a man to raise him, you know. Where is he, Madeline? I want to see him." She heard furniture breaking. The heirloom rocker? More glass shattered beneath his hands. "Do you hear me?"

"Joe, please."

But no, those were just things. Things could be replaced. People couldn't. She had to put Joe back in prison before he hurt anyone else. Keeping him on the line until she could notify the police was a start, even though it meant listening to him destroy precious memories and hard work.

"Joe, please," he mimicked. "Where's my grandson?" he bellowed.

Under the sound of the next crash, Maddie lifted the cordless receiver off Dwight's phone and dialed Cooper's cell.

Please answer. She mouthed the request and prayed that Joe was working himself up into such a rage that he wouldn't hear the detective pick up on the other line.

"Detective Bellamy." His easy, friendly voice was a marked contrast to the vile things she was listening to.

"It's Maddie," she whispered.

"I can barely hear you," Cooper answered in a normal

tone that sounded way too loud under the circumstances. "Can you speak up?"

"Having a boy is the first thing Katie's ever gotten right. You can't keep him from me, you bitch!"

Even with her cellphone at arm's length, Cooper had no trouble hearing Joe's ranting. "Ms. McCallister? Are you all right?"

She could envision Cooper sitting bolt upright behind the wheel of his truck. The bald, young detective would be instantly on alert.

Maddie whispered into Dwight's receiver. "Joe Rinaldi is at my house. Right now. He may have done something to the cop inside the van."

Joe ranted on about taking a knife from her kitchen and knowing the best place to stick it if she didn't tell him what he wanted to hear.

Cooper swore. "He's saying that crap to you?"

"He says it to every woman."

"I'm going to hang up so I can get backup to your place ASAP." She heard his truck door open and close. "Can you unlock Mr. Powers's security grid so I can get into the house without tripping the alarms?"

"I thjnk so."

"Do it."

Maddie cringed as Joe shouted in her ear. "Who are you talking to, bitch?"

She stood. "The police are coming. They're already on their way."

"Ratted me out again, did ya?"

"Joe, you need help." She had to keep him on the line. Had to keep him at the house. "If you surrender yourself—"

"I ain't givin' up nothin'!" She could hear his heavy,

booted feet running down the stairs. "Don't think I'm done with you, Madeline. I will find you. I'll find my grandson."

"Joe!" An ominous click of silence echoed in her ear.

Maddie tucked her cellphone into the pocket of her jeans and ran downstairs to punch in the security code Dwight had given her. Seconds later, Cooper Bellamy charged in, still giving directions on his cell as she bolted the door behind him and reset the grid.

"He's running," she warned him. "He hung up. I couldn't keep him on the line."

Cooper flashed her an okay sign and reported in. "Our fugitive is on the run again. What's your ETA? Damn."

Damn didn't seem promising.

"Well, get someone there faster," Cooper ordered. "And notify Commissioner Cartwright's office. She wants to be briefed on any new developments." He rubbed the top of his head and grimaced. "No, I'm not brownnosing. I'm doing my job. Now go do yours."

He folded up his phone and clipped it onto his belt beside his badge. "A black-and-white is on the way."

"An ambulance, too?"

He nodded. "I couldn't raise anyone in the surveillance van, so I notified dispatch that we might have an officer down." He pointed to the phone in her pocket. "You'd better call Mr. Powers."

"Why?"

"Let him know what's goin' on. He worries about you."

Maddie scoffed. "Where'd you hear that?"

"Word's out about the way he rode to the rescue last night when the authorities announced Rinaldi's escape. Officer Jackson is still catching grief this morning over the way he tried to step between you and Powers. He won't make that mistake again."

Did the whole precinct think she and Dwight were an item? Couldn't they tell a driven man with a sense of duty from a man who truly cared for her? Last night she'd made a humiliating mistake by confusing the two. Men didn't fall in love with Maddie McCallister. They weren't her champion unless there was something else at stake besides her. The men she knew fell into three categories: casual acquaintances who barely noticed she was a woman, good buddies who didn't care whether or not she was a woman, and big mistakes like Joe Rinaldi who made her wish she'd never been born a woman.

There was no knight-in-shining-armor category. She wasn't anything more than an obligation to Dwight Powers—despite the gossip down at the Fourth Precinct.

"Dwight's in court. I can't interrupt him."

"I'm sure he won't mind if *you're* the one doing the interrupting."

She made a valiant effort to change the subject. "Shouldn't we get to my house, too? I want to see how much damage Joe's done. I can report anything that's been stolen. He said he was taking a picture of my sister. If he's taken a recent photograph of Katie, he could use it to find her. Maybe he left a clue, something that could help us track him."

"Us?" Cooper planted his feet in front of the door. "Mr. Powers would have my hide if I let you and the baby leave. He's the man who makes KCPD's cases stick. I don't want to get on his bad side. I promise I'll check out the house as soon as I get a replacement here."

"The sooner we move on this, the better, right? It's *my* home that's been violated. *My* family that's in danger."

"Ma'am, I—"

Maddie spun away and pulled out her phone to search for a number. "Roberta Hays, please."

As soon as she was connected to the DFS caseworker, Maddie headed up to Tyler's room, leaving the befuddled detective standing at the bottom of the stairs.

Roberta had already made arrangements to take Tyler to the doctor that afternoon for blood work and DNA tests. She'd said that the state would require the objectivity of a physician and lab of their choice in order to prove a familial relationship and grant legal custody. Leaving out any information about Tyler's grandfather escaping prison and demanding his grandson, Maddie explained that she had to check her house and report to the police about a break-in. Roberta agreed to let Maddie drop Tyler off early at the DFS office. "Thanks, Roberta. I'll be right there."

With Tyler's carrier hooked over one arm, Maddie descended the stairs and shoved the diaper bag into Cooper's arms.

"Are you going somewhere?" he asked, already suspecting the answer and not liking it.

"We're driving Tyler to the family services office downtown." She gestured to Cooper. "Under police escort." She opened the door and walked straight to his truck, then pulled the passenger seat forward to secure Tyler in the back. "The sooner we do something about Joe, the sooner I can quit jumping every time my phone rings and the sooner you can get back to finding Katie. She's the one in real danger, not me."

The detective locked the house and hurried after her. But when he climbed in behind the wheel across from Maddie, he just sat there. "I don't know that Mr. Powers sees it that way. I'm not going anywhere until you call him."

Maddie huffed in frustration and pulled out her phone. "Fine." The instant she heard Dwight's deep, authoritative voice, she started talking. "Dwight? It's Maddie. Joe Rinaldi…"

"…name and number and I'll get back to you as soon…"

Her impatience fizzled—or maybe that was disappointment kicking in—when she realized she couldn't talk to the man himself. When the recording ended, she left a simple message. "Hey, Dwight. It's Maddie. I heard from Joe again. Call me when you can."

She hung up and looked at Cooper. "Voice mail. Just as well. Shall we?"

Cooper reached across the seat to squeeze her hand, thinking she needed comfort. "Don't give Mr. Powers too much grief for being such a hardhead, ma'am. Since his first family was murdered, you can't blame him for being a little overprotective of the people he cares about."

"But he doesn't care…"

Murdered? Oh, damn. Maddie groaned as she remembered the news clippings from six years ago. She'd worried then about how he'd fare in a domestic-violence case. Could he prosecute the killer of another murdered wife without losing his cool? But Dwight Powers was all about cool in the courtroom. His coldhearted detachment had robbed Joe and his attorney of any emotional sway with the jury.

Katie had seen him as an unbeatable hero back then. And, to be honest, so had Maddie. Especially after Joe's threats on that last day of sentencing.

But the Dwight Powers she'd gotten to know over the past few days wasn't indestructible. He'd lost his wife and son, and had paid a heavy emotional price. She'd heard his nightmares. She'd witnessed his need. And his regret. What had Katie asked of him when she'd left him her child?

It was a miracle that he'd done anything at all to help her and Tyler. The baby, at least, must remind him of his own son. She made no claims to think she reminded him of his wife. "You're right, of course."

She blinked away fresh tears and looked down at Cooper's grasp. It was a perfectly nice hand. But it wasn't as strong, as rough, as seasoned by life as Dwight's.

It wasn't the hand she wanted to hold.

Chapter Six

Maddie knew that glare.

Thank goodness it was directed at Cooper Bellamy, not at her. Dwight ducked beneath the yellow crime-scene tape and made his way toward the detective and the crime-scene technicians speaking with him.

Before he spotted her, Maddie slipped into the gathering crowd of onlookers. She wasn't up for butting heads just yet, not with all the blood she'd seen inside the listening van and on the pavement outside still weighing on her conscience.

She averted her gaze from the gurney that the ME was loading onto her van. Inside the body bag lay the slain surveillance officer. Maddie only had to see the numerous defensive wounds and slit throat to know that Joe Rinaldi was responsible. She'd seen the wounds from one of his knife attacks before.

Forty-one of them, to be exact.

Maddie tucked a loose strand of hair back into her ponytail and hugged her arms around her waist. She ignored the bump of people as her neighbors and a small herd of reporters moved past her for a closer look at the macabre scene. The thermometer at a bank said it was ninety-eight degrees. The humidity had to be higher than that. The afternoon sun beat down on her skin, exposed by the sleeves of her T-shirt, but she was still riddled with ice-cold goosebumps.

"Where is she?" Dwight's tight-lipped question carried across the buzz of conversations and sent a shiver down her spine. "Whatever possessed you to bring Maddie here?"

"Have you ever tried to win an argument with her, sir?" Cooper Bellamy was outclassed if he thought he could bandy words with the master.

From the corner of her eye, Maddie saw Cooper's hands go up in placating surrender.

"Of course, you have. Look, it was either bring her with me or wait for her to sneak out of the house on her own. I did make sure she called you. She said you wouldn't want to be bothered in court, but I knew you'd want to hear about this."

Maddie almost smiled at Cooper's last-ditch effort to smooth things over with a man he truly respected—and was probably even a little intimidated by. She should go rescue him.

"You do realize she's in danger here." Dwight had a way of cutting through the niceties and the BS and getting straight to the point—no matter how painful it might be.

"There are at least twenty cops and state police here," Cooper argued. "Rinaldi's not going to get to her."

"Right. So you know where she is right now, huh?"

Yep, she really ought to go save Cooper.

Maybe later, when she didn't feel to blame for the death and destruction and distinctly unsettled feeling Joe had brought to the people around her. As neighbors and friends whispered about locking their doors, renewing gun permits and even moving, Maddie hunched her shoulders and stayed out of sight.

Maddie traded a sympathetic smile with one of her teenage neighbors, Trent Dixon. He paused and stood beside her to watch the ME van pull away. "Wow. Somebody murdered right on our street in the middle of the day. I thought that stuff only happened downtown."

Right. Just like spousal abuse only happened in low-income families—not between professionals like a university accountant and his wife. Joe had bucked the stereotype with that one, too.

The teacher inside Maddie responded to her young friend's shock. "Violence can happen anywhere—to anyone—if someone's determined enough. We're just not used to seeing it in our front yards. But the police are working very hard to find out who's responsible. Just think about how protected we'll be from here on."

Trent shrugged. "I guess. Some of the girls I hang out with at school won't even go out anymore. Or their folks won't let them date. First, Whitney Chiles leaves, then Katie disappears, and now this. They're afraid."

The mention of Whitney's name sparked a curious chord inside Maddie. She'd been Katie's friend since grade school, and the two had sung in choirs and participated in plays together. Whitney was one of the few peers Katie had trusted enough to talk about her father. "Say, Trent. Did you ever hear anything from Whitney before she transferred schools at the beginning of last semester?"

"She didn't transfer, Ms. McCallister. She quit because she got knocked up." His cheeks burned red with embarrassment. "Not by me."

Maddie pursed her lips together as pieces of the puzzle tried to connect themselves. *Pay it forward?* The line from Katie's good-bye note began to make a little more sense. If her friend had gotten pregnant, Katie might try to help her out somehow—like taking her shopping for maternity clothes or driving her to a doctor. But help in running away?

While Maddie made a mental note to locate a phone number for Whitney's parents to ask about their daughter, she dredged up a reassuring smile for the young man. "I didn't think you were responsible. I just didn't realize Whitney had been pregnant, too."

Relieved that any suspicion had been cast aside, Trent suddenly became very chatty. "Yeah. Her parents freaked. They had her all lined up to go to a performing-arts school in New York after graduation. From what I heard, Whitney went to live with her older sister or sister-in-law, something like that—I guess to keep the other kids from gossiping. I think her folks were gonna pull some strings to get the school to take her second semester—you know, after she got rid of the baby."

Got rid of? Oh, Lord. "You mean an abortion?"

"I don't know. I just heard that her parents didn't want her to keep it. Maybe she put her baby up for adoption."

Wait a minute. Maddie touched Trent's arm. Had she heard right? "Did you say Whitney went to stay with her sister?"

"That's what I heard."

Like Katie, Whitney was an only child.

Detective Bellamy's theory about an adoption clinic where young women checked in but rarely checked out was looking more and more like a dangerous possibility. But how would Katie and Whitney learn of such a place?

The chill of the grisly murder scene began to fade as the chance of getting one step closer to finding Katie filled her head. "One more thing, Trent."

"Yeah?"

"Have you or your brother, Jeff, gotten a new car recently?"

"No."

"Know anyone around here who has? Black or dark-gray. Just a plain old sedan. Big enough to have a V8 engine. Probably a little too big to be cool."

Trent grinned. "You mean like a grandma car?"

Or a murderer's. "I've seen one like that around the neighborhood over the past few days. I thought maybe someone had gone car shopping. Or that it belonged to one of the guys you hang out with?"

He shook his head. "Jeff and I keep a pretty tight eye on who's driving what. There's nothing new like that around here."

"Would you mind keeping an eye out for it? Your mom has my cell number. You can call me if you see it."

"Sure. You think it has something to do with Katie being gone?"

"Possibly."

A large hand clamped over her shoulder and Maddie cried out.

"So now there's a car watching the house and you didn't report it?"

Her fingers flew to her mouth as the volume of her startled yelp registered. Trent's eyes were wide with shock and half the crowd had turned her way. But Maddie recognized the timbre of the voice and the firmness of the grip. She shrugged off Dwight's hand and whirled around. "You need to work on your finesse a little bit, Mr. Powers."

"And you need to tone down the red hair if you don't want anyone to spot you." His coolly observant gaze darted from face to face in the crowd. "Where's the kid?"

After her conversation with Detective Bellamy earlier,

she had no doubt he was talking about Tyler. "With Roberta. He's safe."

He wrapped his hand around her upper arm and pulled her to his side. "Good, then let's do the same for you and get you out of here."

"You're not getting me out of here," she insisted, digging in her flip-flops as he dragged her along beside him. "I'm waiting for the crime-scene team to clear the house and then I'm going inside to see what kind of damage Joe did."

He lifted the yellow tape and pulled her inside the official circle with him. "*Your* message was frustratingly vague, but Bellamy provided a few more details. He said Rinaldi threatened you. That's reason enough to go back to my house, where you'll be safe."

"No."

"No?" With a slew of curious glances monitoring their progress, Dwight shifted directions and steered her toward the surveillance van, using the vehicle on one side and his superior stature on the other to hide her from prying eyes. "You should, at least, change your cell number so he can't harass you again."

"No!" Maddie shook her head, shook his hands off her and planted her feet. "Then Katie can't call me. Dammit, Dwight, I'm tired of hiding and waiting. I'm tired of not being able to do a damn thing to help except baby-sit, pray and wait for the phone to ring." She pointed to the blood-stained concrete at the rear of the van. "A man is dead. Katie might be next if we don't find her in time."

She frowned at the immovable force of his chest, made even broader by the tailored seams of his suit jacket stretching to accommodate his flexed arms and beefy hands propped at his waist. She lifted her gaze, pleading to those storm-cloud eyes for understanding. "I don't care what Joe's done in there. I can handle it. I *need* to handle it. If there's something missing I can point out to the police or something that doesn't belong, then I'm the only one who'd know it. If I can do anything to help, I have to."

His chest and shoulders heaved in a massive sigh that stirred the air between them. "You done?"

Was he angry? Conceding? Even listening?

"I'm not leaving until I check the house," she asserted, though much more softly than a moment before.

To her surprise, Dwight reached out and brushed aside a copper lock that had fallen across her forehead. "At Rinaldi's trial, I had you pegged as this meek, mousy woman who needed a nudge to speak up for herself. But you've got grit, McCallister." He made a face that made her wonder whether or not that was a compliment. "Hell, I expected you to be a lot more cooperative than this."

Not a compliment.

"These aren't times for meek and mousy. Katie and Tyler need a strong advocate right now. And since I'm all they've got, *strong* is the way I have to be."

"No worries there." A compliment, after all. There was nothing flowery or profound in Dwight's words, but he talked about her strength as if he believed it to be a fact. Maddie finally felt a flicker of warmth deep inside, seeping outward to do battle with the chill that had surrounded her. "We'll stay," Dwight said, loosening his tie and unbuttoning his collar. "But I'm gonna be with you every step of the way."

An obstinate urge to grin tilted the corners of her mouth. "I was staying, anyway."

"You wish." She almost glimpsed a line softening beside his mouth.

But before anything resembling a smile could form, a gravelly voice intruded. "Dwight?"

Dwight stepped aside to greet a tall man wearing a CSI vest. He was built on the lean side, and his most noticeable feature was the scarred, blind eye behind the gold frames of his glasses. "Mac Taylor."

The two men shook hands like old friends. "What brings you out into the real world?" Mac asked.

"I prosecuted the murder conviction on Joe Rinaldi four years ago. I'd like to see him back where he belongs."

"That was one of my men the ME just took away. Believe me, I'll do everything I can to help." The blond CSI looked from Maddie to Dwight and back again. Though his good eye sparkled with curiosity, he kept his questions to himself. "I'm Mac Taylor, KCPD Crime Lab. You must be Ms. McCallister?"

Maddie nodded.

Like Dwight, Mac seemed to have a habit of getting straight down to business. "There are fingerprints all over inside. I'm guessing most of them are Rinaldi's. He didn't make much effort to hide his tracks."

"We already knew he was here," said Maddie. "What's to hide?"

Mac adjusted the strap of the camera hanging around his neck. "We're going to need a set of your prints—to eliminate any of the strays we found. If either of the men who helped him escape was here, as well, we might be able to track down an ID."

"My prints are already in the system." She curled her fingers into her palms and tapped them against her thighs. "Take your pick. I'm a teacher in the public-school system, a foster parent...and you guys took my prints from another crime scene."

The movement and conversations around her blurred as her thoughts skipped back in time. She'd known she was too late when she discovered Karen that awful morning. Still, she'd gotten down on her hands and knees and tried to resuscitate her sister's lifeless body. She'd smeared Joe's footprints in the blood and added her own fingerprints to the phone and doorknobs.

A hand, warm and unyielding, wrapped around the fist at her side, startling her back into the moment. Dwight. He stood beside her now, facing Mac. Holding her hand. Sharing some of his abundant strength. "Maddie's sister was Rinaldi's first victim." He didn't elaborate. "My prints will be in the house, too. Are we clear to go in and have a look around?"

Grateful that he'd refocused the conversation and her thoughts back to the task at hand, Maddie looked up to study the stern line of his jaw. She didn't understand how his terse assertiveness and mysterious moods could frustrate her one minute, then touch her heart and make her feel extraordinarily safe the next. She wondered if Dwight's personality was changing, or just her perception of it, as this search for a missing niece, an escaped murderer and lasting justice brought them closer together.

Mac's gaze flickered over their joined hands before he nodded. "The house is clear if you want to go in. Beyond the mess, if you notice anything that seems out of place, let us know, okay?"

"Hey, Mac." Cooper Bellamy had jumped down from the back of the van and circled around to join them. "The circuits in there are fried. Rinaldi really did a number on them." He thumbed over his shoulder, indicating the equipment in the van. "Whatever we had recorded may have been damaged, as well."

"We'll take a look at it, see what we can salvage," said Mac. "If there's anything in the house you want to double-check, Detective, now's the time."

"Thanks."

After Cooper trotted off to do his bidding, Mac switched his attention back to Dwight and Maddie. "I can tell you're anxious to get in there. You two go ahead. I'll catch up."

DWIGHT FELT AN UNEASINESS he couldn't quite put his finger on when Maddie pulled away and hurried up the porch steps behind Bellamy. She'd gotten that distant about-to-faint look when Mac mentioned fingerprints. As the color drained from her face, he'd obeyed the impulse to go to her before thinking of the consequences.

Before he realized how her cold hand would worry him. Before he admitted how the way her skin heated beneath his simplest touch fascinated him. He'd sensed her spirit reviving, her resolve getting stronger. He had to admire the unbeatable resiliency she possessed.

He'd seen the pictures of the crime scene she'd referred to, remembered the details vividly, since he'd used both photos and her eyewitness testimony to describe it to the jurors at Rinaldi's trial. If she remembered that scene half as well as he did, then she'd drifted to a very ugly place in her head.

He'd have to watch himself. He was starting to think like a man around her. No, that wasn't quite right. He was starting to feel things whenever Maddie was around. And *feeling* things for others had been his downfall once before. Because he'd felt too much, Arnie Sanchez had been able to manipulate him by attacking and destroying the things he cared about.

He could care about the investigation, care about Maddie as the victim of a crime. But he couldn't afford to care about *her.*

Dwight moved out to follow her, but Mac's hand on his arm stopped him. "It's bad, Dwight. Rinaldi is one angry SOB. If she's the sentimental type at all, it'll be pretty tough in there."

"Thanks for the heads-up. But Maddie's pretty tough herself." Where had that come from? First, he was holding hands, and now he was defending her? He just had to re-member that she was a package deal—that she came with a mad devotion to a teenage girl and her infant son—to douse any confusing emotions and stick to the business at hand. "Keep me posted on anything you find out."

"Will do."

Ten minutes later, Dwight was dealing with a whole new set of emotions. Namely anger. And, as his friend A.J. had reminded him three days ago, a driving need to ensure justice was served.

Maddie wasn't weak, but she was clearly the underdog in this crazy game of terror and vengeance Rinaldi was playing. There wasn't a stick of furniture in her quaint, old-fashioned home that hadn't been tossed or cut or broken. Sofa cushions had been shredded, their stuffing strewn from wall to wall. Her coffee and end tables were marred by the round, distinctive burns of a cigarette. Her dining room and kitchen tables had gouges where Rinaldi had carved deep, destructive lines with a knife. Glasses were broken. Walls had been punched through. Chairs were overturned. The fridge and pantry doors had been opened and emptied out. Raw egg stuck to the tile above the stove and sink, and thawing meat bled across the vinyl floor.

"Was he looking for something?" Cooper speculated out loud.

"The only thing I see missing are some family photographs," Maddie whispered, almost in a monotone, "and a few kitchen knives."

Cooper recorded the information. The detective made a gentle inquiry about insurance and suggested the name of a cleaning service. But even his cocky tone had gone flat, indicating that the devastation was getting to him, too.

Thank God Maddie hadn't been here or the KCPD might be investigating a double homicide. There were no written or recorded messages, but the hate was clear, the evidence of violence overwhelming and intimidating. It all felt very personal, very vindictive, very punishing.

Dwight inhaled deeply, squeezing his hands into fists to still the tremors pumping through his taut muscles. Walking through the destruction, he felt as if *his* territory had been violated. This shouldn't happen in his city, his jurisdiction. It shouldn't happen to this family, to this woman. He felt sick for her. He felt the need to do some damage to Rinaldi himself.

And all Maddie said was, "He must have been tearing up the place before he ever called me."

Dwight wasn't feeling quite so charitable. He made sure Cooper noted the home invasion in his report to MODOC and the commissioner, upgrading Rinaldi to an armed and extremely dangerous fugitive. And if he ever got that four-eyed freak in his courtroom again…

He forced aside his own thoughts of retribution as he followed Maddie up the stairs to inspect the second floor. Dammit, he was noticing details about her again. She was too stiff-backed. Too quiet. Even more so than she'd been on the witness stand four years ago. He couldn't tell if she was angry, saddened or in shock. She'd worried her copper hair free from its ponytail, and her revealing skin alternately colored and went pale as they moved from room to room. Rinaldi's handiwork was really getting to her, and *that* got to him.

But any suggestion of leaving was met with stony blue eyes and a pursed mouth that refused to either smile or speak.

The upstairs wasn't quite as bad, making him think Rinaldi had started downstairs and worked his way up here before he'd called Maddie and she'd managed to notify the police. The bathroom hadn't been touched. Katie's room seemed intact, except for an empty baby album Maddie reported missing.

He shut his eyes and tried to walk past the nursery, but Maddie's ragged words, "Mother's rocker," prompted him to look inside after she and Cooper had moved on. An antique walnut rocking chair had been mangled beyond repair, but everything else looked and smelled sweetly innocent. A pile of stuffed animals on the dresser reminded him of Braden's tiger. And a border of stenciled alphabet letters made him think of the loving care and design that Alicia had...

"Dwight!"

Maddie's strangled scream jerked him from the nightmarish trip down memory lane.

"Maddie?" Dwight ran down the hall to her bedroom. As soon as he cleared the doorway, she turned and launched herself against him.

"Oh, God, it's awful," she sobbed, sliding her arms beneath his jacket and burying her nose in his chest. "It's awful."

Surprised to feel her burrowing against him, Dwight was slow to wrap his arms around her shoulders. But his eyes scanned the bedroom with a ruthless intensity. It was a warm, homey room of antique lace and colorful embroidery, reminding him of the cool skin and fiery hair of the woman who slept here. But it was clean and tidy, except for the broken glass on the floor and dresser.

"What?" Cooper shrugged behind Maddie's back, equally perplexed by her volatile reaction. "There's just the broken picture frame. We saw worse downstairs. I don't get it."

Maddie shivered against him and linked her fingers behind his waist. "The flowers."

Dwight quickly pinpointed the bouquet of red roses in a vase on the stand beside the bed. Had she finally cracked from the pressure of keeping the understandable grief and horror inside? He patted her back in an awkward effort to provide support without giving away his own confusion. "What's so awful about the flowers?"

"You two have a fight?" Cooper asked.

Dwight glared the detective's curiosity into silence. "They're not from me."

"Oh."

A sob rubbed Maddie's body against his, stirring something male and protective inside him. Dwight slid his right arm down around her waist and tunneled the fingers of his left hand into her hair, pulling her tighter, more securely into his embrace. Though his guard never relaxed, something inside him shifted to a calmer, more focused place. Maybe this was what he'd needed to do all along to ease his own guilty tension. He needed to shoulder some of the burden of this senseless attack from her.

He massaged his fingers against her scalp. "C'mon, Red. You have to talk to me."

"They're from Joe."

Cooper walked over to the vase and looked around it without touching anything. "How do you know? There's no note."

"I just…know."

Dwight let his hands slide to her elbows as she pushed some space between them and nervously toyed with a button on his shirt.

"It's a message from Joe."

Despite her stalwart expression, Dwight could feel her shaking. "Get Mac Taylor back up here."

With a nod, the detective darted from the room. Maddie turned and stared at the roses as if she saw a man with a gun pointed to her head.

"Tell me," Dwight urged.

"Joe never sent Karen flowers—not as an apology, not for their anniversary or her birthday. Never." She swallowed hard. And when she started rubbing her arms for warmth, he came up behind her and took over the job himself. "He told Karen the only time he'd send her flowers was for funeral. The day before…" Her hand found his and squeezed. "He sent a dozen roses to the house. She was terrified. Without a single word, she knew it was a death threat. And then the next day, she was gone. He'd… There was so much blood. The same color as the roses."

Son of a bitch. Rinaldi had some seriously twisted ways of terrorizing the women in his life. Dwight folded his arms around Maddie and pulled her back against his chest. He dipped his head and heard his own growly voice whispering in her ear. "I've seen the pictures. He is not going to get to you like that, I promise."

"What if he gets to Katie instead? Or hurts someone else? What if the police never catch him?"

"One problem at a time, Red." He threw his jacket

around her shoulders and guided her to the door. "Will you let me take you home now? You'll be safer there and I can start making some calls, pulling in some favors, so we can get this bastard off the streets."

"We have to pick up Tyler first."

He must have made a sound or flinched—something to betray his unwitting reaction to the kid's name—because Maddie turned to block his path. Her eyes were dark with compassion, and the apology that crooked her mouth was as evident as the terror that had lined her face a moment ago. "It's okay. You don't have to go. I can do it myself. I remembered this morning about your wife and son. I'm so sorry if having Tyler around reminds you of them. If Joe trying to hurt us reminds you of…what happened."

"I'm not going to talk about that right now." Not when he needed to concentrate on piecing together the details of Rinaldi's plan and how he could best keep Maddie safe. He was still processing the aftershocks of holding her so tightly against him. He didn't need to deal with pity right now, too. He stepped forward, hoping she'd take the hint and get moving.

But she braced her hands against his chest and nudged him back a step. "I know Tyler's crying upset you last night. But he's two weeks old. He's gonna do that."

"Can we go now?"

Short of knocking her over in the narrow hall, he had to stop and listen. "I'll pick up Tyler on my own and meet you at your house. I still have to stop by the doctor's office and get blood drawn for the DNA tests anyway."

"No. Not by yourself."

"When I'm done with that, I can talk to Cooper about setting up guards around here—"

"No."

·"Or moving us to a safe house so we aren't such an imposition."

Dwight grabbed her by the lapels and let her know he wasn't budging on this. "You're not going anywhere or doing anything on your own. Not after what Rinaldi's done here. We'll put the kid in my car."

THE ELEPHANT WAS on her head again.

"Give her another dose."

"No!" The ground beneath her shook. Wait. It was a bed. She was lying in a hospital bed. "If you keep doping her up and giving her stimulants without any consideration for her weight or body chemistry, you'll risk brain damage. After that, even if she *wants* to talk to us, she might not remember anything. She's coming around on her own. Just be patient."

The scuffle beside Katie's bed ended and the familiar smell of halitosis burned through her brain, waking her to the muted darkness of her room without fully rousing her from the dreamy meanderings of her thoughts. Didn't they pay their electric bill in this place? Aunt Maddie was always so responsible about making sure the utilities were paid before anything else.

Her aunt might be a little challenged in the fashion department, but Katie had been working on her. She'd gotten her the golden highlights to soften her red hair. Introduced her to clothes that fit her full figure instead of hiding it. She'd learned all the practical, responsible, loyal things she knew from Maddie. In return, she'd taught her aunt a little about having fun and taking chances.

Oh, man, how she missed Maddie. An understanding smile. A big hug. A fierce protector. A true friend. Without ever giving birth, she was everything a mom should be. Everything Katie had hoped to become.

But that was before.

Something firm gripped her wrist and lifted it. "Her pulse is racing. I warned you to leave the doctoring to me."

"Blow it out your ear. It's your fault either one of them got out of here in the first place."

Katie's wrists were still bound, her bladder was full and the argument ensuing from either side of her blotted out fond thoughts of home. The tenderness in her breasts was finally subsiding, but the ache in her belly where Tyler used to be throbbed. Whether the pain was real or imagined, the emptiness inside her brought tears to her eyes.

"There. See? I told you she'd come around on her own."

Was that the midwife's voice? She'd been so kind during the delivery and had seen to all of Tyler's needs.

Katie reached out to that voice.

"Help me. Please." Her appeal sounded faint and scratchy to her own ears. Maybe no one had heard her.

Or the wrong person had.

Stinky Pete's lips brushed against her temple as he whispered, "No one's gonna help you, sweetheart, until you help us. Where's the boy?"

Thank God. They still hadn't found Tyler. Mr. Powers would keep him safe.

"Stand back, Morales." A new voice joined the nightmare. It was articulate in enunciation, gravelly in tone and no kinder than the others. "You. Get out of here."

It must be the voice of authority. The odors of garlic and sweat receded as the short, wiry man who answered to Morales moved away from the bed.

"Don't let him give her anything else," the woman's voice requested. "She's already too weak to put up any kind of fight, and I won't have another kid's death on my hands."

"Go," the authoritative voice repeated.

With a huffy sigh, the woman hurried out of the room, leaving Stinky Pete on Katie's left and the voice of authority standing at the foot of her bed. Between unfocused eyes and the dim light of the room, Katie couldn't make out the shape, age or even the gender of the figure silhouetted against the glare from the hallway. It could be a woman with a low-pitched voice or a man with a higher pitch. The only identifiable trait that got through her muddled brain was the odor of cigarette smoke wafting from the boss's clothes.

"Miss Rinaldi, you've cost me a great deal of money. I provide a needed service for women in your unfortunate situation. I can't allow the irresponsibility of one impulsive teenager to ruin my reputation or jeopardize that service. I have a client waiting for an infant boy. *Your* infant boy. Your little disappearing act has put me in an awkward position. It's all about good business, you see. The clients create a demand and I supply what they need. Their money reimburses me for my investment."

"Plus a nice profit," Morales emphasized.

The boss nodded. "That *is* what makes it good business. But I can't give them what they need or help anyone else in your position unless you cooperate with me."

There were too many words for her foggy comprehension to get around. The boss could go screw himself. She wasn't telling him what she'd done with Tyler. Katie rolled over onto her side and curled up into a ball.

"I thought that might be your reaction. Bring him in."

"Right, boss. Hey, Fitz!" Morales's voice receded, leaving her alone to give into the sleep that wanted to claim her.

"You see, Miss Rinaldi, you can either do the mature, responsible thing and tell me where your son is so that you fulfill the terms of your contract with us—" the boss paused long enough that Katie roused herself to pay attention to the threat in his voice "—or I'll be forced to resort to—how shall I say this?—less desirable tactics? There are other people besides yourself whose welfare you should consider."

What other people? Whitney had escaped. Tyler was safe. Her mother was dead. The only family she had left was Aunt Maddie, and Katie had made sure to keep her aunt in the dark so she couldn't be forced by the police or these lowlifes to tell them anything.

"What are you talking about?"

"He's here, boss."

"Invite him in."

Morales was back, along with his hulking buddy, Fitz. And someone else. She tried to focus on the tall, narrow silhouette in the doorway. When she finally did, she sank back into the pillow and prayed that the oblivion would suck her in again.

Katie didn't think her imprisonment could get any worse.

She was wrong.

"Hey there, Katie. Daddy's home."

Chapter Seven

"And I thought *I'd* had a bad day."

Maddie paused at the bottom of the basement steps and watched Dwight duke it out with a giant punching bag suspended from a steel beam in the ceiling. The bag was losing.

He bounced on the balls of his feet, swiped the perspiration from his face with the back of his dark red glove and spared her a glance. "What do you need?"

"Some company?"

His stormy gaze raked her from head to ankle, taking note of the oversized terry cloth robe she'd borrowed from him to cover her old nightgown so they wouldn't have any more misunderstandings if they should run into each other tonight. Dwight turned away, positioned his arms and punched the bag with an echo-absorbing thud that made her jump. "I don't do chitchat. Go back to bed."

"I can't sleep."

"You're safe here tonight. Rinaldi doesn't know your location. A black-and-white unit is parked out front. I've called in favors from detectives I know, so this house will be guarded 24/7." He breathed deeply, expanding his chest before the bag absorbed another volley of punches. "And for what it's worth, I've cleared my calendar for the week so I'll be around to keep an eye on things, as well."

He let loose a flurry of jabs and punches while he danced around the bag. Maddie flinched at the controlled violence, wondering at the fury of it even as she admired his strength and fluid coordination.

"Is that bag anyone in particular?" she asked, hearing her lame effort at a joke fall flat in the damp basement air.

Dwight stilled the swinging bag and glanced over his shoulder. "It's called boxing. I do it for exercise—" he adjusted the gray sweats he wore around his waist "—and stress release."

He rolled his neck to loosen some kinks, butted his knuckles together and resumed his methodical attack on the bag. Exercise, huh? More like *exorcise.*

Though she understood that he had dismissed her, Maddie shoved her hands deep into the pockets of the robe, where she'd tucked her cellphone and a tissue, and sat on the step to watch him work. It beat pacing the hallway upstairs or lying in bed, replaying the gruesome images from Karen's murder and imagining what torturous way Joe would carry out the threat promised by those roses.

Whatever demons Dwight was laying to rest through this late-night workout, Maddie felt an unexpected release herself. It was more than a distraction from her troubled thoughts, though; it was a glimpse into a kindred spirit— another soul who had seen far too much ugliness in his life. Maddie doted on her family. She had her teaching and music to help her cope. Dwight had his courtroom—and this subterranean hideaway to pummel away the loneliness and guilt.

This choreographed workout explained the sturdy boxer's body beneath the suit and tie. The man had a little silver on top and some distinct lines beside his eyes and mouth that gave him an air of intellect and authority. But the strength and power of his shoulders and torso added a quality of danger that left Maddie battling with the instinct to keep her distance and the foolhardy urge to walk right up to him and be cradled against that chest.

Like this afternoon. And last night.

It had been ages since a man had held her. And none of those rare embraces had suffused her with the raw energy Dwight possessed. Dwight was definitely a man of contrasts. Tailored suits and bun-hugging sweatpants. Icy detachment and turbulent emotions. He wasn't her protector by choice, but he'd gone out of his way to keep her safe.

Dwight Powers was a man she could truly be afraid of, and yet she wasn't. With every punch that landed on the bag, she became more certain that he would never hurt her. Or Tyler. Even if he couldn't bring himself to say the kid's name or touch him, he would never intentionally do anything to harm Tyler—or allow him to be harmed.

"Where did you learn to box?" she asked.

"You don't give up, do you?" Though he was shaking his head, he never varied his rhythm. "Mean streets of Chicago. The U.S. Army fine-tuned my skills."

"You're not from Kansas City?"

"No. Went to law school at Mizzou after my ROTC stint. Met my wife and moved to K.C. after graduation. Alicia was from here…." The workout came to an abrupt halt. Dwight grabbed the bag and stilled its rocking.

Maddie suspected his ragged breathing had as much to do with the deeply grooved frown that tightened his expression as it did with the fast-paced workout. She gripped the wall for balance and slowly rose to her feet.

"I'm sorry. It's a shyness thing. I run on at the mouth when I get nervous and don't know what to say. Sometimes I think it's easier to keep talking than to get lost in the silence. But I didn't mean to bring up a painful topic. I'm sorry."

While she rambled on, he stripped off his gloves, reached for one of the white towels and turned to face her. "Get lost in the silence?"

She watched him blot the perspiration on his face and chest before rolling the towel and looping it around his neck. As his breathing evened out, hers seemed to catch and stutter. "Yes. Usually all these thoughts are spinning around inside my head. Worries, concerns—trying to figure out the right thing to say or do, wondering how others will react to what I say or do. Shy people can be quiet on the outside, but usually it's pretty noisy in here. You can get lost inside your head with all that going on. Of course, I don't seem to be having that problem tonight."

He opened a bottle of water and drained half of it before taking a breath. Maddie tried to look away but couldn't help being fascinated by the muscles working up and down his throat as he swallowed. "Do I make you nervous?"

Her gaze settled on two beads of condensation that trickled along his hand and forearm. Her skin seemed to catch fire and make the cozy robe seem unbearably warm. Oh, yeah. Definitely nervous.

Dwight had held her out of comfort this afternoon. He'd held her last night because he hadn't been thinking straight after that nightmare.

She was the only one who kept forgetting that this unlikely alliance was for practical purposes. Not for any sense of attraction or compassion or... She closed her eyes. *Stop thinking. Stop thinking.* She opened them, vowing to keep her hormones in check. "I'm on edge about a lot of things lately."

"That's understandable." He tossed the empty bottle into the trash and moved toward the stairs. "You get the kid to sleep?"

"Yes." Maddie instinctively moved up a step as he approached. "I suppose we should do the same."

"I suppose." He stopped at the base of the stairs.

Standing two steps above him, she was only slightly taller. But his shoulders seemed to fill the stairwell, nearly side to side. She inhaled the essences of heat and soap rising off his skin.

His gaze hooded and dropped to her mouth. "What are you doing to me, Red?"

"I'm not doing…anything." Her heart thudded in her chest. What was *he* doing? She'd come downstairs to find someone to talk to, a place to feel safe. But *safe* wasn't exactly what those gray-green eyes were promising her right now. "I haven't seen any pictures around the house. What was your wife—Alicia—like?"

Maddie retreated a step.

Dwight followed.

"Smart. Gorgeous. Exotic."

And she thought plump and pale could compete with a memory like that? Maddie tucked a brassy lock behind her ear. She must be misreading his intentions. Wishful thinking.

She moved up a step. "I'm not anything like her."

"No. You're not."

The closer he came, the more she rambled. "You know, I have to take umbrage with that. The smart part, I mean. I have two college degrees. I read almost anything I can get my hands on. I work with teenagers and they keep me current on the latest technology. *Umbrage.* That's a funny word, don't you think?"

Her back hit the doorjamb at the top of the stairs, trapping her. His strong, craggy face kept coming toward her. His lips moved in a growly whisper. "Shut up."

Maddie braced a hand against his chest, tangling her fingers in damp terry cloth and crisp gold-and-silver hair. "That's pretty damn rude, even for you."

But his smile took away the offense. At least, she thought that was what the dimpling crease beside his mouth meant. "Sometimes silence is okay."

When Dwight pressed his lips to hers, Maddie caught a startled breath. Then she couldn't seem to exhale. His mouth was warm, firm. The tip of his tongue was as cold as the water he'd drunk a moment ago. He brushed it across the seam of her lips and urged her to open for him. She did.

Dwight was kissing her. *Her.* Maddie McCallister. Hair too red. Hips too full. Shy English schoolmarm who'd needed a teenage niece to move in with her to learn how to dress halfway pretty, halfway sexy, halfway...

His tongue slipped inside her mouth and Maddie gasped in startled delight. There was nothing halfway about her pulse hammering in her ears or the delicious tingle that teased the tips of her breasts and made them heavy with want. Instead of pushing him away, her fingers clutched at his slick skin and dug into the muscles beneath. He tunneled his fingers into her hair, angling her mouth to deepen the kiss. His palm rested against the side of her neck, caressing the pulse point and igniting a flame that bloomed along the surface of her skin and spread into her limbs, her toes, the very heart of her.

Last night, he'd wanted to kiss her. She'd wanted him to. But the baby had cried and he held back. The rejection had hurt and she'd pushed him away. Nothing was stopping him now. Nothing was stopping her.

Thoughts of toxic roses and missing loved ones and senseless deaths went silent for a few moments as her head filled with the scent of his skin, the taste of his lips, the heady knowledge of all that strength channeled into this gentle burst of passion.

The sound of the William Tell overture playing in her pocket.

"Damn." Dwight cursed, shocking Maddie back to her senses. The phone.

"Umm…" Eloquent. She wasn't used to functioning in the aftermath of a steamy kiss.

Dwight's blunt fingers brushed across her sensitized lips as he pulled away. She was half a beat slower to release her death grip on his shoulders, and when she reached into her pocket, his hand was already there.

"Hey!" But he was already taking the last step into the kitchen. Maddie hustled after him. She snatched at his arm but came away with nothing. "Give me that."

He read the Unknown Caller ID. "It might be Rinaldi."

"It might be Katie."

"It's after frickin' midnight, Maddie. *I* will answer it." He punched the talk button, his face a grim mask. "Yes?" His brow furrowed. Maddie clutched the robe together at her neck, feeling the fire of Dwight's kiss quickly abandoning her. "Who is this?"

"Can I answer my own phone?"

"Dwight Powers." Maddie stood in front of him, studying every flicker of expression on his face. His jaw tightened like a fist and he swore.

"What?"

He scrubbed his palm across his beard stubble and

turned away. Oh, that was *so* not a good sign. "You're sure?"

Her chill seemed to be catching. She lay a hand on his forearm and he shivered. "Dwight?"

"I'll tell her." He glanced down at her fingers, maybe evaluating the difference between her tentative touch now and her needy grab a few moments ago on the stairs. "Yeah, we'll be there."

The instant he disconnected, she asked. "Tell me what?"

He handed her the phone. "That was the medical examiner, Holly Masterson."

"Is it about the police officer Joe killed?"

As always, Dwight made no effort to sugarcoat the truth. "She's got a Jane Doe she'd like you to take a look at to see if you can identify her."

Oh, no. Please, God, no. Maddie backed away until her hips bumped the counter and she had nowhere else to go. The intense focus of those gray-green eyes locked on to hers was the only thing keeping her standing.

She didn't want to ask. She didn't want to know the answer. "Why call me?"

"It's the body of a teenage girl."

COOPER BELLAMY MADE the funkiest damn baby-sitter Dwight had ever seen. The kid had more hair than he did. But with a Glock on his belt and a burp rag over his shoulder, the detective had finally given Maddie enough reassurance that they could leave and get this hellish task over with.

Dwight steered his Mercedes through rush hour traffic to the southern edge of the city, where the main crime lab was located. The sun had come up with an unforgiving intensity, turning the pavement hot and raising chimeras of heat that reminded him of kissing Maddie.

He didn't regret a second of that kiss, though he knew he damn well should. She'd looked so vulnerable, sitting there on the steps, drowning in his robe, her blue eyes luminous with fatigue and worry. The same blue eyes that, moments later, had darkened with interest as he put his old body through its paces.

She'd asked about Alicia and he'd been stunned to hear himself answer without thinking—without filtering his words and memories through a sharp grip of pain. His therapist would have called it a breakthrough moment, but he'd just felt lighter—as if a bit of the weight that burdened his heart had been lifted.

For the first time, he'd been able to think about their marriage in the past tense. Without missing her. He treasured what they'd had, remembered how he'd loved her, still knew he was responsible for her death.

But he'd been able to set the memories aside and keep himself in the moment. He'd imagined Maddie's lush body, hidden beneath the folds of his robe, and felt something stirring in his blood. He'd savored her spicy orange scent that clung to the soft terry cloth. He'd listened to her husky voice and knew he wasn't cooling down the way he should after a workout.

He'd tested his theory about moving on by kissing her. He hadn't batted one eye at how she'd opened for him, clutched at him, responded to him. He hadn't felt such a rush—in his veins, in his head, in his groin—for ages. God, he was out of practice. He'd cornered a woman on the stairs in his basement and told her to shut up. Even with Alicia, he hadn't been much of a romantic, but that had seriously lacked in style.

But it hadn't lacked in passion. Kissing Maddie had been the truest connection he'd had with a woman since Alicia.

If the phone hadn't interrupted them, he might have picked her up, carried her to the sofa or his bed and tested his theory in a way that would probably shock the good Ms. McCallister.

But the phone *had* rung. And despite the frissons of lust still thrumming through his body, this morning, *she* was a different person. As he drove, he glanced across the seat at Maddie. She'd pulled that glorious hair back into a tight no-nonsense bun. And the soft skin that had fired beneath his touch last night looked chilled and pale, except for the light dusting of makeup she wore.

This morning, Maddie McCallister was back to stoic and subdued, the way she'd been four years ago at the trial—as if keeping her fears and doubts and questions locked inside was the only way to prevent her strength and perseverance from rushing out along with them. Though he'd complained about her incessant need to argue a point, he liked the chattier version of her better than this. Even when she was rambling on, jumping from one topic to the next, at least he knew what she was thinking. At least—like she'd said last night—he couldn't get lost in the silence, worrying about her.

As he pulled into the parking lot outside the lab, he tried to prep her for what to expect. "A couple of homicide detectives are going to meet us first. A. J. Rodriguez—you met him at the precinct—and his partner, Josh Taylor."

"Can't I just see if it's her and go?"

"You'll have to check in, get a visitor's pass. The ME will meet you and give you a little speech."

Maddie angled her gaze toward him. "You've done this before?"

Oh, damn, this was tricky. Dwight managed to park the car and kill the engine before the haunting images overwhelmed him. The long metal tables, shiny with their sterile cleanliness, cold to the touch. The crisp, white sheets. The tags on the bodies to match the label on the doors and the paperwork.

The neat bullet hole in Alicia's temple.

The gray bruises on Braden's round, sleeping face.

Dwight's breath caught in his chest. He ached as if he'd taken a blow straight to the sternum.

He hadn't forgotten one harsh detail.

"Dwight." A cool, gentle hand curled around his fist on the seat beside him. "Your wife and son?"

He nodded.

"You don't have to go in with me. The memories must be horrible for you."

He reversed the grip of their hands and clutched hers tightly within his. He selfishly absorbed the comfort she gave him but wanted her to know everything he hadn't been prepared for. "It'll be a shock. Make sure you know where the bathroom is before you talk to Holly. There'll be some paperwork—I'll help you with that—and probably some more questions afterward."

"Maybe it will give me a sense of closure to finally see Katie again. To know."

Dwight shook his head and climbed out of the car, denying himself the contact with her, putting space between them before he roared something terrifying. Like there was no closure when a loved one was murdered. Like seeing her dead body was only the beginning of the nightmare. Like putting away the bastard responsible for the murder appeased only your sense of justice. It didn't assuage the guilt that you might be partly responsible. It didn't mend the hole in your heart or piece together the shreds of your soul.

Sure, you could function in the world, you could do

your job, you could learn to lust after someone new. But you couldn't… *He* couldn't…

"Dwight?" He started when he felt her hands on him again. Twin medallions of soft heat at the middle of his chest. He blinked his eyes open and looked down into a sea of deep, shadowy blue. "You wait out here. Or with your detective friends inside. I can do this on my own. I'm the one who has to make the ID, anyway. I won't let Katie down."

If she hadn't tried to smile, he might have been low enough to let her go into the morgue without him. But her soft lips curled, trembled, failed. He touched his fingers to the tremulous pout of bravely checked emotions, silently called himself every name in the book for not having the guts this woman had, then grabbed her hand and led her inside.

A. J. RODRIGUEZ had taken Dwight aside while Maddie signed the registry and got her visitor's pass. "Hoped I'd never have to see you in this place again, amigo."

A.J.'s partner, even bigger and taller than Dwight, had introduced himself as Josh Taylor. He'd expressed his condolences about her missing niece, then joined the conversation with Dwight and A.J. while the ME, Dr. Holly Masterson, came out of her office to explain the procedure to Maddie.

Though shaded by his personal grief, Dwight had already given her a pretty good idea of the identification process. So while she appreciated Holly's business-like demeanor and the kindness in her hazel eyes, Maddie turned her ear to pick up snippets of the conversation between Dwight and the detectives.

"Found her in an alley in No-Man's-Land, though Holly says the body had been moved from the original crime scene."

"Probably a drug overdose. Though whether accidental or intentional, self-inflicted or…"

Maddie could answer that one. Katie didn't do drugs. And she wouldn't take her own life. That left *intentional*. That left murder.

"Ready?" Holly asked.

Maddie nodded. Her knees quavered like gelatin and her stomach sat like a rock inside her. But she could do this. She had to do this. For Katie.

Holly looked over her shoulder to Dwight. "You coming?"

Seeing the stark, unblinking pain in those gray-green eyes, Maddie knew she couldn't force him to relive a nightmare.

"It's okay," she assured him, then turned to follow Holly's white lab coat down the hallway through a set of swinging and glass-and-stainless-steel doors.

When they reached the proper square of stainless steel that looked like a refrigerator door, Holly hesitated. She rested one surgically gloved hand on Maddie's arm. "Remember. All you have to do is look at the face and tell me if you recognize her or not. It won't take long."

Maddie nodded. "I'm ready. Wait." She wasn't. "There will be a face, right?" Panic welled in her throat. Tears burned in her eyes. "When I found my sister," Maddie said, splaying her fingers and touching her cheeks where some of Karen's wounds had been, "part of her face was…" She couldn't say it.

Could she survive looking at Joe Rinaldi's handiwork again?

"Ms. McCallister." Dr. Holly Masterson's voice remained very calm, but Maddie could hardly hear her from the panic roaring in her ears. "This girl wasn't stabbed."

"But he sent the roses."

"What roses?"

A warm suit coat draped over Maddie's shoulders. A sturdy arm curled around her. Long, blunt-tipped fingers laced with her own. And a familiar, growly voice gave the command. "It's a complicated story, Doc. Let's do this."

Having Dwight beside her to lean on short-circuited her panic. His warmth surrounded her and gave her strength. Feeling the tight clutch of his hand reminded her of what supporting her must be costing him.

She tilted her face to his. "You don't have to be here."

"Yeah, I do." He pressed a kiss to her forehead, then nodded to Holly. "Do it."

Maddie nodded her consent, then stepped back as Holly opened the door and slid out a long, narrow gurney. Squeezing Dwight's hand between both of her own, Maddie held her breath and prayed.

With care and respect, Holly folded back the sheet, exposing the teenage girl's body down to her shoulders. "Is this your niece?"

Her hair was dark, her face pale and unblemished. "Oh, my God."

"Is this Katie Rinaldi?" Holly clarified.

"No." The stiff anticipation in Dwight's body eased on a deep breath. But Maddie wasn't so quick to relax. She raised her gaze to Holly's hazel eyes. "It's Katie's friend, Whitney Chiles."

AT FIFTY, SHAUNA CARTWRIGHT was not only one of the youngest acting commissioners in the KCPD's history; she also had to be the prettiest.

Not that Dwight was paying that kind of attention to the authoritative blonde in the navy-blue suit. His focus was on the curvy redhead in blue jeans, pacing at the back of the Fourth Precinct's conference room, stopping with each pass to check the sleeping baby in the carrier on the counter.

A paranoid sense of responsibility, of doom lurking just around the corner, made him reluctant to let Maddie out of his sight. He'd buried one woman already, had seen another life snuffed out far too soon today. He wasn't sure he had it in him to bury anybody else.

At Commissioner Cartwright's request, a veritable brain trust of sorts had gathered to discuss what now seemed to be several converging cases. She wanted to compare notes and plan a strategy for moving forward in a direct, organized assault to uncover and close down what she'd dubbed the "Baby Factory."

Detectives from homicide and the SVU, as well as Dr. Holly Masterson and Mac Taylor from the Crime Lab, were there. Plus one surly assistant district attorney and a frantic aunt who was ready to tear Kansas City apart, building by building. All in order to find the niece Maddie loved like a daughter before she wound up on a slab in the morgue like her unfortunate friend.

The precinct had brought in sandwiches and coffee to keep them going through dinner, but Maddie hadn't eaten a thing. She'd answered official questions at the morgue, dug a card out of her purse with the number for Whitney's parents so they could be notified. She verified that she'd never known Whitney to take any of the lethal combination of drugs that had been found in her system—and that fists and knives were Joe Rinaldi's stock in trade, so he was an unlikely suspect in the girl's murder.

They'd climbed into the front seat of his car before she said anything about what she was feeling. "Thank God it wasn't Katie." She'd pressed her fingers to her lips to hold back the tears he heard in her voice. "I feel like a horrible person for saying that. Someone else has lost a child they love. But I'm so glad it wasn't me." Her eyes glittered like sapphires as moisture gathered there. "That means there's a chance Katie is still alive."

"You're not a horrible person," Dwight whispered. "We'll find her." He was beginning to think that hope was a real thing and that more than fools believed in it. In the presence of Maddie's determined faith, he might even consider believing in hope himself one day.

"Thank you for being there with me. I know it wasn't easy." When she made a hesitant move toward him, Dwight reached across the seat and pulled her into his arms. He freed her hair from its spinsterish bun and buried his nose and fingers in the free-falling waves. He held her tight, finding more healing comfort for his own wounds than he was sure he had to offer her.

"So we're ruling this a homicide?" Commissioner Cartwright plucked her reading glasses off the bridge of her nose and directed the question to Mac and Holly.

Dwight brushed at the lapels of his jacket. Even now, the tan cotton carried Maddie's spicy citrus scent. That constant hint of her stirred his blood, made him edgy to do something, solve something, make something right for her.

The best place to start would be to pay attention to the details of the conversation.

Mac opened his copy of the report the commissioner had been reading. "The blood we found in Dwight's office belongs to Whitney Chiles. We found trace levels of a sedative in those samples but nothing matching the toxic amount or combination that caused her death. There's no evidence to suggest she was a user, and the drugs that were in her system were hospital meds—they're hard to find on the streets."

Shauna Cartwright jotted a note. "That fits the clinic theory. We need to track down whether any hospitals or doctors' offices are missing supplies."

"Already on it," Mac assured her.

Maddie stopped her pacing. "That wasn't Katie's blood on Tyler's things?"

Dwight could tell by the blush on her skin and her thoughtful pout that she didn't know whether to be relieved that Katie wasn't hurt or worried that they no longer had any clear indication of where her niece might have been.

"Are you saying that Whitney left Tyler in Dwight's office?" Maddie joined the others at the two front tables. "But the note was in Katie's handwriting."

Mac offered an explanation that Dwight was curious to hear, as well. "All we know is that Whitney bled in his office. Katie could have been right there beside her."

"Maybe that's why Katie didn't stick around. If her friend was injured, she'd try to help her." Maddie circled the group, winding up behind Dwight's chair. "When she ran away, she said she had something she needed to do. That I'd helped her and she wanted to help someone else in return. Like that movie."

"That motivation fits a teen's psyche," Shauna agreed. "So you're suggesting an escape attempt from this clinic. The girls deposit the baby someplace safe, then try to get help for the one who's injured."

"A classmate of Katie's—a boy who lives across the street from me—said that Whitney had been pregnant, too."

Holly Masterson chimed in. "Whitney's body indicates a healthy delivery. But there are no signs that she'd been breast-feeding or even that her milk had come in. It's not conclusive, but it doesn't look as if she'd been taking care of her own child."

"How could she if she was stoned?" Bellamy asked.

"She wasn't taking those drugs by choice," Maddie argued. "Whitney wanted to go to New York to pursue a career in music theater. She sang and danced. She took good care of her body."

Dwight began to see a pattern forming. "It makes sense that she'd want to give the baby up for adoption if she was about to launch a career in a new city."

"Where were her parents through all this?" Josh Taylor asked.

"Busy hiding news of her pregnancy and creating a cover story from the sound of things," answered Bellamy. "They didn't even report her missing for two weeks because they'd bought her a train ticket to Phoenix to attend a special boarding school for unwed mothers. It wasn't until the school called to find out if they'd gotten the arrival date wrong that they suspected she'd probably never left K.C."

"How awful." Maddie hugged her arms around her waist and frowned. "I can't imagine sending a child away when she needed her parents most."

A.J. agreed. "That kind of desperation would make her easy pickings for the Baby Factory to approach her. Having a nest egg to live off until she got her big break would make life on the Great White Way a lot easier."

"Are we sure this is an adoption-ring murder?" Though it was in Dwight's nature to play devil's advocate, he found himself hoping it wasn't true. He didn't want Maddie to have another reason to visit the morgue. "Maybe this is an old-fashioned relationship-gone-bad issue and there's no bigger conspiracy. Do we know anything about the father of Whitney's baby?"

Bellamy nodded. "The parents aren't sure of the father

but said Whitney had gotten involved with a theater producer who was conducting a talent search in the Kansas City area. Maybe he got her on the casting couch and got her pregnant."

Forget the stomach-churning idea of statutory rape; they were looking for a murderer now. "Do we have a name for this guy?" Dwight asked.

"According to her mom and dad, Whitney only referred to him as Roddy. He was with a company out of New York. We don't even know if he's still in the area."

Shauna checked off something in her notes. "Find out. The Chileses sound like stage parents. If they don't know the name, I'll bet they know the company and the audition site—things we can track to find Roddy."

A.J. nodded. "Got it."

Commissioner Cartwright folded up her glasses and closed her notebook. "I wish I could get somebody on the inside and set up a sting. Catch these bastards in the act of trading lives and selling babies."

Detective Bellamy laughed. "I don't think we have anyone on the force who's pregnant and can pass for a teenager."

"What about infiltrating the ring from the other direction?" Dwight suggested, pointing out the one facet of the investigation they hadn't discussed.

Maddie caught on quickly. One hand that had rested on the back of his chair settled on his shoulder. "Get two people to masquerade as a wealthy couple, eager to adopt. Desperate to find a baby."

A.J. glanced at his partner, Josh. "We can work on Zero. Get a name on where he heard about this clinic. As we get closer to the source, he could start dropping hints about our couple looking for a baby to adopt. Zero could use a few brownie points with the department."

"I'll work the boyfriend angle with the Chileses," Bellamy volunteered. "See if we can find this mysterious Roddy."

"Now all we need is a well-to-do couple."

"You look the part, ma'am," Bellamy suggested.

The commissioner laughed. "My name and face have been in the paper too much recently, with the Baby Jane Doe funeral and task force. Until the department solves that murder, I'm too hot a topic. I'm afraid my days of undercover work are behind me. Besides, I don't believe I could convince my ex to play along."

Everyone's gaze gradually settled on Dwight and Maddie and the familiar way her hand rested on his shoulder.

Dwight rose to his feet, quickly putting the kibosh on what they were thinking. "Maddie's a civilian. You're not putting her in the middle of any undercover op."

"Technically, you're a civilian, too, counselor," Shauna pointed out.

A.J. defended him. "Dwight's one of us. He can handle himself, think on his feet. He keeps a nice behind-the-scenes profile, so he's not a recognizable face. I could give him a few pointers on undercover work."

Ignoring the fact that he was the last man in the world who could convince anyone that he wanted to adopt a baby, Dwight pointed out one very dangerous sidebar that they'd all overlooked. "What about Joe Rinaldi?"

The commissioner topped off a chorus of curses and scoffs about the bastard they suspected had killed one of their own. "Let's get that man on death row, where he belongs."

Her efficient tough-lady image softened with a thoughtful pause. She tapped the earpiece of her reading glasses between her lips as she studied Dwight.

"I'm pretty sure I don't like that look." He splayed his hands at his waist and subtly positioned himself to shield Maddie from both view and consideration.

"I think I might just have an ingenious way to keep your girlfriend safe."

Dwight didn't know if he was more stunned to hear Maddie referred to as his girlfriend or worried about what danger *ingenious* might entail.

Chapter Eight

"I need something nice for court tomorrow," Maddie insisted, shivering as the car's air-conditioning hit her damp skin.

They'd stayed at their meeting long enough for the sun to drop low on the horizon and disappear behind a squall line the same gray-green color as Dwight's eyes. She shook the rain from the jacket Dwight had held over her while she'd buckled Tyler into his car seat and draped it on the headrest behind him.

Dwight might have thought the discussion ended the moment the storm hit, but Maddie still had a point to make. "I can't go in front of the judge looking like this."

"You'll dry out." Dwight turned on the headlights and windshield wipers and pulled out of the Fourth Precinct's parking lot. He headed past the block-sized city park that had been recently landscaped just south of the new Federal Court Building. The gleaming glass, steel and concrete of the semicircular high-rise seemed as cold and foreboding in the eerie green cast of the storm as the man sitting beside her.

"You know that's not what I mean." Lightning over the river just a few blocks away charged the air and pricked goosebumps all along her arms.

Dwight adjusted the temperature to defrost the windows

and warm the Mercedes's gray interior. "I think we just need to get home right now, don't you? Maybe after the storm passes, we can drive over."

It wasn't much of a concession, but, at least, he'd finally given his opposition to Commissioner Cartwright's proposal a rest. Personally, Maddie could see the sense in taking on a new name, dressing like an upper-crust attorney's wife and moving into a recently seized estate home across the state line in Mission Hills, Kansas.

She eased back into the cushy comfort of the leather seat. No one would expect to find inner-city schoolmarm Maddie McCallister setting up house in the swanky suburb. Especially with a distinguished husband who commanded authority and oozed masculinity with every word, every look, every move at her side. Joe Rinaldi would never think to look for her there. He'd never think to look for a married woman.

It truly would be an ingenious way to hide from the escaped fugitive. And with Tyler securely tucked away at a safe house out of harm's way, Mr. and Mrs. Dwight Payne could be setting up an undercover sting. As an older, wealthy—childless—couple, they would certainly be taken seriously if word got out that they were desperate to adopt. They'd be invited to meet with the proprietor of the Baby Factory—or a representative—because they could pay the going price for instant offspring. And if they could finagle an invitation to the clinic itself, if she could get inside and search for Katie…

Maddie was willing to consider the idea. She would consider anything that might help Katie.

She looked across at the granite jaw of the man behind the wheel. *No way* was still etched in his face. Dwight had insisted that going undercover would put her at unnecessary risk. Despite the growing rumors circulating around the precinct, maybe he worried that they wouldn't be convincing as husband and wife and that their cover would be easily blown.

She'd wondered if he wasn't ready to even pretend he was part of a couple. Standing by her side at the same morgue where he'd identified the slain bodies of his wife and son had used up his emotional reserve. Dwight had made it clear more than once that he had no interest in being part of a family again. That die-hard sense of justice flowing through his veins had given him the power to stand beside her and support her when she'd needed his strength. But he probably didn't have it in him to give a repeat performance. It was too much to ask that he play the part of the loving husband, especially when *she* wasn't the wife he loved.

Maddie ached for the pain locked up behind that unsmiling profile. She marveled at the way the words tumbled out of her mouth when she was around him—as if shyness had never been part of her character. An unfamiliar yet exciting tension thrummed through her whenever he turned the force of his personality on her. Just like the sultry humidity had finally erupted into this summer storm, that kiss on the stairs had been the brief ignition of the desire simmering in her veins. By first light tomorrow, the heat and humidity would return to Kansas City.

This push-pull hunger to feel Dwight's passion again had already returned.

Maddie was beginning to think she could play the part of Dwight's loving wife. But one kiss, endless debates and the most amazing set of arms and chest a woman could turn to for comfort didn't make them a couple.

No matter how well she acted her part, she couldn't allow these growing feelings for Dwight to become real. Because acting as though they cared for each other didn't make it so.

Maddie shivered in her seat and hugged her arms around her waist. Dwight, ever observant, reached out and cranked the heater up another notch. She smiled and nodded her thanks, though she knew darn well that the chill of emptiness she felt right now came from inside, not from the car or storm.

Pushed once more to take action before the waiting overwhelmed her, Maddie turned and glanced at the seat behind her. There was still one little man in the world she could love as much as she wanted without pretending a thing.

Tyler was awake but content to watch the swirl of colors and movement outside the window as they drove through downtown. He needed his mommy around to teach him that these things were buildings and lightning and rain. He needed his mommy to teach him about love and family.

"I'll get her back for you, sweetheart," she promised. Her throat burned with the tears she didn't want to shed anymore. Seeing Whitney's body had really shaken her faith in the belief that she would have Katie home—alive and in one piece—soon. Guilt fisted in her stomach that she could even think in terms of *if*, not *when* she'd have her niece in her arms again.

Tyler pursed his lips in an instinctive suckling rhythm. He startled as he saw his fist flail in front of his face. Maddie reached back and guided his delicate little hand up to his mouth. The thumb found its way in and he settled back into contentment once more. She couldn't help but smile at his unshakable trust that all would be right in his world.

Renewed determination turned her around in the seat. She might not be able to convince Dwight to take a risk on the undercover sting idea—and she certainly couldn't pull it off on her own—but she could use his refusal to budge on that point to persuade him to relent on another.

"We're not that far from my house," she reasoned. "If you'd just turn around and head north, we could be there in ten minutes. I could grab what I need and we'd be heading to your place in twenty. You wouldn't have to worry about going back later tonight."

"Couldn't we just go shopping in the morning?"

"Oh, right. You look like the type who loves to shop."

"I don't mind if it's for a good cause and you make it quick."

"I have two perfectly good suits at home."

He glanced across the seat, his gaze passing over the spots where her damp shirt clung to her shoulders and breasts before returning his attention to the traffic narrowing through a construction zone. "Wear that pretty, flowery blouse you had on the other day."

"With what?" Was that a flash of heat she glimpsed in his eyes? Or just her own body's helpless reaction to Dwight's attention? Now wasn't the time to get sidetracked over whether or not that was a compliment or just a practical observation. "I'm not going to jeopardize my claim to be a fit parent for Tyler by showing up in front of the judge in a pair of blue jeans. Either you take me or I'm calling a cab when we get to your house."

His shoulders swelled in a huff, sending ripples of displeasure through the air between them. There was no mistaking what *that* look meant when he turned her way again.

"Fine." He signaled and eased into the turning lane, then whipped around the block and headed back north. "Twenty minutes. Then we're back at my place under KCPD's watch."

Maddie doffed a salute at his grumpy order. "Yes, sir."

When he opened his mouth to take issue with her sarcasm, she cut him off with a thank-you.

"Yeah...." There. She'd deflated that argument. He shook his head, grumbled something under his breath and fixed his attention on the road once more. "Twenty minutes."

Maddie allowed herself to relax for a moment, knowing she and Tyler were in good hands as the storm blew past and ebbed into a steady rain and the sky turned to night.

It took him less than ten minutes to reach her home a few blocks north of Independence Avenue. As Dwight pulled into the driveway, he was already giving instructions. "Get your keys out. Pick up whatever you need and we're out of here."

Ignoring the steady drumbeat of rain that took the edge off the heat and filled the air with the scent of ozone, Dwight climbed out and surveyed the house and the spaces on either side of the detached garage at the end of her driveway. He walked down to the sidewalk and looked up and down the street.

Matching his wary tension, Maddie got out beside the car and turned a slow 360, looking for signs of anything out of place. There was no police van now, no crime-scene tape. Just the familiar houses and vehicles and trees. With the curtain of rain adding its own camouflage, the illumination from the street lamp across the way seemed to create more shadows than it erased. A shiver of unease followed the water that dripped inside her collar and trickled down her back.

Maybe she didn't want to be back here, after all. The very normalcy of her surroundings made the violence that had happened here seem that much more shocking. Still, for Tyler's—and Katie's—sake she would do this.

"Let's go." Dwight nodded toward the porch as he strode back up the driveway, appeased that all was safe.

Maddie blinked the moisture from her lashes and reached for the backdoor. "It'll take me a minute to get Tyler out of the car." She stopped the protest forming on his lips. "I can't leave him out here alone."

"Of course not." The streetlight revealed an interesting play of ridges and hollows as it reflected off the rain that plastered Dwight's shirt to his skin. "Why should anything be simple with you?"

Maddie knew his grinching was the result of that protective state of alertness that kept him on guard and on edge, so she took no offense. But he did surprise her when he took the carrier from her grip. He draped his jacket over his arm to keep Tyler dry, then hooked his free hand around her elbow and hurried her up the front steps.

"I wish I had the porch light on so I could see what I was doing." Maddie did a little grinching of her own. She shoved her soggy hair behind her ears, then squinted into the shadows. With her key in one hand, she used her fingertips to find the center of the dead bolt.

"Today, Red."

She found the slot and inserted the key. "Ha!" But her victory was short-lived. Her cellphone rang in her pocket and she jumped inside her skin. "Damn."

"Easy." A broad hand flattened at the small of her back, its steady presence making her realize how badly she was shaking.

Maddie forced herself to breathe normally, in and out, before pulling the phone from her pocket. "It's getting to where I don't want to answer it anymore."

"You want me to?"

"Not if it's Katie." She tilted her face and mustered a

smile, whether he could see it or not. "That big bad wolf voice will scare her."

"Big bad—"

"Oh, wait." She recognized the number on the lighted screen. "It's Mrs. Dixon across the street. She probably saw us pull up and wants to make sure that everything's okay." Able to take a real breath without thinking about it, she pressed the talk button. "Hello?"

She turned around and waved toward her neighbor's porch light. Maddie went still, her arm frozen in the air, her fingers slowly curling into a fist.

"Ms. McCallister?" Trent Dixon's familiar voice conveyed only a margin of the concern that kept her peering into the shadows farther up the street. "I saw a black car, like you described, parked in front of the Dooleys' house when I got off work at five. There was some man sitting in it, but he's not there now."

"I see it."

Dwight did, too. "Get in the house."

He slid in front of her, blocking her view of the black sedan and keeping her out of its view. Adrenaline sped up her pulse, chasing the chill from inside her. She tried to spy around him, but he moved to keep her trapped between him and the house. "Thanks, Trent," she spoke into the phone. "I'll handle it from here."

"You'll handle nothing." Dwight reached around her and twisted the key in the lock.

"I want to know who's been creeping around my home like some kind of ghost."

Dwight shoved the baby carrier into her hands and opened the door. "Get in the damn house. Lock yourself and the kid inside. *I* will check it out."

As he backed out of the doorway, Maddie grabbed his

arm. "Maybe we should call Cooper. Or your friend A.J. Or just 911. What if it's Joe? He's already killed a cop and a prison guard. He won't have any qualms about killing again."

Dwight took her by the shoulders and backed her into the foyer, calmly refusing to listen. "Don't turn on the porch light until I'm around the corner of the house. Then I want every light inside this house blazing."

"Dwight."

He pulled the door shut. She brushed aside the curtain, but even with the barrier of a window between them, there was no arguing the point. "Lock it."

As soon as she slid the dead bolt in place, he dashed down the stairs into the rainy night and was gone. "Bully," she accused, not really meaning it. "How come it's okay for you to risk your life but not me?"

Hearing her fears echo off the glass, Maddie pressed her fingers to her lips and drew in a more rational breath.

"Be safe," she whispered, praying the appearance of the black car was just an unfortunate coincidence. She counted to five after Dwight's silver-and-gold hair had disappeared from sight before turning on the porch light. Her pupils contracted at the sudden brightness, reminding her of Dwight's order to turn on the interior lights, as well.

The eight pounds of weight in the carrier registered. Maddie pulled off Dwight's coat and smiled at her grand-nephew. "Besides, I have you to take care of, don't I, sweetheart?" She blew him a kiss. "That'll be my job, okay? We'll pack our bags as fast as we can so that we're ready to go when Dwight gets back."

Bracing herself to face her violated home, Maddie walked from one light switch to the next. The mess in her living room had been picked up, the entire sofa removed. Her kitchen had been sanitized to removed the smell of rotting food, though the stains embedded in the linoleum remained. She flipped on the dining room light, the back porch light and even the light in the downstairs bathroom before getting into the hall closet and pulling out a garment bag for her suit. With the bag draped over one arm and Tyler's carrier hooked over the other, Maddie climbed the stairs and turned on the second-floor lights, as well.

Dwight wanted security? She'd see that he got what he wanted so he'd quit worrying about her and concentrate on watching his own back.

As Maddie flipped on the light in Katie's room, the vaguest hint of cigarette smoke in the air gave her a shiver of unease. But then she sniffed again and sensed nothing but the pines and polishes of the cleaning crew that had come in that morning.

Maddie shook off her suspicions and smiled at Tyler. "It's nothing, sweetie. Let's go get some fancy duds for court tomorrow."

With Tyler cooing in imaginary agreement, Maddie headed for her bedroom. The stale scent lingered here, too. But even as she crinkled up her nose, she rationalized that it could be from one of the cleaning crew or one of the detectives or crime-scene investigators who had swept through her house over the past few days.

She pushed open the door to her room and hit the light switch, more relieved than she cared to admit to see that the vase of roses had been removed. Exhaling a breath she hadn't realized she'd been holding, Maddie set Tyler's carrier in the middle of the bed and unzipped the garment bag.

Before she could turn around, the door closed behind her with an ominous click that thudded through her heart. *No.*

Yes. The cigarette smell.

Her scream strangled and caught in her chest as a voice from her past turned her veins to ice.

"Zat my grandson?"

DWIGHT ACTUALLY SPARED a full stomach-clenching minute waiting around the corner of Maddie's house to ensure that she wasn't hardheaded enough to come after him. The kid was actually doing him a favor this time—what Maddie wouldn't do to take care of herself, she'd do for him.

"Good girl." Once the interior lights started popping on, Dwight was on the move. He hadn't seen the threat coming that had taken his family from him six years ago. Hadn't believed anyone could get to him and the things he cared about until it was too late.

He wouldn't make that mistake again.

He intended to stop this threat before it got any closer to Maddie. Or the kid.

And the notion that *caring* had gotten mixed up in his thoughts about the redheaded schoolmarm went unnoticed.

After ducking through the shadows of the neighboring houses, Dwight followed a hedgerow out to the street beyond where the black car was parked. He swiped his palm down his face to clear his vision. The rain made it difficult to get a good fix on anything at this distance, but that would work to his advantage, too, giving him the element of surprise as he approached the car.

Hiding behind the hedge, Dwight waited for the headlights from a passing car to disappear before hunching down and dashing across the street. As he came up on the Impala's blind side, he began processing details. Black. Faded by sun and wear and rusting at the wheel wells. Local plates. And unless they were midgets, dead or asleep, no one was in that car. No one was watching.

Dwight paused. Was the idea of an unidentified stalker a manifestation of Maddie's imagination? He quickly dismissed the idea. Fanciful didn't describe the redhead he knew. The woman was down-to-earth. Practical. Sure, she was a bit naive in the heart-on-her-sleeve love-and-loyalty department. And she was way too stubborn. But she lacked the ego to make up stories about anyone making her feel afraid.

So Dwight sidled up next to the car behind the Impala and squinted through the rain for other signs of movement. There. Skulking down the sidewalk toward his position. A tall man in dark, baggy clothes. The man turned his head and looked straight over his shoulder at Maddie's glowing house before dropping his chin to his chest and slinking closer to the car.

So the guy had gotten tired of sitting at his post.

Dwight balanced his weight over the balls of his feet. He flexed his fingers into loose fists, breathed deeply and lunged from the shadows.

The perp got in a "Hey!" and a curse before Dwight plowed into his gut and took him down. The two men slid across the wet grass, rolled across the sidewalk and into a puddle of standing water before Dwight could flip him onto his stomach and get an arm bent behind his back. The perp was taller, skinnier and younger, but he wasn't putting up much of a fight.

"Wait! Stop! I'm on your side."

Dwight froze. Ah, hell. The guy wasn't putting up *any* fight. "You're that kid across the street." Dwight rolled onto his feet and extended a hand to help the young man up. "Sorry about that."

"No problem." Yeah, tackling innocent pedestrians less than half his age was a problem. But the dark-haired kid seemed to brush off any offense as he brushed the grass and mud from his soggy jeans. "You're Ms. McCallister's boyfriend, right?"

Now there was some unintended payback. "For the record, I'm too old to be anybody's *boyfriend*. I didn't hurt you, did I?"

"Nah. I play football. I know how to take a hit." He shook Dwight's hand in a solid grip. "Trent Dixon, sir. Sorry if I surprised you. I was coming to check the car, too. Ain't nobody been in it for a couple of hours now."

Dwight didn't know if that news should relieve him or make him worry more since the enemy he sought was nowhere in sight. Ignoring the mud and grass staining his own khaki slacks, he pulled out his cellphone and punched in A.J.'s number. He could run the license plate. If the car wasn't stolen, they could ID an owner. "You don't know who it belongs to?"

"No, sir. Ms. McCallister asked me to watch for it and let her know when I saw it again."

Dwight had to give the kid his props for vigilance. "How old are you?"

"Seventeen, sir. I'll be a senior this year."

Lucky senior class. The phone rang, but Dwight looked at Trent. "Appreciate you helping out."

"No problem, sir. Ms. McCallister's cool. She used to baby-sit me when I was a kid."

"You can drop the sir. I'm not *that* old."

"Yes, sir—"

The scream from Maddie's house cut through the rain and set every nerve on edge.

A.J. answered, but Dwight was already pushing the phone into Trent's hands and moving toward the house. "That's Detective Rodriguez. Get inside your house and lock the door. You give him my name and the make, model and plate of this car. Tell him there's another break-in at Maddie's house. Then stay on the line until the cops come."

"Yes, sir. I mean…"

But the rest of Trent's words faded into a blur. Dwight charged across the street, pushing his body as fast as it would go through the yards and up the wooden steps to Maddie's porch.

"Maddie!" Dwight twisted the knob. "Son of a bitch!" With all his planning and paranoia, he'd locked her inside with the danger and couldn't get to her. He pounded on the door. "Maddie!" Something crashed upstairs. He heard muffled shouts—Maddie's. And a man's.

"Damn. Damn." He turned his pockets inside out. He had his own keys and a billfold and not one other thing to defend her with. Dwight whirled around. He tossed the welcome mat aside, searching for a key. He lifted flower-pots and checked inside the mailbox.

"Stop it!" Maddie screamed. "Leave him alone!"

"He's mine. You McCallister bitches owe me a boy."

Dwight could see them through the sheer curtains at the top of the stairs now. A tall, skinny man wearing black glasses with the baby carrier in one hand—and a knife in the other.

Joe Rinaldi.

"Maddie!" Dwight hefted one of the big clay pots and smashed it through the front window.

"Dwight, no! He'll hurt Tyler!"

"Shut up, Madeline!" Rinaldi shoved and Maddie flew back against the wall upstairs. He lunged toward her and Maddie sank to her knees and rolled out of sight.

"You son of a bitch! Rinaldi!"

Desperate to distract his attention from Maddie, Dwight ignored the shards clinging to the rim of the window and thrust his arm inside. Jagged glass ripped through his sleeve and skin, but he blindly found the dead bolt and released it.

"Dammit, Rinaldi! You deal with me!"

The challenge was enough to divert his attention, and Joe altered course and ran down the stairs. Blinded by a raging need to get to Maddie, Dwight shoved the door open. He crushed glass and clay and geraniums beneath his feet and blocked Rinaldi's escape at the base of the stairs.

"Oh, ho, ho. Well, if it isn't Mr. Badass Attorney who twisted the truth and used all his pretty words to send me to prison." Rinaldi slowed his descent with each deliberate step.

"Maddie?" Was she alive? Hurt? Dead? Dwight didn't dare take his eyes off the man with the knife.

"Did Madeline finally land herself a man? What does she do for you? Cook? Clean? Can't be the sex. She's too prudish to put out. I ought to know. I had her first, you know—" the bastard winked "—before I found something better."

Dwight seethed. He wouldn't be baited. He wasn't budging, either.

"If one hair on her head is out of place…"

Joe laughed. "You got the wrong sister, you know. Karen's the real catch. Unless you gotta thing for extra meat on a woman's bones."

Maddie's head appeared at the top of the stairs and Dwight's heart pounded with relief. "Karen's dead, thanks to you." She was crawling on her hands and knees, heedless of his insults. "You used me. You murdered your wife. Terrorized your daughter. You have no right to take Tyler and destroy his life, too." She pushed her hair off her face and Dwight swore.

The shape and size of a man's hand was marked out in blushing-red relief on Maddie's cheek.

Adrenaline poured through Dwight's system, sharpening his senses, deepening his breath and bracing every muscle for a fight. The blade of the long, thin stiletto flashed in the foyer light, granting him a split second's relief to see that the blade was clean.

He hadn't cut Maddie or the kid.

He wasn't going to get another chance to try, either.

"You won't get past me," Dwight warned, retreating a step and leaving room to maneuver as Rinaldi hit the main floor. He could take a man with a knife. Hell, once upon a time he'd been able to. But with Rinaldi swinging the baby carrier between them like a shield…

Rinaldi grinned through the black scratch of his beard as if he could read Dwight's thoughts. "Trying to impress the lady, lawyer man? Now back off or I will cut this baby."

"Tyler!" Maddie screamed and charged halfway down the stairs.

Rinaldi flicked the knife in her direction. "One step closer, Madeline, and I'll do it."

She froze, gripping the railing and breathing hard, every terror shining in her face. "He's your grandson."

"He's my ticket to freedom."

Dwight flexed his fingers. He never took his eyes off Rinaldi's. "Is the kid strapped in, Maddie?"

"Yes." He heard the breathy catch in her voice.

"Good and tight?"

"Yes, but—"

Dwight slammed his right forearm against Rinaldi's knife hand, knocking it up in the air and giving him the opening to smash his fist into Rinaldi's jaw. The skinny man staggered back against the wall, but his grip on both the baby and the knife held fast.

"Dwight! What are you doing?"

He got another left into Rinaldi's gut before the fugitive got his feet beneath him. The knife slashed down. In a split second decision, Dwight knew dodging the attack wasn't an option. He snatched the carrier handle and jammed his shoulder between the knife and the baby to absorb the blow.

He roared as steel sliced through skin and muscle. He pried the carrier loose and tossed it aside, spinning it across the wooden floor.

"Tyler!"

Dwight was only vaguely aware of Maddie shooting past them to check the kid. His ears were full of grunts and curses and deep, pained breaths. A lip split beneath his fist. A warm river of blood oozed from his forearm. He drove Rinaldi into the dining room table and toppled chairs. He absorbed a kick to the gut and stumbled back into the foyer, slipping on the rain-slick glass from the broken window.

Before he hit the floor, Rinaldi was on him. Maddie was a blur of coppery-red. He glimpsed the chair she raised over the back of Rinaldi's head, but Dwight was quicker. He locked his fist around his enemy's wrist and rolled him onto his back, pounding the hand with the knife once, twice against the hardwood until Rinaldi's fingers popped open and the weapon skittered across the floor.

In his mind, he shouted, *Grab it!* But his arm burned, his ribs ached and a high squealing sound filled his ears.

But Rinaldi was fading, too. Dwight heaved a deep breath and dragged the bastard up to his knees. "Enough," Dwight ordered on his next gasp for air. He searched for Maddie in his peripheral vision. "Get something to tie him—"

The dining room window exploded.

"What the hell?"

"Tyler!" Maddie ran to the baby carrier nestled in the corner beside the coat rack.

He identified the distinctive pop of gunfire an instant before the window beside the door shattered. "Maddie!"

She curled her body over the kid as glass showered down around them. "What's happening?"

"Stay down!"

More shots fired. Dwight shoved Rinaldi aside and dove for Maddie as glass and rain and bullets sprayed the foyer. He dragged her as close to the wall and as low to the floor as he could, wrapping her and the carrier up in his arms and shielding them with his body.

Rinaldi staggered to his feet and lurched toward the door. "Wait. Stop." He swung the door open and raised his hands in surrender. "I found—"

Rinaldi crumpled to the floor.

The screech of tires on the pavement outside told Dwight that the assault was over. The thudding of Maddie's strong heart beating against his chest told him she was still alive. The kid's high-pitched cry told him he was unhurt, as well.

The pool of blood spreading beneath Joe Rinaldi's body told him the intruder was dead.

Dwight crawled over to verify that the murdering son of a bitch had no pulse. Straight through the heart. Either someone was a hell of a lucky shot or Rinaldi was the specific target.

There were plenty of details he needed to process, but his brain was a little fuzzy. He should get up to see if he could still spot the car the shooter had driven. He didn't know if the Impala belonged to Rinaldi or whoever had taken him out of the picture. He could call Trent, see if the football-player-turned-neighborhood-watchdog had seen anything. Sirens blared in the distance—he should be collecting his thoughts to make a statement to the police.

But right now, he needed two seconds to catch his breath. He sat on the floor, propped his elbows on his knees, his head in his hands, and let the emotions locked out by adrenaline finally work their way through him.

Rinaldi had gotten to Maddie. He'd hit her. Hurt her. Threatened her with a knife. He'd tried to kidnap the kid. And where had he been? Off playing detective. He should have left that to the cops and stayed here to protect Maddie. Not that he'd done such a whizbang job of that.

"Oh, Dwight."

He blinked his way through the rage and regrets. Of course. Maddie needed comforting right now. Her home was a shambles. A man was dead.

But when he looked up to say something pithy and reassuring, she darted into the kitchen. She'd left the kid crying in the corner. Left the kid alone with him. "You okay? Hey."

"He's fine." Maddie reappeared. She knelt beside him. "Physically, anyway. You? Not so much."

"Agh." Dwight bit back a curse as she pressed a towel against his forearm. Oh, yeah, more evidence of the adrenaline rush wearing off. His sleeve was soaked with blood and his forearm burned like hell.

Maddie hadn't been looking for comfort; she'd been looking out for him. "We need to get you to a hospital."

"We stay here until the cops arrive."

She brushed her fingers across his tender cheekbone, where a bruise to match the mark on her face must be forming. "I don't even have any ice. You'll need stitches and antibiotics. Maybe a tetanus shot."

And then she surprised the hell out of him by looping her hand behind his neck and pulling him in for a sweet, wild, all-too-quick kiss. When she pulled back, he felt his own blood warming like the shy blush that crept up her neck. "What was that for?"

"I wanted to do it before I lost my nerve."

Dwight laid his hand over hers, where she stanched the wound in his forearm. "Red, there's one thing you've got in spades, even if you don't realize it. And that's nerve."

The blush along her skin deepened. "You saved us, Dwight. Tyler and me both. If there's anything you ever need…"

Dwight wanted to touch his fingers to the thoughtful pout of her lips. No, he wanted to put his mouth there and kiss her again. Thoroughly. Deeply. He wanted to see where else a kiss could lead.

But he checked his libido and did nothing.

"There's a dead man in your house. If you think I'm doing a decent job of keeping you and the kid safe, then you'd better think again."

She didn't argue. Instead, her attention shifted to the floor. "Dwight."

Her skin went ashen. She reached down beside him and picked up a small ring on a silver chain that had fallen out of Rinaldi's pocket during the fight.

"What is it?"

She sank back on her haunches and stared at the filigree circle between her fingers.

"Maddie?"

She snapped out of her daze and laid the ring necklace in his palm. "It's Katie's. It was her mother's. I gave it to her after Karen was killed so she'd have something to remember her mother by. She was wearing it when she ran away."

Dwight understood the implication. "Rinaldi saw Katie before he died."

He closed the ring inside his fist and looked down at the man who had terrorized this family for too many years. It was no coincidence that Joe Rinaldi had escaped so soon after his daughter had given birth and disappeared.

He's my ticket to freedom.

Rinaldi hadn't broken out of prison to find his grandson.

The proprietors of the Baby Factory had helped him escape. So that he could find Tyler for them.

Chapter Nine

"Where's the baby?"

Katie roused herself to wakefulness. The voice wasn't talking to her, was it?

"We went to the aunt's place, like you said. Put Rinaldi inside to get the information out of her. Then we left because the cops were sending regular patrols up and down the street."

"And?"

"And nothin'." That was the hulk's voice—big, loud and more than a little worried. "Somebody shot up the place. By the time we got back, the house was swarmin' with cops. Rinaldi's dead."

"I knew that murderer was nothin' but trouble." Stinky Pete added his own whine. "He's been a liability from day one."

"I'd be careful tossing around words like *murderer*." The boss was mad—way beyond mad. Katie could tell because his voice had dropped in volume and he was articulating like nobody's business. "You're telling me this maiden aunt shot and killed a convicted murderer who broke into her house?"

"Why not? You've seen how much trouble the niece is.

She had to get that from somewhere. If Auntie Em knows where the baby is, we're gonna have to find another way to get to her."

"That's right, boss. There's just too much bad blood between Rinaldi and these women. When things get personal like that, it's bad for business."

"I'll tell you what's bad for business. Expecting you morons to carry out simple instructions. Now instead of Rinaldi bringing us the baby and taking the heat, I have nothing to show for it. Nothing!" The boss's voice carried clearly through the walls of the clinic. "I am not losing a quarter of a million dollars because of those two women. If I have to contact her myself, I will."

"But you said we couldn't afford any direct—"

The voices were arguing next door. In the clinic's posh office. Katie remembered that now. There was the office, the hidden room behind the janitor's closet, where she was kept, the nursery and then Whitney's room.

The elephant sitting on Katie's head had taken a vacation for a few hours, leaving her more alert and able to think than she'd been for a couple of weeks. Or however long she'd been kept prisoner in this state-of-the-art hellhole.

A snippet of memory flashed through her brain. The boss had wanted her awake enough to understand the threat that had come to visit her. Daddy. A free man. Walking around the city in spite of what he'd done to her mother.

The memory wasn't a pleasant one. After her protests had fallen on unsympathetic ears, the midwife had given her a shot of something to counteract the sedatives in her system, leaving her flying high enough to transform Joe Rinaldi's appearance into a surrealistic nightmare. He knew where Aunt Maddie lived, he'd said. If she wasn't a good little girl and told him what she'd done with Tyler, then Aunt Maddie would have to pay the consequences.

But Katie had lied. She'd given her son to Whitney, she'd said. To replace the daughter the clinic had stolen from her. What Whitney had done with the child was anyone's guess. She and Whitney had been found together, hitching a ride to Truman Medical Center because her friend was bleeding internally again. But there was no baby. And Whitney was too ill to answer questions.

The lie had fooled her father. Had fooled the boss. There was no reason to hurt Aunt Maddie—she didn't know where the baby was, and Katie had told them all she knew.

She reached down and stroked her shrinking abdomen. Tyler was safe with Mr. Powers, wasn't he? Unfortunately, alertness allowed her to feel the fear again, too.

Katie rolled over in bed and took stock of her surroundings in the dim light, fighting to recall more of the past few days of her life.

She was ravenously hungry but didn't feel ill beyond the lingering disorientation. She traced the line of her IV up to the bag of fluids hanging beside the bed and wondered what all the chemical symbols meant. Maybe they were feeding her that way. Certainly, they were keeping her hydrated.

They.

A remembered feeling of dread shivered across her skin. Fitz and Morales. The hulkster and Stinky Pete. Her keepers. The men who'd captured her and Whitney on their way to find a real hospital and dragged them back here to the boss. That was the three of them now, arguing behind closed doors.

Katie pushed herself up to a sitting position, but it wasn't easy. By the time she'd rediscovered the plastic cuffs that bound her wrists together and the throbbing inside her head had receded to a dull headache, the argument had faded into a conversation that she could only catch snatches of.

"Rinaldi was a loose cannon from day one."

"He diverted the cops' attention away from us, didn't he?"

"For a few hours. Do you think he tipped the aunt about us before she shot him? I say we cut our losses and move on."

"*I* say when we move on. And any losses will be cut directly from your share of the profits."

Katie frowned. Did she understand them right? Her father had gone after Aunt Maddie? Joe was dead? She felt no remorse. She felt no sense of relief, either.

"That ain't fair. We're the ones doing all the dirty work while you prance around makin' nice with folks."

"I'm crying. Now go back there and get me some answers. If you have to, bring the aunt here. That'll make the girl talk."

Katie's own rusty voice scratched through her throat. "No."

They knew about Maddie and where she lived. These men were as great a threat as her father. Katie plucked the IV from her arm and dropped her legs over the side of the bed. She needed to find a way to call Maddie. To warn her. If it wasn't already too late.

Katie swayed on her feet when they hit the icy floor and took her weight. She grabbed the steel guardrail on the bed and held on until she could stand on her own. Once the room stopped spinning, she stumbled toward the door. There was no reason to lock it. With Fitz and Morales on patrol, they assumed she had nowhere to go.

She opened the door into the black hole of the janitor's closet. Here, the pungent odors of ammonia and pine-scented cleaner bit through her sinuses and cleared away the last of the leaden cobwebs in her head.

With her outstretched hands leading the way, she found the outer door and turned the knob. The bright light from the hallway burned through her retinas and she drew back inside. She reached inside her collar for the comfort of her mother's ring and nearly cried out when she remembered it was gone. Daddy had it. According to his twisted way of thinking, if it had belonged to her mother, it belonged to him.

But Katie had learned some of Maddie's practical ways. A ring she could live without. Her son and her aunt she could not.

Moving at a slower pace, Katie let her eyes adjust to a crack of light and listened for signs that someone might be approaching. But other than the boss barking orders to Fitz and Morales, no one was around.

Using the same blend of caution and daring that had helped her escape the first time, Katie slipped out and tiptoed down the hall. She couldn't resist stopping a moment to look through the glass windows of the nursery. There were no babies inside, but two plastic bassinets had been prepared to receive a boy and a girl. Her initial excitement at the prospect of welcoming two new babies into the world was quickly tempered by the lies she knew the expectant mothers had been told. *Here's a lot of money. Give us your baby and we'll send him or her to a nice home with a loving family.*

They left out the part about not being able to change your mind. About never being able to have contact with your child, even when he or she turned eighteen. They preyed on the desperation of women with too little money or too much shame, said nothing about the whole process being illegal or that you could be charged with a crime for taking part.

They neglected to say that to keep you from breathing a word they'd fry your brain with drugs. And if you were still tempted to talk, then they would use more permanent means to silence you.

Whitney had changed her mind. Fearing her family's reaction to becoming a criminal on top of being pregnant, she'd turned to her friend for help. Katie, knowing the precious gift of having someone to depend on no matter what, had been there for her.

Katie had come to Whitney's aid. Now she had to help her aunt.

Steeling her resolve to find a phone if she couldn't get out of the building, Katie crept down the hallway. When she came to Whitney's room, she had to find out if her friend was okay.

She slipped inside the dimly-lit room. "Hey, Whit. You awake?"

A fluorescent light over the bed clicked on. Katie shielded her eyes and squinted into the brightness.

"Who are you?"

Forcing her eyes to focus, Katie looked across the room at a pregnant girl with long blond hair. Katie shrank back against the door. This wasn't right. Did she have the wrong room? "Where's Whitney?"

The blond girl stuffed pillows behind her back and sat up. "My name's April. I don't know any Whitney."

Katie searched for a second bed, a hidden door, anything to help this make sense. But her head was clear. She knew what she was doing. She hadn't made a mistake. "This is her room."

"I've been in this room for two weeks."

That meant... Katie lifted her hands in a beseeching position and charged the bed. "Are you sure it's been two weeks?"

April flinched and reached for something beside her in the bed. "Yes."

"You haven't changed rooms?"

"No."

Katie saw it now. April had pressed the call button to summon help to the room. "Don't do that." She reached across the bed to snatch the button from April's hand.

April covered her swollen belly in a protective gesture. Her eyes were riveted on the plastic bands around Katie's wrists. "Is there a crazy wing in this place?"

Katie shook her head. Tears stung her eyes. Whitney was gone. She hadn't saved anyone, after all. Tyler. Maddie. She'd endangered them all. For nothing. "These people aren't who they say. You're in danger here."

"They're going to help me have my baby. I can't afford it on my own."

"No. They'll destroy you. They destroyed my friend." She pulled back April's covers. "You have to come with me."

April snatched them back. "No, I don't."

"Please."

"Get out of here." She pushed the call button again.

"You're making a mistake. A huge mistake." Katie backed toward the door. They were coming. She had to get to a phone. She had to escape.

With the whole idea of stealth blown by April's panic, Katie swung open the door and ran into the hall.

"There she is!"

She didn't get far before a rough set of hands wrapped around her from behind and picked her clear off the floor. "No!"

Katie screamed and kicked. But the foul odor of stale breath laughed in her ear. "Damn, you're a lot of trouble, girl. Give us the boy and I'll put us both out of our misery."

"Get the box," the boss ordered. "Sedate her while I calm this one down."

"Right." Fitz grabbed her flailing legs and helped Morales wrestle her to the floor.

"No! You can't do this! You killed Whitney!"

She got a glimpse of the boss in the bright light of the hallway before the tip of the needle pricked her arm. He looked about as normal and unassuming as a man could be. His refined clean-cut image didn't jibe with the ruthless orders or the lack of conscience in his eyes.

As her arms and legs started to numb and her brain began to fog over, she thought of how her father had had the same kind of eyes. "You were supposed to help me. I trusted you."

The man squatted down beside her. "That's the whole idea."

MADDIE PACED HER ROOM at three in the morning, unable to relax. She'd fed Tyler an hour ago and had rocked him to sleep. She was weary to the bone. The nerves that Dwight had praised were fried. The storm had passed and they had survived.

Joe Rinaldi was dead. Shot by an unknown suspect driving away in a black Impala.

She should be feeling relief. Instead, she was plagued by the notion that the real nightmare was just beginning. Had Joe been nothing more than a dangerous diversion to keep the police from focusing on the bigger picture? Had they aided his escape so that he could wield his personalized brand of terror against Maddie—or Katie herself—in a desperate effort to retrieve what they wanted most.

Tyler.

How could one precious life be the cause of so much pain and death?

"You couldn't sleep, either?"

Maddie caught her breath in a slight start at the low-pitched rumble of Dwight's voice behind her. She hugged her arms around her middle, self-consciously aware that she wore the old gown he'd asked her to keep covered up. She reached for the robe he'd loaned her, slipped it on over her shoulders and cinched it around her waist.

Her breath caught again, deeper this time, when she turned to face him. He filled her doorway, wearing nothing but blue pajama pants and the gauze bandage that wrapped the twenty-three stitches along his right forearm.

"I'm sorry if we woke you," she apologized.

"You didn't. Seems we both have a lot on our minds." He invited himself in a couple of steps, and the muted light from the lamp beside her bed caught in the golden shimmer of his hair and beard stubble, emphasizing the purple shiner beneath his left eye. He inclined his head toward the bassinet without drawing any closer. "Everything all right?"

"Dr. Grant in the ER said he was fine. She said *you* needed your rest."

"Actually, she recommended I stay the night for observation." A deep sigh lifted his chest. "I needed to be here."

"Joe could have killed you." Maddie had never appreciated timing the way she had when she saw Dwight breaking down her front door. She'd been crippled by anger and grief at the thought of Joe walking out of the house with Tyler. Her pleas had been useless, her threats ineffective. She couldn't outfight or outwit her ex-brother-in-law. But Dwight had stopped him.

"He could have killed you, too."

An awkward silence left Maddie fidgeting on her feet and suddenly sensitive to the temperature rising in the room. She stared at the center of Dwight's broad chest, wishing she could be closer yet seriously afraid of just how close she wanted to get.

Dwight's deep sigh broke the quiet and whispered across her skin. "You don't believe those things Rinaldi said about you, do you?"

"What things? Oh." Maddie flushed with embarrassment and turned away. "I've gotten used to his insults over the years." Tonight, she'd barely heard the snide innuendos, she'd been so focused on getting Tyler back and keeping Dwight alive. But she *was* the plain McCallister. The plump one. The one men asked out so they could get to her sister. Just like Joe had. "Karen was a beautiful woman."

"*You're* a beautiful woman."

"Trust me. I pale by comparison."

"The man had a twisted mind." Dwight's voice drifted closer. "He couldn't see the beauty in any woman. He couldn't appreciate your glorious red hair or smooth, milky skin. He sure as hell never looked below the surface to see the fire inside you."

Maddie tried to laugh off this miserable effort at sweet talk. "C'mon, Dwight. I rely on you to always tell me the truth. That's one of the things I like best about you."

"You *do* believe him." He sounded disappointed.

"I'm just being a realist."

His hands closed over her shoulders and his breath brushed against her ear before he whispered, "I have never lied to you. I will never lie to you. If I can't promise anything else, I promise that."

The vow in his voice seeped into her bones and tempted

that shy, fragile confidence buried inside her. She turned to gauge the sincerity in his eyes. "Don't try to flatter me, okay? Or make up for anything Joe might have said. I've had too many secrets and false hopes in my life to deal with. I don't need any more from you."

Dwight held up his right hand. "I promise to tell the truth, the whole truth and nothing but the truth, so help me God."

She couldn't help but grin. "That's quite the cliché, counselor."

"You're quite the woman. I had to make it good." His gaze left hers and glanced at Tyler. "If we leave the doors open, will he be all right in here?"

Not the question she'd expected. "I think so."

Dwight took her by the hand and led her into the hallway. She wasn't naive enough to question where they were going, but she was having a hard time understanding *why* they were heading to his bedroom. True, there was an undeniable heat simmering between them. But tonight, they'd cheated death. Dwight needed his rest.

And she was, well, she wasn't what a man like Dwight really wanted, was she?

Still, the words to argue her point stuck in her throat. He tucked his fingers inside the knot of the robe and untied it. His gaze went to the shadowy gap as it fell open. "Dwight, I—"

"Shh." Dipping his hands beneath the collar, he slid the thick terry cloth off her shoulders, caressing her skin with its rough texture. The robe caught in the crook of her elbows and his hands lingered there.

Maddie squeezed her eyes shut as he looked his fill at the translucent white cotton and whatever extra curves were revealed underneath. Without seeing it, she felt his scrutiny like a gentle, insistent touch. Her nipples hardened and shamelessly thrust against the soft material. She felt the usual embarrassment and something less familiar, more hopeful, engorging her breasts, warming her skin, rising along her neck.

She sucked in a heated breath as Dwight's cool hand splayed across her chest. Two fingertips soothed the throbbing pulse at the base of her neck while the heel of his palm rode the top swell of her breast.

Opening her eyes, she saw his hooded gaze taking in every stuttered breath, every turn of color, every heated response—every detail.

"What are you doing to me?" she whispered through parched lips, echoing the same question he'd asked her last night.

He blinked and his storm-colored eyes were focused on hers. "Understand this." His voice was as hushed and still as the night around them. "Any man who doesn't see what I see is an idiot."

"Don't do this. Please don't say anything to spoil—"

He pressed a finger to her lips to silence her. "The way you respond to a look or a touch is pretty heady stuff. Makes a man feel like he might not be so far over the hill as he thought." Three more fingers followed the first, brushing across her mouth in a callused stroke that made her want to open her lips and catch a finger between them. A lazy smile spread across his face. "Yeah. Just like that."

"You're not over the hill, Dwight," she protested. A few gray hairs couldn't erase the power of that body or personality.

His boxer's knuckles had been bruised up in his fight with Joe, but his fingers were amazingly gentle as they touched the bruise swelling her own cheek. Dwight's smile faded, but the intensity of his pinpoint gaze did not. "I'm forty-three years old, Maddie. Older than that inside, where it counts. I've loved and lost everything a man can. You stir things up inside of me that I thought were dead. I don't know that I want to feel them, but they're there."

"What are you saying?"

"That I'm done talking." His fingers slid from her cheek into her hair. He palmed the back of her head and pulled her onto her toes for a kiss.

Maddie's palms sizzled where they braced against his chest. She tilted her mouth and let him plunder. He slipped his tongue inside to slide against her own. Maddie moaned at the seductive discovery of his direct approach and tried to wind her arms around his neck. But the robe caught and bound her, frustrating desires that were awakening and growing and eager to be released.

Dwight swept his hands down her arms, taking the robe with them and tossing it aside. He guided her arms back and pulled her against him, pillowing her breasts against the wall of his chest. The pearled tips caught in the crisp hair there, even through her gown, tugging and rubbing and making her want.

He skimmed his palms down her back, igniting a delicious friction that fired her pulse. Maddie slipped her fingers into the short fringe of his hair and pushed it against the grain, loving the prickly feel against her palms.

When Dwight skimmed lower and squeezed her butt, she gasped her first startled breath. "No."

With a self-conscious haste, she reached behind her to move his hand to someplace a little less endowed.

"Yes." He grabbed her bottom again. Grabbed it with both hands. And then, with an almost feral growl in his throat, he added, "I want the whole package."

When he lifted her off her toes, up into the heat of his body, there was no way to lie about where this was leading.

He dipped his head and pressed a kiss to the hot pulse at her throat. "Here comes that honesty part." He laved the same spot with the rasp of his tongue and Maddie shivered in anticipation. "I can't get it out of my head that Rinaldi got to you." He gently kissed her cheek. "That he hurt you." He bent even lower and stroked his lips across the swell of her breast, where the neckline of her gown pulled taut across her skin. "That he made you feel afraid."

Maddie dug her fingers into his shoulders, seeking purchase. "It wasn't your fault." Was he shaking? The molten heat flowing through her veins chilled with concern for a moment. "Dwight, put me down."

Instead of setting her on the floor as she expected, he sat on the edge of the bed, pulling her into his lap so that she straddled him. Leaving them both very vulnerable to the need that filled the night around them.

Dwight's hands ran aimless circles against her back and shoulders. Maddie stroked her fingers against the bold line of his unshaven jaw and waited for the emotions that racked deep breaths through his chest to subside.

When he was ready, he reached up and framed her face between his hands and looked her straight in the eye. "I haven't made love to a woman since Alicia died. I haven't wanted to. Until you. Until tonight. Somehow I can't get it out of my head that I can only keep you safe by getting closer to you."

"You want to make love to me so you won't worry about me getting hurt?"

"Real romantic, huh?"

"What, like a bouquet of roses?" Maddie matched his position, framing his face between her hands before the glower in his eyes could take hold. "I didn't ask for romance. I asked for honesty."

"Say no and I'll walk you back to the kid, tuck you in and deal with it. Say yes and…" He brushed his thumb over her kiss-swollen lips and, just like that, her body was alive with hunger again. "Say yes."

It wasn't a profession of love. She probably wouldn't have believed it if it had been. But Dwight was attracted to her on some level. For some reason. And he needed her.

A man like Dwight Powers. Needing *her*.

Heady stuff, indeed.

Maddie nodded. "Yes."

With a sound that was half relief, half joy, Dwight tightened his arms around her and fell back onto the bed, claiming her mouth in a kiss. Their legs tangled together and she squeezed her thighs around his, gasping at the instant pool of heat that rushed to her feminine core. He slipped his hand beneath her gown, beneath her practical pink panties, and palmed her, skin to skin.

He lifted her higher in the bed, giving his mouth access to her breasts. He caressed them with his hands, then took one aching tip into his mouth, sucking hard through the cotton until she quivered and whimpered and begged him to do the same to the other breast.

And when the self-conscious echo of Joe Rinaldi's cutting words tried to steal the pleasure of Dwight's mouth and hands on her body, she cast the memory aside and made a few bold moves of her own. Laving her tongue around Dwight's taut male nipple. Palming his pulsing erection through the tented cotton of his pajamas. Kissing a spot on his throat and listening to him groan in response.

"Now, Maddie." He sat up, spilling her into his lap. "Now."

In a flurry of need, he pulled her gown over her head and peeled off his pants and her panties. He pushed her back into the pillows and covered her body with his. His fingers were there between them, slipping inside her, testing her slick readiness. Maddie squeezed her eyes shut and twisted beneath him as the pressure built around his touch and drove her closer and closer to the edge of a dangerous, maddening precipice.

Every nerve ending became a supersensitive trigger, firing a ribbon of molten heat to the juncture between her thighs. A prickle of hair against her aching breast. A heated murmur against her throat. The musk of their sex filling the air with its intimate smell.

He propped himself up on his elbows above her. "Open your eyes, Red. I want to see your beautiful eyes. You're so responsive. I can look at you and know when I'm doing something right or wrong."

She did as he asked and he entered her in one long, smooth stroke. Maddie gasped as she stretched to accommodate him. He was so much. She felt so full. So complete.

Yet she wanted…more. All. Now. "Dwight," she gasped. "Dwight."

Feeling feverish, she dug her fingertips into the base of his spine and murmured her need. She turned her cheek into the pillow to find cooler air. Dwight's fingers traced the heat she could feel rising along her skin. They trailed around a taut, dancing nipple. Along the length of her throat. Across her lips. He took her by the chin and forced her gaze back to his while he pulled out and entered her again.

She moaned as he dangled her so close to the edge of what she craved.

He smiled. "So far, so good, hmm?"

Maddie could only nod her pleasure.

His jaw clenched with the power of his own need. "I can't make this last."

"Don't." Wrapping her arms around his shoulders, she pulled him back down to reassure him, to keep him close as they careened toward the edge of that precipice. "This is right. It feels right."

He ground into her a third time, crying out harshly against her throat as he poured himself into her.

But Maddie barely heard him. The fire inside her erupted in a cascading heat that rolled over her in waves, tumbling her over into the abyss so that they were falling together. The wind roared in her ears. The ground rushed up to meet her.

But there was no hard landing, no shock to destroy the moment. She was simply drifting. Soft, husky praises whispered against her skin. Strong, sure hands stroked her hair and lips, slowly guiding her back to her senses and laying her gently in the circle of Dwight's arms.

She was still a little dazed when Dwight pulled back the covers and crawled underneath them with her. He tucked her in up to her chin and spooned behind her. He wedged one muscular thigh between hers and claimed her breast in a proprietary hand. Brushing the hair away from the dampness of her skin, he kissed the back of her neck. "Earlier tonight, you asked me what I needed. Just this. Holding you close."

He wanted to hold her. Close enough so he could drop his guard and sleep. She was an antidote to stress and nightmares—a release for a very physical man, that was all. He needed her, all right. She wondered how she could feel elated and disappointed at the same time.

"Thank you for giving me this," he whispered, the rhythm of his breathing relaxing into sleep.

Maddie nodded. He was talking about her body. About sex.

But as she snuggled down into the haven of Dwight's arms, she feared she had already given him much, much more.

Chapter Ten

Dwight followed Maddie out of the sixth-floor courtroom, carrying a diaper bag and a truckload of guilt.

The woman should be sky-high after Judge Ellison had granted her temporary legal guardianship of Tyler. Lab work had proved that she was a relative. Roberta Hays had given her the recommendation of DFS. And a half dozen character witnesses, from Trent Dixon to Police Commissioner Shauna Cartwright herself had been on hand to testify that nobody came any finer than Maddie McCallister.

He could testify to that fact himself.

If she'd let him.

Despite her pasted-on victory smile, Maddie had been in a somber mood all day. That morning, Dwight had awakened to cold arms and an empty bed. The spicy scent of her lingered on the pillow beside him and on his skin. But he couldn't savor the moment or the memories it triggered. The most contented night's sleep he'd had in ages had been negated when he found her downstairs in the kitchen, snuggling with Tyler and singing some dopey song about fish and birds.

As if this were any other day.

As if nothing had happened between them.

As if he'd taken what he needed and left her wanting.

He could handle the singing. He understood the responsibility to a hungry child and even the trepidation about appearing in court.

What bothered him most was that Maddie hadn't looked him straight in the eye since she'd come apart in his arms last night. Not once. Not really.

And why the hell was the woman who gave him such a hard time about everything else not talking to him about this?

She'd tied up her sexy hair in a prim little bun and shut down every effort at a conversation by...shutting down.

There was no sassy backbone, no nervous prattle, no challenging banter. At first, he thought the stoic silence was a dignified act for the judge's benefit. But now Dwight had a sick feeling in the pit of his stomach that this shy, sparkless retreat was his fault.

Last night, Maddie had asked for honesty from him. She'd come to his bed with eyes open. He'd tried to make it good for her and hadn't been disappointed in any way. She'd brought out the randy adolescent in him, just as surely as she'd tapped into something wiser, deeper inside him. Ultimately, he'd felt the humble satisfaction of a man who'd found everything he'd wanted and more. He thought he'd made that clear—she had a sexy body, beautiful skin and hair, an amazingly sensual mouth. She had a compassionate heart and a passionate soul—and he'd wanted it all.

Nothing Joe Rinaldi had said about her was true. He thought she'd believed that. There should be no regrets.

But as the sensuous sway of breasts and bottom inside that staid navy-blue suit disappeared around the corner ahead of him, Dwight admitted that he wasn't being entirely honest with himself. *He* was the one with regrets.

He was falling for Maddie. But he might not be falling for the woman she truly was.

Last night, he'd claimed he wanted the whole package. He *had* wanted her body, her kisses, her hardheaded demands and gentle understanding. He'd wanted the solace of holding her close, the healing of losing himself inside her.

But that was Maddie the lover, Maddie the listener.

What about Maddie the mother? The rock who refused to let a child in her care be hurt in any way? She deserved a family, a home. A wedding cake and lots of babies of her own.

She was a giving lover. A stubborn fighter. A better friend than he deserved.

Maddie was a long-term kind of woman, not a one-night stand.

Dwight didn't have any forevers to offer her.

She was smart enough to know it.

So why was her apparent willingness to move on and forget about last night bothering him so much?

"Ms. McCallister."

"Ma'am."

"Detectives."

Dwight picked up his pace as he heard familiar voices.

Cooper Bellamy's. "Congratulations on the custody hearing. You and Mr. Powers planning to celebrate?"

"I doubt it," Maddie answered. "I won't feel like celebrating until Katie's home, too."

Dwight hurried around the corner to catch up. Detective Bellamy and A.J. Rodriguez waited in front of the bank of elevators. But despite their polite greetings, Dwight could tell that this wasn't a social call.

Striding up beside Maddie, Dwight rested his palm against the small of her back in a protective gesture of support. Did she stiffen because it was *his* touch? Or was it the stress of the day, compounded by armed detectives with grim expressions? He didn't mess with pleasantries. Or let go. "What?"

Bellamy's gaze darted to Maddie. "I'm sorry, ma'am, but you might not want to hear this."

Maddie wouldn't be put off by anyone trying to spare her feelings. "If this has something to do with Katie's disappearance, I'm staying."

"We have a legal matter we'd like to discuss with the ADA." A.J., a veteran undercover officer, delivered the lie with such cool veracity that Dwight almost believed it.

"Oh." For a brief second, her resolve gave way and Maddie sagged against his hand. "I was hoping you'd found out something. But, of course, Dwight has other cases."

Considering Maddie's plea for honesty, Dwight was on the verge of telling her to stay put. But then Tyler grunted in his carrier. Using the demands of the baby as an excuse, Maddie not only moved away from Dwight's touch to push the elevator's call button but also reinstalled that fake smile that never reached her eyes.

"I'll leave you to your business, then." She turned her attention to Cooper. "You'll keep me posted on anything new you *do* find out, right?"

"Yes, ma'am."

"You know, Coop, you don't have to keep…"

Oh sure, for Bellamy, her smile softened into the real thing.

"Call me Maddie. You make me feel a decade older every time you *ma'am* me."

"Yes, ma'am, um, Maddie." Bellamy's neck colored to match the renewed glow in Maddie's expression. "Sorry."

Dwight noted the stab of jealousy that bristled through him at their shared laugh, but he filed it away to deal with later. She could make friends with every man at the Fourth Precinct if that's what she wanted. He got that he wasn't the kind of man who inspired smiles and laughter. And he got that, despite the unexpected alliance that had formed between them, he had no claim to where she bestowed her smiles or kisses or any other damn thing.

He just had to get past wanting to make that kind of claim.

By now, the distinct odor of a diaper that needed changing had wafted up between them. Maddie shifted her gaze to a vague point near Dwight's chin. "We'll meet you downstairs in the parking garage by your car."

She turned to the elevator and Dwight took a step to follow her. "Give me five minutes and I'll go down with you."

She tugged at Tyler's yellow blanket, knowing the best deterrent to keep him at a distance. "The two of us need to make a pit stop. Like I said, do your thing and meet us downstairs."

But her safety was the one issue he wouldn't budge on. "Show your visitor's ID to one of the security guards on the parking level. Give him my name and tell him to walk you to my car."

"We'll be fine."

She could think him any lowlife name in the book for not offering her a marriage proposal or whatever she'd expected after making love, but 'tude or no, she was going to be safe. Dwight looped the diaper bag over Maddie's shoulder and, in the same motion, palmed the back of her neck. He slipped his fingers into her hair, loosened a couple of pins and turned her face up to his for a kiss.

The lush shape of her mouth softened beneath his almost instantly, casting aside guilt and concern in a mini-burst of passion. He kissed her squarely, succinctly, leaving no room for doubt that he cared about her welfare and he meant business. Just as quickly as it had started, though, he lifted his head. Better. *Now* she was looking. "Straight to my car," he ordered.

The intoxicating pools of midnight-blue blinked their vulnerability. "You shouldn't do that. We have an audience."

"I don't care." Two weeks ago, he would have minded his decorum. Hell, two weeks ago, he wouldn't have considered kissing a woman anywhere, much less in public. Today, he tangled his fingers a little farther into Maddie's hair because he hated this distance that had come between them. "I'll tell you if they say anything that pertains to Katie or the kid. I promise." He pulled his keys from his pocket and held them out in his palm. She curled her fingers around the keys and he caught her hand in his. "Rinaldi might be out of the picture, but whoever killed him isn't. The people who want Tyler are still out there. Let the guard walk you to the car."

"If I don't, will you send these two detectives after me?"

The elevator dinged and the doors opened behind her.

Dwight reluctantly loosened his grip and watched her back into the empty car. "I'll come after you myself," he promised, not quite able to match the teasing in her tone. "I'll be down as soon as I can."

"Wait! Hold the elevator, please." Instinctively, Dwight reached out and blocked the doors to keep them from sliding shut. Roberta Hays's smoky aura reached him a split second before the DFS caseworker dashed past him into the elevator. "Thanks."

"No problem." Good. Someone to keep Maddie company and make sure she reached her destination.

Still huffing to catch her breath after her sprint, Roberta braced her hand on her skinny chest and turned her attention to Maddie. "I'm so happy Judge Ellison sided for you and Tyler. Knowing who your brother-in-law was, I must say I was a little worried. I can't tell you how many babies I've worked with over the years who get lost in the system and wind up just taking up space in someone's home. You're really fighting for him, and I admire that."

"Thanks."

"Sometimes, the teenage mothers I work with get into trouble and don't think of anyone but themselves. It's a death sentence for these little ones."

"Mrs. Hays," Dwight snapped. *Death sentence* seemed a pretty callous metaphor to use, no matter what point she was trying to make. When had the woman who'd been too tired to do her job last Saturday gotten to be so chatty, anyway? Still frowning, he glanced down at the infant in Maddie's carrier. Bright blue eyes looked up at him and sparkled as if they were mature enough to focus and communicate. Maybe it was the memory of another baby that seemed to transmit an unspoken message. Right. Shut the noisy lady up.

"Mrs. Hays, it's been a long day for Ms. McCallister. A long week. Maybe you could save the commentary for another time," he suggested. He lifted his gaze to Maddie's pale face. Her eyes were as blue as the kid's and filled with a plea he didn't have to imagine. "I won't be long."

Maddie nodded. "Remember, you promised to tell me the truth. Anything they say. Even if it seems insignificant."

"I promise."

But Roberta wasn't done apologizing. "I just meant that Tyler is very fortunate to have someone step up to become a real family for him. I've been in this business thirty years. Believe me, I don't see nearly as many happy endings as I used to." She caught a deep breath and continued on. "As soon as all this mess gets settled, you and I can set up a time to—"

The doors closed on Roberta's voice and Maddie's blue eyes, looking at him as if she didn't hold much stock in Dwight's promises. It was a look that twisted the guilt in Dwight's stomach every bit as much as Alicia and Braden's deaths once had.

Dwight turned to A.J. and Bellamy. He didn't intend to keep Maddie waiting long for whatever truth they were about to share. "Maddie's not an idiot. What's going on?"

Bellamy hooked his thumbs in the front pockets of his jeans and nodded toward the elevator. "You want me to run down and keep an eye on things while A.J. fills you in?"

Dwight considered the offer for about two seconds, swallowed any lingering jealousy and nodded. "You mind?"

"I wouldn't have offered." The young detective doffed a salute and jogged toward the emergency stairs.

Feeling a margin of relief as the door closed behind Bellamy, Dwight swiped his hand over the tension in his jaw and confessed to his friend. "Maddie will be glad to see a new face. She thinks I'm overprotective. I *am* overprotective."

"A man broke into her house intending to kill her last night," A.J. reasoned. "He took the child she loves and he wound up dead at her front door. I think you're entitled."

"Yeah. Thanks for pointing out what a slam-bam job I'm doing of keeping her safe." Hell, he wasn't even earning any points at protecting her from himself and *his* moods. But there was still something too raw and unsettled about his feelings for Maddie to confess that much. "Now talk to me so I can get downstairs before she gets it in her head to go after this Baby Factory on her own."

A.J. didn't waste time or words. "We traced the black Impala from the plate number the kid across the street gave us."

"Stolen?"

A.J. nodded. "The owner said it was taken from a Mission Hills address. That gives us a place to start our search for the shooter."

"That junker isn't a Mission Hills car."

"The owner works construction. Remodels old homes and buildings around the city. He said he was on a job when it was taken."

Dwight tuned in to one more detail. "You said *shooter.* You don't think it was the same two guys that helped Rinaldi escape the prison transport?"

"That's what we got from the neighbor, Trent Dixon. Physical evidence backs up his story. The lab retrieved bullets and fragments from only one gun."

"So there's another player in this case?" Dwight pushed the call button to retrieve the elevator. He'd already been away from Maddie for too long. News that someone besides Rinaldi might be after her made it seem even longer. "Are you sure Rinaldi was the intended victim? Did they know that Maddie and the kid or even that I, was there?"

"You're asking the same questions we are, counselor. Did you tell anyone where you were going last night?"

"No one knew. Hell, that wasn't even our destination until Maddie changed my mind."

"So whoever was driving the Impala *was* looking for Rinaldi."

"But Maddie had seen that black sedan before. That first night she was home with the kid. *Before* Rinaldi escaped."

"Maybe the perp knew Maddie's would be a destination for Rinaldi once he was out. You said he'd threatened her after the trial." A.J. pulled out his notepad and jotted a line. "We're looking into any grudges against Rinaldi— inside prison and on the outside. So far, we've come up empty."

"I need answers, A.J." Dwight turned to his friend, his voice almost a plea. "Things are getting complicated. I can't have anybody else's death on my hands. I put my wife and son in the ground. I can't…" What was he trying to say? What twisted emotions were trying to get into his head now? "I can't let anything happen to Maddie and that kid."

"You still can't call Tyler Rinaldi by his name, can you, amigo?"

Dwight was sure that he didn't want to hear whatever insightful observation A.J. had made.

"You still believe that caring about somebody means they're going to die, don't you?"

"It isn't that. It's… Ah, hell." Sorting through his emotions wasn't on his list of priorities right now. He squeezed his hand into a fist and smacked the call button. "Where's the damn elevator?"

A.J. pocketed his notepad and turned to face the elevator, standing shoulder to shoulder with Dwight. "I heard what Maddie said about telling the truth. You have to be honest with yourself and what you're feeling before you can be honest with her."

"If I want philosophizing, I'll go back to my therapist. Why don't you stick to what you do best."

"Lovin' my wife?"

Dwight looked down into A.J.'s golden eyes and glared. But the detective's smug smile remained unflappable. Pulling back the front edges of his jacket, Dwight splayed his fingers at his hips and relaxed his defensive posture. He couldn't begrudge A.J. the happiness he'd earned with his wife, Claire. But that didn't mean he could completely understand it. "You have a dangerous job. There have been threats against you and your family a dozen times over. How do you live with that?"

"I think of the alternative—never having known Claire. I was just going through the motions of living before I met her. I had my job. I brought in the bad guys. But I didn't have a purpose. Now, every day's richer. Every moment means more." The elevator doors opened and A.J. followed Dwight inside. "I still bring in the bad guys. But now I understand why I do it. I know why I get up in the morning and why I watch my back. Because I've got something to go home to, something worth every scar, every stakeout, every phone call from an old friend in the middle of the night."

The doors slid shut as the devil's advocate inside Dwight had to be heard. "And if you lose her?"

A.J. punched the button for the parking level before answering. "Would you have loved Alicia and your son any less if you'd known you were going to lose them?"

Three floors passed while Dwight considered the answer to that question. "I thought being a cop was what you did best."

A.J. laughed, a sound Dwight couldn't recall hearing before the detective had met his wife. But he took the hint and let him change the subject. "I still get the job done. That's why I thought you'd be interested in a couple of new developments on the investigation."

"Such as?"

"I had a heart-to-heart chat with Zero this morning."

"Zero the pimp?" It still curdled in Dwight's gut to think of Maddie pounding the streets in No-Man's-Land on her own, demanding answers about her niece from pieces of scum like Zero.

"He gave us a name. From a friend of a friend who recommended that if any of Zero's girls got pregnant, they could contact a man named Roddy, maybe Radé. He could get them some quick cash in exchange for their babies and silence about the whole setup."

Dwight was already processing the details. "Whitney Chiles had a sugar daddy named Roddy. A Broadway talent scout, according to her parents. Zero's claiming this guy's local?"

A.J. nodded.

"You get a number or a last name?"

"We're working on it."

The elevator dinged, announcing their arrival at the first level of the parking garage. "You still haven't told me anything that Maddie wouldn't want to hear about her niece."

Pausing long enough for Dwight to look at him and worry, A.J. answered. "We found some hairs caught in the chain that was attached to the ring you took off Rinaldi. They're Katie's."

"Maddie said she'd given the ring to her. Rinaldi probably took it as a souvenir."

"That's not the disturbing part."

Dwight pushed the button to keep the doors closed until he heard what A.J. considered *disturbing*.

"The hairs show traces of the same drugs that were in Whitney Chiles's system."

"The ME said that combination of drugs is what killed Whitney."

A.J. didn't have to spell out the connection for him. Dwight jabbed the open button and pushed his way out as soon as the doors split apart. He had to get to Maddie. Not just to keep her safe but to keep her from hearing the news that Katie might already be dead.

THE DRONE OF ROBERTA HAYS'S conversation beat like a steady hammer against Maddie's temples.

The older woman had followed her into the main-floor bathroom while Maddie changed Tyler. Then she'd joined her on the ride down to the parking garage along with Dwight's bodyguard-in-training, Cooper Bellamy. Maddie didn't for one minute think Cooper's appearance was an accident, nor that his offer to lug Tyler's carrier down the concrete ramp to the middle level of the parking garage where Dwight's car was parked was just a friendly happenstance.

"Yo, slugger." Cooper was having his own conversation with the baby he carried. "Next time I come over, I'm gonna show you some more of those yearbook pictures of your mom. There's one in there from a musical where she's wearing this tight pink jacket. I tell you, she's a fine-lookin' girl. I'll bet you get all that dark hair from her."

"Coop!" His appreciative tone compelled her to reprimand him. "My niece doesn't turn eighteen for another six months. Don't you have a girlfriend your own age? One who's legal?"

Cooper's cheeks turned bright red. "Oh, no, ma'am. Maddie, I mean. A few pictures aren't gonna give me the hots for Katie. Not that she isn't hot. But I'm not…" He'd stopped halfway down the ramp and was apologizing with every bit of body English he possessed. "I just think it's important for Tyler to hear about his mom and see pictures of her so he knows her when they meet again. My dad was a career military man. Mom used to do that for my brothers and me whenever he was deployed."

"Oh. That's sweet." The tension in Maddie eased a fraction. She reached out and squeezed Cooper's hand at his consideration. "I hadn't even thought of doing something like that. Thanks."

"Yeah, *sweet* is what every man's goin' for. I promise you, I can be tough if I need to be."

Maddie grinned. "All right, tough guy. I believe you."

She turned to resume their descent and saw that Roberta was already on the middle level, casting darting glances to the left and right along the rows of cars.

"Just watch using terms like *tight* and *hot* when you're talking about my niece, okay? Maybe when she's twenty-five and you're thirty-three or so I won't freak out about it quite so much, okay?"

"Yes, ma'am." He scrunched his face in apology. "Maddie."

"You're parked on the middle level?" Roberta asked the question over her shoulder. Then she turned to survey the catacombs of cars and concrete barriers again. "Which way?"

Maddie frowned. Had Roberta just smoked her way through a whole pack of cigarettes? If she wasn't on some kind of nicotine high, then what was making the older woman so nervous? "Is something wrong?" Maddie asked. "Did you forget where you parked? Or do you need a lift?"

Roberta hugged her purse to her chest and shifted her distracted glance to Cooper as he paused beside Maddie. "You'll walk her and Tyler to their car, right? You or the guard?"

"Yes, ma'am."

Maybe it was Roberta's almost-frantic state of paranoia rubbing off on Maddie, but she was suddenly aware of the subtle nuances of her surroundings. In the late afternoon, with the sun blazing outside and leaking through metal ventilation grates and the rampway arches that led to the surface, the interior of the parking garage was striped with a hazy pattern of artificial light and shadow. But it wasn't the pockets of cool air or the intermittent squeal of tires from the level below them that warned her to pay attention.

Cooper sensed it, too. "Where's the guard?"

As he scanned the garage with watchful eyes, Maddie did the same. The guardhouse at the base of the ramp stood empty, with no indication of where the uniformed sentry had gone.

A ripple of unease shivered along her skin beneath the polished cotton of her suit. Maybe Roberta was right to worry. "Dwight said to meet the guard here."

"Maddie!" The gruff call of Dwight's voice in the distance jolted through Maddie. Part of her wanted to grab Tyler and run to the source of that voice. But another part of her curled her toes into her low-heeled pumps and held her ground. There was nothing to panic about. Roberta's nervous energy made her jumpy but not incapable of making her own decisions. And the guard's disappearance probably had a rational explanation. There was no need to grow any more dependent on the sense of security that Dwight's strength gave her.

Roberta tucked a spike of her black-and-white hair behind her ear. "Is that Mr. Powers?"

"Sounds like it," Cooper answered. He pushed Tyler's carrier into Maddie's hands, handed her the diaper bag and opened the door to the guard's shack.

"Maybe we should go back and stay with him," Roberta suggested, craning her neck to see around a barrier to the floor below them.

"Probably not a bad idea." Cooper frowned at the empty interior and pulled out his cellphone. "Let me call it in first, then I'll walk you back up. Could be nothing more than the guard is helping someone with a flat tire." He dialed a number once, frowned, then dialed it again before shaking his head. "There's no reception down here. You—" he took Maddie by the shoulder, opened the guardhouse door and ushered her inside "—in here."

"Don't be ridiculous."

She heard the scrape of footsteps on the floor above them.

"Maddie?" Dwight called out again.

"Down here, sir!" Cooper yelled.

Maddie couldn't tell if Cooper's wary alarm or her own fear and fatigue made her jump at the slam of a car door nearby.

She breathed deeply to ease the rapid rate of her pulse and reminded herself not to create enemies where none existed; she had plenty of real ones to contend with. "Dwight's car is right over there." She pointed to the silver Mercedes with the keys she pulled from her pocket. "I'll lock Tyler and myself inside. Like you said, it's probably nothing."

"And if it is something and I leave you alone, the ADA will have my hide."

The screech of tires careened around a corner below them.

"He's right," Roberta added, snatching Tyler's carrier. "Let's go back up and wait for Mr. Powers."

Maddie tugged the carrier back into her hands. "Where are you taking him?"

"Where he'll be safe."

"I appreciate all your help, Roberta, but he's not your concern anymore. I have custody, not the state."

"Make a decision, ladies," Cooper urged.

"It's made," Maddie insisted. A mewling sound, soft and low like the whine of a wounded animal, echoed through the garage. "Did you hear that?"

"Okay, that's it. We're going." Cooper replaced the phone on his belt and plucked the carrier from both their hands. "Something's hinky here and until I figure it out—"

"Roberta?" Another man's voice joined the debate. As he circled the security booth, Maddie could see that he was tall and slender and wore a crumpled suit and loosened tie that indicated a bureaucrat at the end of his workday. "Is that you? What are you doing here?"

"Where did you come from?" Roberta asked in a shaky whisper.

"Tan Cadillac, two rows over." The fiftyish man laughed at his own answer. The receding points of his peppered hairline shifted back even farther as he caught sight of Tyler and smiled. "Hey there. What a cutie-pie."

Cooper angled himself between Tyler and the stranger, flashing his badge. "Excuse me, sir. I'm going to have to ask you to continue this conversation later. We were on our way inside."

The man pushed up his sleeve to check his watch. "It's awfully late in the day for a court appearance, isn't it?" Unfazed by Cooper's brush-off, the man shifted his briefcase to his left hand and extended his right. "Craig Fairfax, officer."

"It's Detective. Bellamy."

After shaking Cooper's hand, he raised his own in apology. "I recognized Roberta and wanted to stop by and say hi. We're old friends, aren't we? Haven't seen her recently. Of course, she's been out of the office a lot."

Maddie turned to the older woman, whose expression had gone as pale as the white in her salt-and-pepper hair. She'd seen that same look of fearful recognition in Karen's face more than once. "What's wrong? Who is this guy?"

The questions startled Roberta and, while the other woman smoothed her ruffled composure, Maddie picked up Tyler's diaper bag and secured her greatnephew firmly in her own hands. She was beginning to have her suspicions as to why Roberta had become such a friend after this afternoon's custody hearing. Maybe she'd expected to run into Craig at the courthouse and didn't want to meet him alone. The man could be an old boyfriend, an exhusband.

"Yes, um, Craig," Roberta stammered. "He's my supervisor. It's good to see you."

Liar.

An engine gunned in the distance and the feeling that something was off in the world around them intensified. She glanced over her shoulder toward the floor above. What was taking Dwight so long? He'd recognize this man if he worked at the courthouse.

Maddie's momentary distraction gave Craig an opportunity to reach down and stroke his fingertip across Tyler's cheek. "I have a new granddaughter about the same age. My son and daughter-in-law just adopted her."

"Hey." Maddie flinched away at the uninvited caress, but she needn't have bothered.

Roberta had snagged Craig by the wrist. "Don't touch him."

Cooper's hand closed around Maddie's arm just as Craig twisted out of Roberta's grip. Any pretense of a friendly reunion had vanished. "You disappear for two whole days without a word? And now I find you here?"

"Roberta?" The woman needed someone to stand up for her.

But Cooper was already dragging Maddie up the incline. "This isn't our fight."

"We have to help—"

The next several seconds ticked by in slow-motion clarity.

The squeal of tires became the roar of a beat-up white truck, picking up speed as it whipped around the corner and barreled toward the security booth.

"Roberta!" Maddie screamed.

"Run!" Cooper shoved her up the ramp.

"No!"

Craig Fairfax's eyes widened like saucers as the car barreled toward him. "Crazy moron!"

Maddie craned her neck to see around the barricade of Cooper's shoulders. "Look out!"

Roberta spun around. Craig pushed.

Saving her? Or killing her?

Cooper swore and leaped off the ramp, diving in front of the oncoming truck.

"Cooper!"

His arms snapped around Roberta's skinny body and the two flew through the air as the truck's fender clipped them both. Maddie's scream was drowned out by the deafening sounds of the truck slamming into an SUV, then squealing to find traction. Burning rubber stung her nose as the truck ground through its gears and cut back up the ramp, racing straight toward her.

"Maddie! Move!"

She was already running when strong arms lifted her, spinning her and Tyler out of harm's way. A breeze stirred around her legs as the truck zoomed past. She heard the groans of injured people before the hardness of the concrete wall at her back and the unyielding strength of Dwight's chest registered.

"Officer down! Repeat. I've got two men down." A. J. Rodriguez's distinctive accent drew her attention to the crumpled body of a black man in a dark blue uniform, lying behind the SUV the truck had bashed into. A.J. had pulled the officer's radio off his shirt and was calmly relaying instructions about the situation, the location and an urgent need for backup and medical attention. Then he was on his feet. He lay a hand on Dwight's arm, glanced at Maddie and then back at Dwight. "You got things under control here?"

Dwight nodded. "Go."

Then A.J. was off. Making his own shortcut, he scrambled from one concrete tier to the next, climbing his way toward the surface of the parking garage in an effort to catch the speeding truck.

Maddie fought her way through shock and confusion to focus on the cold fury in Dwight's stormy eyes as he cupped her face and demanded she talk to him. "I'm fine," she managed to say. She glanced down to see Tyler in his carrier, secured in Dwight's fist. "We're both fine."

"Do you suppose there's any way in hell you could stop throwing yourself in harm's way?" Maddie heard the desperation in Dwight's voice and heard it echo in her own.

"The others—Cooper, Roberta, Mr. Fairfax—are they all right?"

"You're my main concern."

She clutched at Dwight's lapel, pressed her fist against his heart. "No. I can't be. We have to help them."

With a jerky nod, Dwight moved his hand to hers and squeezed. "You're right. I'll check Bellamy and Mrs. Hays.

You look after the guard. And don't—" He squeezed harder, then lifted her fingers to his lips and kissed the back of her hand. "Do not leave my sight. You or the kid." He released her and hooked the carrier over her arm. "Understand?"

MADDIE MADE HER WAY to the groggy security guard. Beyond basic first aid, there wasn't much she could do. But she checked the reaction of his pupils, tested the evenness of his breathing and pulse and pressed his white handkerchief to the back of the man's head. "Who did this?" she asked. "Did someone hit you?"

"A man coldcocked me from behind."

With his slurred speech, Maddie didn't want to push for a clearer answer.

She'd seen a man driving the truck, too. But it had all happened so fast she couldn't give any better description beyond short and dark-haired.

She gladly moved aside as the paramedics arrived. As police units and ambulances pulled up and other guards blocked off the area with yellow tape, the scene took on the same feeling of organized chaos that had overwhelmed her when the TAC officer had been killed outside her house. The same pall of heartless violence filled the air and seeped into her bones.

Cooper was sitting up, complaining to the paramedics trying to tend to his injuries that he had a job to do and that they were keeping him from it. Roberta was tied down to a body board, her neck and head framed by an immobilizing brace. The DFS caseworker's hand felt cool when Maddie tried to hold on and offer words of comfort. And though the paramedics insisted that Cooper had saved her life, Roberta's eyes never opened. Her lips never moved.

And her alleged supervisor and probable ex never once asked how she was doing.

In fact, as Maddie stepped back to let the paramedics load Roberta's gurney onto an ambulance, she slowly turned to scan the uniformed figures and curiosity seekers alike. What had happened to Craig Fairfax? And why had Roberta been so afraid of him?

Maddie inhaled the familiar scents of pressed cotton and musk an instant before she was enfolded in a layer of warmth.

"Penny for your thoughts?" Dwight's deep voice rumbled against her ear.

"You haven't got enough money for what I'm thinking." Neither one of them laughed. "Have you seen Craig Fairfax?"

"Who's that?"

"Roberta's supervisor. We met him just before that truck…" Maddie swallowed, not wanting to recreate the images the words would conjure. "You've probably seen him around the courthouse. Older gentleman. Receding hairline."

"I don't know any Fairfax. But you just described half the men I work with. You should mention it to A.J." Savoring the comforting weight of Dwight's jacket settling across her shoulders, she didn't protest when he draped his arm around her and pulled her to his side. "C'mon, he needs your statement."

He took Tyler's carrier from her a second time and hauled it at his side while he guided her to the security office that KCPD had taken over as a command post. As soon as they were inside, he set Tyler on a desk and pulled out a chair for her.

"He wants us to wait here until he's done talking to Bellamy," Dwight said, explaining the empty room. "He says Bellamy's a regular hero—just what that young pup needs to give him a swelled head."

"He's a good kid," Maddie insisted. "He's going to be a great cop."

"Yeah, well, we'll hire him to baby-sit for a few days, then."

"I don't get it, Dwight."

He pulled out a chair to sit across from her.

She reached for his hands and pulled them into her lap. "Why is this happening to me? To my family? I'm just a high-school English teacher. I've never broken the law or anybody's heart. The most rebellious thing I've ever done is let Katie talk me into putting highlights in my hair." She traced her thumb along one scarred-up knuckle. "But people around me are dying. People I care about are getting hurt."

Oh, God. She was going to cry. She could feel the tears stinging her eyes and she was too tired to stop them. "All I ever wanted was a family. Someone to love. Someone who needs me. How did I get mixed up in all this? How can I make it stop and get back to my boring old life?"

"First of all, I doubt that life with you would ever be boring." Dwight shifted his grip so that he was holding on to her now. She studied his bruised and battered boxer's hands that had always been so gentle with her. "You're mixed up in this because you give a damn. Criminals are threatened by people who care, people who take a stand against the things that are wrong in this world. If courageous people like you didn't stand up to bastards like Joe Rinaldi and that Baby Factory, then I'd be out of a job. And they'd be running this city."

Maddie frowned and sat back in her chair. Dwight's vehement argument made logical sense and should have been a comfort to her. But those weren't the words that registered.

"Wait a minute. Go back. Why are we hiring Cooper to baby-sit?"

Dwight's deliberate pause should have prepared her. Nothing could have.

"Because I want you to marry me."

"What?"

Maddie heard the words. She knew Dwight's voice, recognized the intensity of his gray-green eyes.

And though her heart expanded with an unexpected joy, it contracted just as quickly as common sense and experience kept her from believing that the words were sincere. "Did you say *marry you?*"

"Not for real." Dwight released her hands and stood, towering over her for a moment before pacing to the opposite side of the room. "But if half of the KCPD believes we're a couple already, then I think we can pull it off."

"Pull what off?" Maddie stood as well. She'd never been proposed to before, but she was pretty sure this wasn't how it was supposed to happen.

"We're going to try this Commissioner Cartwright's way." He pounded his right fist into his palm. "We're going to take the fight straight to whoever this Roddy and the Baby Factory people are. We're going to find Katie and bring her home."

"By getting married?" she repeated in robotic disbelief.

Dwight nodded.

Oh, God, the man was dead serious.

"You and I are going to adopt a baby."

Chapter Eleven

"You're sure I have to keep this on the whole time?" Maddie asked, squirming to adjust the wire that had been taped beneath her breasts and at her waist.

"Yes," Dwight answered unequivocably. Though she'd directed the question at the female TAC officer who had shown her how to attach and conceal the listening device, Dwight wanted Maddie to understand that, although he'd finally agreed to Commissioner Cartwright's plan, he still wasn't going to take any more chances than necessary with her safety. "That's the only way backup can monitor your situation and location at all times."

He held out Maddie's suit jacket to slide it over her shoulders and further mask the wire hidden beneath her sleeveless cotton turtleneck. He held on longer than necessary, smoothing the tan linen down her arms. Massaging his fingers into her soft skin, he wondered if the faint trembling he felt were her nerves or his own.

"Dwight." She reached up and lay her hand over his, giving him the reassurance he should be giving her. "I can do this. I won't let Katie down."

And *he* wouldn't let her down. Not the way he'd dropped his guard with Braden and Alicia.

He leaned forward and pressed a kiss to the copper silk at Maddie's temple, sealing that vow. "You're not the one I'm worried about, Red."

Dwight pulled away before he changed his mind about this whole charade. In the mirror above his mantel, they looked every inch the image of a well-to-do professional couple who took what they wanted from the world and bought whatever else they couldn't get their hands on. Maddie's hair had been tamed into a sleek style, and her makeup had been applied in such a way as to play down the lush shape of her lips. Her pretty blue eyes were less pronounced, her features as pale as he'd ever seen them. They'd erased the vibrancy that turned Maddie from ordinary to irresistible and left a coolly untouchable sophisticate in her place.

While part of him longed to comb his fingers through her hair and muss it up to reveal the real Maddie again—the one who smiled and laughed and rambled on at the mouth when she got nervous—another part was thankful that the undercover experts at the KCPD could alter her appearance so dramatically. Joe Rinaldi might be dead, but there was no knowing if the man who'd killed him—or tried to run her down in the parking garage yesterday—knew Maddie. *He* could recognize her by the sway of her hips or the pursing of her mouth, but another man wouldn't notice those select, sensuous details on this Stepford woman.

Wearing a microphone and going on the streets to make contact with the mysterious Roddy from the Baby Factory wasn't Dwight's first choice when it came to uncovering the illegal-adoption ring, locating Katie and putting an end to these dangerous attacks that kept forcing Maddie into the line of fire. But he'd been a fighter for enough years—in the boxing ring and in the courtroom—to understand that the best defense often meant going on the offensive.

The only way Maddie would stop risking her life and making him nuts with the fear that he couldn't protect her was to reunite her family and eliminate the threat to them.

Tonight, he intended to do just that.

Dwight adjusted his striped silk tie to camouflage the monitoring devices he wore. "You're picking up everything we say?" he asked, dipping his chin toward his collar, where a chip-sized microphone had been hidden.

"Just talk naturally." A.J. slipped around the corner from the kitchen. A small, curling wire ran from his ear to his collar and disappeared beneath his black T-shirt. "We'll hear everything you say. I already have men posted around No-Man's-Land so we can keep a visual and auditory lock on you at all times. Neither you nor Maddie have receivers. You won't be able to hear us. But we'll be in constant contact among ourselves and the van as we follow you."

"That'll keep Zero from hearing you, too," added Bellamy from his perch on the couch, where he'd elevated his strained knee. Tyler lay beside him on the seat cushion, gurgling and cooing through all the last-minute preparations. "Do you remember the panic word in case you or Mr. Powers runs into trouble or you think your cover's about to be blown?"

Wearing a big smile, Maddie scooped the kid up in her arms and gave her answer to him. "It's Mr. and Mrs. *Payne*," she corrected, reminding herself and Dwight not to make the easy slip in names. "And the word A.J. and his men will be listening for is *TKO*. We're gonna knock those bad guys out and bring your mom home, aren't we?"

She buzzed Tyler's cheek with her lips before cuddling him against her shoulder.

Technical knockout. They'd chosen the boxing term

assuming that the sport wouldn't come up in any discussion about adopting babies. Dwight refused to see it as an omen, either good or bad. He didn't rely on luck when he entered the courtroom and he wouldn't rely on it now to help end this craziness. The direct threat of Joe Rinaldi might be lying in the ME's morgue, but there was still someone out there willing to kill in order to reclaim a baby and cover his or her tracks.

Bellamy limped to his feet and tucked a burp rag between Maddie's shoulder and Tyler's chin. "You concentrate on what you need to do and don't worry about Tyler here. The Royals are playing tonight and I intend to teach him the finer points of baseball. We'll be locked up snug and tight."

"Thanks, Coop."

Once the bald detective lowered his bruised body back onto the couch, Dwight became aware of a set of tiny blue eyes fixed on him. Maybe it was just the position Maddie held him in over her shoulder. Maybe his memories were playing tricks on him again. But he'd be damned if the kid wasn't looking right at him.

So what was he trying to say?

Get it right this time.

Bring Mommy home.

Take care of Aunt Maddie.

"I will," he promised.

"You will what?" Maddie asked, catching him in the snare of expectant blue eyes.

Damn. How did he explain that fanciful lapse in judgment? A grown man answering a baby who was probably just passing gas. Yeah, he was a real sharp-witted asset to this operation.

He took a deep breath and steeled his mind against anything resembling weak or distracted or *fanciful*.

"Put the kid down," Dwight ordered, checking his watch and glancing out the front window to verify that the evening was darkening into night. When Maddie's hands were free, he reached for one and folded it in his grip. "C'mon, Mrs. Payne. Let's do this."

"Keep your wits about you," A.J. advised, following them out the door as Bellamy locked it behind them. "Make sure the other guy does more talking than you do."

Dwight opened the car door for Maddie, then looked over the roof of the Mercedes at his friend. There were no second chances on this sting, no room for mistakes, no detail that could be overlooked. "Just make sure you're there to get her out in one piece if anything goes south."

"THAT'S WHERE I MET Zero before." Maddie pointed toward the sidewalk opposite the abandoned Wingate Mission as they walked by a second time. Each pass left her more nervous than before. If Dwight circled the block a third time, she might not be able to control the angry butterflies that were tying her stomach into knots.

Even though most of downtown Kansas City closed by 9 p.m., these few blocks of 10th Street off of Broadway seemed even busier at night than they'd been the day she'd first come searching for Katie. The slow flow of traffic, the glare of headlights, the competing thumps of bass from more than one boom box and car radio all made it difficult to focus on picking one man out of the crowd.

"Maybe we should get out and walk," she suggested, though she could tell from the silent swell of Dwight's shoulders that he didn't like the idea.

Finding a parking space along the street would be difficult but not impossible, and there was no parking garage or other protected lot where he could leave the silver Mercedes. "Your car should be safe if we lock it." Though she hadn't spotted even one face she recognized yet, she was determined to keep faith that A.J. and his team were already in position. "There are plenty of good guys around to keep an eye on things."

"They'd better be keeping their eye on you."

"And you."

"Yeah, right." Dwight slowed as he passed an empty parking space, then turned on his signal and looked over his shoulder to back into it.

"You can't just dismiss *my* concerns because you're so over the top with your own. This is dangerous for you, too." She snatched at the cuff of his charcoal jacket, where it rested across the back of her seat. She shoved the sleeve up past his wrist to reveal the end of the gauze bandage that marked where Joe had sliced open his arm. "There's proof that would be admissible even in your stubborn court of law."

Those butterflies hammered against the wall of her chest. If Dwight hadn't deflected the blow, if Joe had struck anything vital, they wouldn't be having this conversation. If Dwight hadn't deflected that blow, Tyler might be dead, too. "If anyone recognizes you as an assistant district attorney or tries to mug you for that Rolex—"

"I can handle myself if something comes up." He pulled his arm from her grasp, adjusted the sleeve and set the gear into Park.

She sat back in her seat. "So can I."

"This is not a competition."

"You think I don't know that?" The people on the sidewalk in their partylike bustle paused in their conversations, taking a curious interest in the sleek new car parked in their neighborhood. "Whitney Chiles is already dead. I don't want to see Katie in that morgue, too. Joe's dead. A cop's dead. My sister's dead." By now, her hands were flailing in the air, making her point. "Roberta's in the hospital in a coma. Cooper's on desk-duty-slash-baby-sitting detail because he threw his knee out diving in front of that truck. Believe me, I have a pretty clear idea that this is *not* a game we're playing."

"Okay, okay." Dwight reached out and caught her wild hands, pulling them down to his lap. He turned partway behind the steering wheel to face her. "Truce," he offered in a deep, calm voice. "I know this hasn't been easy for you, either. But I believe you're made of stronger stuff than you give yourself credit for." He stroked his thumb across her knuckles, kindling a fire between them that seeped into her skin and warmed the blood inside her. "I should respect that strength."

She nodded, losing her will to argue with him as a different sort of tension ignited between them. "You should."

"Tell you what." He raised his right hand, keeping it out of sight from the windows so that the oath was for her alone. "I promise to watch my own back. As long as you don't deny me the pleasure—or the need—to watch yours, too."

"And don't deny me the need to watch yours."

That crease deepened beside his mouth and he almost smiled. "Well, you are my wife for the next couple of days. I guess that's what wives do."

"Yeah." He'd knocked the argument completely out of her with that sobering reminder. Though whether it was a real concession or just a clever lawyer's trick, she couldn't tell. Then the clench of hands between them registered. "Wait a minute."

Maddie held up her naked left hand and stared at the most obvious part of their costumes that they'd forgotten. "Wedding rings."

"Damn." Dwight flipped his own hands for inspection. "I don't wear mine anymore."

Now *that* was a sobering reminder. She turned and studied the sidewalk outside her window. Any relationship between her and Dwight was short-term. A charade. He'd already loved another woman completely. Loved her and lost her and didn't intend to love again.

But Maddie only needed to see the teenage girl with too much makeup and too few clothes strutting past the Mercedes and sizing up its occupants for potential customers to be reminded that she was here for Katie. Her own feelings and longings and foolish dreams weren't important.

A practical solution presented itself as she tried to comb her fingers through her oversprayed hair.

"Here." She pulled her mother's silver filigree ring—similar to the one given to Karen and then Katie—from her right hand and slipped it onto the ring finger of her left hand. She waved her fingers in the light from a passing car. "Ta-da! Now we're married."

Dwight laced his big fingers through hers and squeezed her hand. "I'm sorry I didn't think of that. Usually, I have a better eye for detail. I don't want anything to give you away."

Maddie dredged up a game smile. "Just act like you love me and you can't wait to have a baby."

Then she quickly withdrew her hand and slipped out of the car into the humid night air. She didn't want to read on Dwight's face which lie would be harder for him to pull off.

"It'll cost extra for two of you with one of my girls."

Zero adjusted the six rings he wore on his left hand, his

nonchalance only increasing Maddie's shock at what he was suggesting. "Oh, no. I'm not interested in your girls."

He flashed a smile that revealed a diamond-studded gold tooth. "Then I've got nothing to say to you."

Zero turned and ambled down the sidewalk, out of the circle of lamplight where Maddie had finally caught up with him. But he stopped a few steps later at a deep, distinct voice that made even Maddie shiver. "Listen to the lady."

Rolling the tension from his neck, whether real or for show, Zero slowly turned and stepped back into the light. He hung back at the fringe of illumination, though, studying Dwight, who'd come up to circle his arm around Maddie's waist. Idly, Maddie wondered if it was the expensive, tailored cut of Dwight's suit or the muscular threat of the boxer inside that ultimately convinced Zero that he should do business with them.

"So whaddya want?" Zero asked.

Dwight glanced down at Maddie. When A.J. had first briefed them, they'd decided that she would take the lead on this conversation—unless Zero showed signs of recognizing her from before. He didn't. She knew the pampered socialite with a virile man at her side was a far cry from the panicked spinster who'd shown him Katie's picture more than two weeks ago.

Maddie flipped her stiff hair off her collar and began her speech. "I've heard from some of my friends at the club that you might know a man who can help us have a baby."

Zero raked her from head to toe and opened his mouth. But any suggestive comment about how he might personally help her make a baby died on his lips at Dwight's unblinking glare. "I don't know what you're talkin' about lady." He swept his arms out to either side. "As you can see, we're not exactly a family neighborhood. Maybe you should check with your doctor."

"I don't want to get pregnant," she lied, forcing herself to laugh. She patted her hips. "God, no. It's too hard to keep my shape as it is at my age. I'm talking about adopting."

"Talk to a lawyer." Zero's dark brown gaze slid to Dwight, as if he suspected that might be his profession. "Or family services. I don't do charity work."

Dwight added enough to the conversation to convince Zero that they meant business. "We're tired of dinkin' with the system. The older we get, the further down the list of acceptable parents we become. My wife's tired of waiting."

Maddie squeezed her hands together in a pleading gesture. "Sure, they'll fix us up with a teenager or some special-needs kid who's hard to adopt. But I want a baby. A perfect, pretty little thing I can hold in my hands and dress up and…spoil."

As if sensing that the lies were getting harder and harder to eke out, Dwight dipped his head and kissed her temple. "I know how badly you want a little boy or girl, sweetheart. I'll get you one, I promise."

"Can you help us? Money isn't a problem for us. We've both had our careers for so long…." Forget that a teacher would never be able to afford the hundreds of thousands of dollars it would take to finagle an illegal adoption. She was playing the part. She had to remember that. Still, she could feel her lips quivering with the stress of trying to convince this criminal that she was just as heartless and opportunistic as he was. She turned her face to Dwight to mask the nervous habit. "Isn't that right, sweetie? You said I could spend whatever it took to get a perfect little baby, right?"

"That's right." Dwight's eyes narrowed on hers. He was worrying about her now, she could tell. He pressed his thumb to her lips and brushed across them in a heated caress. "It'll be your birthday and Christmas all rolled into one."

Maddie felt his warmth and strength deep inside and summoned a brave smile on steadier lips to give him the reassurance he sought. She fixed the smile in place to look at Zero again. "If you can help us, that is. My friend said I should ask about someone named Roddy. That you might be able to arrange a meeting?"

Zero shrugged. "I may know a guy."

Dwight reached into his pocket and pulled out the flash-wad of bills that A.J. had given him. "How much will it take for you to remember where this guy lives or how to reach him?"

"I don't know, big man." Zero had taken the bait. "How much are you willing to pay to make the little lady happy?"

Dwight leaned inside the driver's side window and gave his wife a kiss.

Not again.

He thrashed in his bed and willed the nightmare to leave him alone.

"Da-da-da-da-da."

He'd been so thrilled to have a son. Braden had made his love for Alicia complete. He had it all. A career. A loving wife. A family. For a tough guy from Chicago whose own father had been killed in Vietnam and who'd never seen what a whole, loving, successful family could be like, it had been everything. Wife. Baby. Love.

He had it all.

"No." He moaned the word in his sleep.

He didn't want to see this. He didn't want to live through this again.

But the nightmare sank its talons into his mind and wouldn't let go.

Dwight let his gaze slip to his son in the backseat.

There was something different this time. The kid was smaller. The eyes were bluer. He wasn't fussing about the stupid tiger.

"No."

His subconscious was a sick, twisted thing and he couldn't fight it. "Don't do this."

The kid's blue eyes looked at him. Looked deep inside him as if those innocent eyes believed in something that wasn't there.

Dwight rolled over. He tried to get away. "I can't save you. I can't give you what you need."

But the blue eyes still believed.

"Dwight?" He heard the soft whisper, like a caress in his ear.

"Don't tempt me, sweetheart."

Alicia's brown eyes should have flashed in his head. But the eyes were blue. The hair was a wild disarray of coppery silk.

He leaned inside the car window and kissed her.

Kissed Maddie.

"No." He snatched at the covers, kicked them aside, fighting to wake up, dreading where his mind was taking him. "Don't do this."

He was going to lose them.

They backed out of the driveway. The last things he remembered were Maddie's kiss—and the kid's blue eyes, watching him, knowing...

"Dwight." A hand was on his shoulder, shaking him.

"Mr. Powers? Mr. Powers?"

Dwight turned and glared at the young security guard. No one, but no one interrupted him before he gave his opening statement. "Later, Smitty."

"But, sir, I think you need to read this now."

"No!" Dwight came up off the bed, roaring himself awake.

"Dwight."

He wasn't alone. She wasn't dead. "Maddie?"

She sat on the edge of his bed, her hair rumpled with sleep, her blue eyes tortured with concern. "You were having the nightmare again. I tried to wake—"

"Maddie." Relief thundered through him, clipping at the heels of the nightmare that left him shaking and feverish. "You're alive." He lifted her onto his lap and crushed her in his arms. "You're alive." He covered the startled *O* of her mouth with his own, driving his tongue inside, tasting her, feeling her, verifying that she was here with every sense he possessed. She was real. She was safe. "God, babe." He could barely catch his breath as he tunneled his fingers into her hair and laved his tongue against the spicy heat of her throat. "I thought I'd lost you."

"Dwight." Her fingers dug into his shoulders. "It was a nightmare." She gasped as he palmed her breast through that whisper-thin gown and squeezed its full bounty. "It wasn't real."

"This is." He nibbled at her ear. Kissed her eyelids. Reclaimed her lips. "You are."

"Dwight." She flattened her palms against his shoulders, pushing some distance between them, even as her lips nipped at his. "You're confused," she tried to reason.

But every fear, every doubt, every haunting image that had ripped through him had transformed into a crystal-clear passion. A driving need to affirm life and reality pulsed through his blood, making him hungry and hard.

His anxious fingers fumbled with the buttons on her gown, then grew frustrated and tugged the white cotton over her head and tossed it aside. He cupped her breasts, loving the warm weight that filled his palms. "You have such a beautiful body."

The large, luscious globes flushed with the color of her arousal. The rosy tips beaded and beckoned to him. How could a man *not* want to feast his eyes on her? How could he *not* want to touch and taste her responsive heat? Dwight lowered his head and laved his tongue around one engorged nipple. She shivered in response. Her fingers clutched at his chest. Her husky moan of pleasure danced against his ears and went straight to his groin.

"But Alicia's the woman you want. She's the woman you miss."

Did she have to argue every point?

Dwight had no doubt about what he wanted. About what he needed. Right now. With Maddie.

"Don't ask me to prove myself every time I want to make love to you." He framed her sweet, blushing face between his hands and looked deep into her eyes, groaning at the restraint that this was costing him. "I loved my wife. I miss her. But I've packed away her memory and I've moved on." Dwight knew the words were true. The grief that had once consumed him was gone. "I want you. Madeline McCallister. You."

She slid her hands behind his neck, linking them together despite the shades of doubt lingering in her eyes. "Are you telling me the truth?"

"Always."

Her fingers slid through his hair and she smiled. "You don't have to prove anything to me."

When she leaned forward and kissed him, the passion that had been simmering on hold instantly reignited. Dwight pulled her in tight and fell back into the pillows, kissing and stripping and touching anything he could reach. He rolled her onto her back and slipped inside her, sinking into her lush welcome. Her fingertips dug into his spine, eliciting tremors that matched the same rhythm pulsing inside her. He claimed her lips with his own as she cried out her release. Dwight knew a moment of complete perfection as he emptied himself into her and collapsed beside her on the bed.

The nightmare was gone. The dream was in his arms.

He didn't even bother with the modesty of covers this time. He loved the look of her pale, curved body lying next to his harder frame.

"Don't leave me in the morning," he begged, fearing that holding her right here in his arms, skin to skin, was the only way he could keep the nightmare of losing someone else he loved at bay.

"Don't leave me," he whispered, finally relaxing as Maddie snuggled against him.

The silent admission that the man who could never fall in love again had done just that was a detail he overlooked as a calm, contented sleep quickly claimed him.

Chapter Twelve

The ringing of the telephone woke Dwight from a deep, dreamless slumber.

For one disoriented moment, he wondered why his left arm had gone to sleep. In the next moment, he smiled at the sleepy woman cuddling against him for warmth. He palmed the cool skin of her exposed backside and waited for her eyes to blink open. "You stayed."

The incessant ringing kept him from enjoying the treasure of her drowsy smile. With a grumpy curse of annoyance, he reached across her body and snatched the phone off the nightstand. "Hello?"

But the damn thing was still ringing.

Maddie's body tensed beneath his. She pressed her palm against his shoulder, her eyes suddenly and fully awake as he questioned her reaction. "Dwight."

And then he knew. The secure cellphone A.J. had given him last night—the number they'd given Zero so he could set up a meeting with Roddy—was ringing.

Dwight hung up the phone and glanced at the clock. It was 6 a.m. "They're calling early to catch us off guard."

But everything about Dwight was completely alert and ready to resume the charade by the time he'd scrambled out of bed and snatched the phone off his dresser. Maddie sat up, pulling up the sheet to cover her nakedness, her lips pursed in nervous anticipation as he opened the phone and answered. "Payne residence."

Dwight listened to the succinct instructions at the other end of the line.

"Can't we just meet at the clinic?" he asked, hating the idea of leaving his car at one location and being driven to the real meeting place. He didn't give a damn about the car. He just didn't want to be at a disadvantage if something came up and he and Maddie needed to make a quick escape.

"If you want me to expedite the adoption, you'll have to do things my way." The mysterious Roddy revealed nothing about himself, his background or his identity, either through his words or his smoothly politic accent. "And don't bother with a personal check. I only deal in cash. Half now, half on delivery. If you meet my requirements, that is."

"One of the reasons we came to you was so that we didn't have to go through all the checks the government agencies insist on."

"Trust me, Mr. Payne. If you and your wife are suitable parents—" by that, Dwight could guess he meant that the Paynes' personal assets met his asking price "—then you'll have your baby within twenty-four hours. Do you have a preference for a girl or a boy?"

Dwight thought of the little boy sleeping down the hall and Maddie's unconditional love for him. If they were really adopting a child together, she'd love the kid no matter what the gender or skin color or health issues. He wondered if her heart was big enough to work any other miracles—maybe one that included him.

Maybe Maddie could tell him what the kid meant when he looked at him with those knowing blue eyes.

"Mr. Payne?"

Dwight tore himself away from his thoughts and got his head back in the game. "Doesn't matter. We'll be there."

After hanging up, Dwight knelt on the bed, facing Maddie.

"Well?" she asked.

He touched a finger to her lips, easing the anxiety stamped there, regretting that last night had come to an end. "We're on, Mrs. Payne. I'll call A.J. to get the money and explain the setup."

She nodded, dutifully stepping into her role. "I'll call Cooper. He promised to watch Tyler."

"As soon as we're dressed and everyone's in place, we'll go."

"And bring Katie home," she insisted.

"And bring Katie home." Dwight leaned in and kissed her. He hadn't lied to Maddie yet. He prayed he wasn't lying to her now by promising something he couldn't deliver.

Because he knew that if he couldn't return Katie to her alive and safe—if he couldn't restore her family—then last night would be…their last night.

"Comfy, ma'am?"

Maddie had nearly leaped out of her skin when the short, wiry man who'd identified himself as Morales had driven up to their rendezvous at the Independence Center Mall in a white pickup truck. Some of the events in the parking garage two days earlier were hazy in her mind. The truck had been so fast she couldn't clearly identify the model. And from the protective barrier of Dwight's shoulders, she'd only been able to catch a glimpse that there was no plate to trace. Like this truck. While she would never forget the horrible sound of the speeding truck hitting Cooper and Roberta, visually, everything—including the driver—had been a blur. She couldn't recall if she'd seen Morales before or not.

Perhaps if she'd gotten a chance to smell him, she'd have remembered him more clearly. The man seemed to have an aversion to soap and a liking for foods that were heavy on the garlic.

He didn't seem to recognize her. Still, Maddie sidled closer to Dwight on his side of the pickup's bench seat and kept her eyes averted to the proprietary grip of his hand on her knee.

"I'm fine, thanks." She finally managed to eke out a few words when she realized Morales was waiting for a response. Beyond that, she let the two men talk as they bounced along a county highway leading north toward Liberty, Missouri, and hoped that Dwight's casual questions could elicit some useful information for the detectives and tacticians listening at the other end of their hidden microphones.

Once upon a time, she'd thought of Dwight as hard and invulnerable. He did have the cool, calm don't-mess-with-me routine down pat, as he did right now, chatting up Morales. She'd seen it in the courtroom, nailing the case against her brother-in-law. She'd seen it in the way he challenged a killer with a knife in order to protect her and Tyler.

But she'd also seen a side to Dwight Powers that she suspected few people ever did. The private man. The man who knew grief and guilt and emptiness on a very personal level. The man who hurt and needed and loved with a depth of emotion that was raw and humbling.

Men like Morales and Zero—and strangers who never got to experience the well-guarded personal side of Dwight Powers—would never know that he was more human than his reputation let on. She ached for the pain and need she'd seen in his eyes and felt in his touch. She rejoiced in the rare smiles and even rarer glimpses of humor. And she vowed that she would protect the heart and soul of this man she secretly loved—just as fearlessly as he'd always protected and watched over her.

"So we're not heading into Liberty proper," Dwight observed, more for A.J. following somewhere behind them in his black Trans-Am than out of his own curiosity.

"Nah." Morales steered the truck onto a twisting gravel driveway, apparently a back entrance to their destination. "The boss likes his privacy. That's what the mothers expect, too, when they come here. A lot of them don't even tell their families they're pregnant because no one cares."

Maddie felt the calming squeeze of Dwight's hand on her knee before she could even get the words to deny Morales's sweeping claim out of her throat. Her nod of understanding was masked by the bouncing of the truck. She wouldn't give them away by getting into an argument about her love for Katie.

"How sad," Maddie responded instead. "Will we get to meet any of these girls? Or see their babies so I can choose which one I want?"

Morales laughed. "You can't be too choosy. There's just one mother in the clinic right now. She gave birth last night to a little girl."

Maddie's hope plummeted a notch. One mother? Katie had given birth three weeks ago. Surely, he didn't mean that she…that Katie wasn't…Maddie squeezed her eyes shut, feeling the sting of tears. She couldn't do this now.

She couldn't give up when they were so close to finding out the truth.

She felt Dwight move beside her. "Here." He pushed his handkerchief into her hand and urged her to dab her eyes. When Morales questioned what was going on, Dwight had a ready explanation. "She gets emotional whenever we talk about this baby stuff." They traded manly-man winks. "You can see why I'm so anxious to get this adoption done."

"I hear ya, man." Morales stopped the truck at a black wrought iron gate and pressed a button on the visor above him. The gate slowly rolled to one side, revealing rows of trees surrounding a tall red-brick building. "We're here."

Maddie couldn't help glancing over her shoulder as the gate closed behind them. Would A.J. and his men still be able to track their whereabouts? Could they get inside the iron gate and perimeter fence if she or Dwight needed their help?

Ten minutes later, she wondered if the police could find them, even if they got inside the building, after following Morales through so many twists and turns of white-paneled hallways that she'd lost her sense of direction. He took them to what must be the front of the clinic building, past closed patient rooms that she longed to peek into, past the window of a nursery where a lone infant in a pink knit cap slept in a plastic bassinet. He led them past the janitor's closet and into a well-appointed office. He offered them both a plush chair to sit in, poured them each a glass of water and asked them to wait while he fetched Roddy.

As soon as they were alone, Maddie popped out of her chair and paced the room. "Do you think there are any hidden cameras watching us?"

"It's hard to tell." But Dwight had stood, as well, and

was turning a slow circle, studying the perimeter of the room. "We just have to make sure we're good guests who mind the rules, Mrs. Payne."

Maddie nodded, understanding his coded reminder not to panic and blow their cover. She set her glass on the corner of the dark walnut desk that filled a good third of the room and let her gaze wander over the contents on top as she carefully worded her questions. "Did you see those patient rooms? Do you think Roddy would let us go in and meet some of the expectant mothers? It would give us a better idea of what the babies were going to look like."

"Don't push it, Red. We'll get what we came for, I promise."

"Dwight, look." Her gaze fell on the open *Kansas City Journal* spread across the center of the desk. "He's reading the article about Roberta Hays."

Maddie picked up the paper and folded it into a manageable square to study the government ID photo of Roberta that had been printed beside the article about the unfortunate accident at the courthouse garage. "The reporter says that some of the witnesses he interviewed worried that Roberta's accident was some kind of terrorist attack."

She knew the truth and felt a twinge of suspicious recognition gnawing at her. That accident hadn't been any random act of terror. The truck barreling toward them had been very deliberate, very personal.

Suspicion became a full-blown connection as she homed in on the name beneath the photograph. "Roberta Fairfax Hays. Fairfax is her maiden name."

"You find something?" Dwight asked, coming to her side and looking over her shoulder at the paper.

"The man Roberta introduced me to yesterday, the one she was so afraid of—his name was Craig Fairfax."

"You asked me if I knew him. There's nobody working at the courthouse with that name. Unless he's somebody brand-new."

Maddie crumpled the paper in her hands as suspicion transformed into all-out dread. "I don't think so."

Without invitation or concern about any sort of hidden surveillance, Maddie tucked the paper beneath her arm and quickly sorted through the items on the desk. "If Roddy is Craig Fairfax, he'll know me. Even if my face doesn't look quite the same, he'll remember me." She opened one drawer after another and searched inside. "He recognized Tyler. I'm sure of it now. He touched him. It was creepy. But I couldn't figure it out. Roberta knew that Craig knew Tyler. They must be in this together. But she had Tyler that day she took him to the doctor. If she's part of this, why did she bring him back to me?"

"Whoa, whoa." Dwight's hands stilled her frantic search, urging her to remain calm. "You're rambling again. You think this Craig Fairfax and Roddy are the same person?" Apparently, he believed the possibility enough to risk direct communication through his microphone in his collar. "A.J., check it out. Find out how Fairfax and Roberta Hays are related."

Maddie found a box of business cards and pulled one out. *"R. Craig Fairfax. Attorney-at-law."*

"We can run his name through the bar association."

She pulled out another card when the words on them changed. *"Rodney Craig, PhD. Young adult therapist.* Oh, my God." A counselor for young adults? Like someone a confused, pregnant teenager might go to for advice? "Dwight." Maddie hugged her arms around her stomach, feeling sick. "Between him being a counselor and Roberta working for DFS, they could have their pick of pregnant girls."

He circled his arm around her shoulder and pulled out the next card himself. *"Roddy Craig. Talent agent."* Dwight stuffed the cards back into the box and closed each drawer. "We're going to need a search warrant for any of this to be usable in court. And I want the charges against this guy to stick."

Maddie finally got a grip on her fears and helped Dwight straighten the desk back to its original, pristine condition. "Okay. But we have to get out of here. He'll know me."

"We're going." He shut the last drawer, grabbed her hand and hurried to the door. "We'll let A.J. run the aliases."

"Wait." Maddie stopped in her tracks and pulled the newspaper from under her arm. She tried to unfold it as she hurried it back to the desk. "What about Katie? Can't we search the rooms? The grounds? See if she's here?"

"Leave that to A.J. We have to get out of here. Now." He tossed the paper onto the desk and dragged her toward the door. "Hell, A.J., while you're at it, see if Fairfax ever owned a black Impala."

Maddie heard the soft swoosh of the door swinging open and plowed into Dwight's back before she realized he'd stopped. Before she realized they had company.

"I never did, actually. But my sister, Roberta, does." The twin points of Craig Fairfax's receding hairline deepened to resemble devil's horns when he smiled. "She had a hissy fit when I borrowed it to do some construction work in Mission Hills. When she took it back, I reported it stolen just to remind her of who was really in charge in this family."

"TKO." Maddie muttered the panic word.

"What were you doing in Mission Hills?" Dwight asked, as coolly as if this were some kind of cross-examination. "Sizing up potential customers?"

Fairfax tapped a finger to his nose, apparently impressed by Dwight's astute deduction. "My business runs strictly on word of mouth. So I have to make sure I'm drawing in the right sort of clientele. I've decided that the two of you aren't exactly what I'm looking for."

"Funny," Dwight countered, sliding between Maddie and the black steel gun Fairfax pulled from beneath his jacket. "You're exactly what *I* expected. Little man who thinks he's clever. No heart, no guts. Where are your bullies? 'Cause I know, even with that gun, you don't have the guts to take me on by yourself."

"Dwight." Maddie tugged at his sleeve, wishing she wasn't feeling the same tightening of muscles she'd seen when she'd found him punching out his demons in his basement gym. "Maybe you shouldn't push."

"He preys on vulnerable teenage girls, desperate parents and innocent babies." A fist flexed at Dwight's side. "Hell, Red. I'll bet *you* could take this guy one-on-one."

Take this guy? Was that some sort of undercover code? Was she supposed to do something?

Fairfax tilted his head to the side and shouted. "Now, you morons!"

A panel in the office wall opened behind her and Morales and a dark-haired man bigger than Dwight himself stepped out.

"Told you he was afraid of a fair fight," Dwight drawled.

"TKO!" Maddie clutched fistfuls of the back of Dwight's jacket and huddled close as the two men advanced. The big man held a gun like Fairfax, but Morales carried a small, black leather box. The smaller man unzipped the box and pulled out a syringe filled with a clear liquid. "What's that?" she asked.

Morales grinned. "Wouldn't *you* like to find out?"

"Not yet," Fairfax cautioned. He looked straight at Dwight. "Double the dosage."

"You can't have drugs like that—much less administer them—without a medical license." Maddie said, not knowing whether to be more afraid of the gun or the syringe. But a little of the fire Dwight was trying to taunt out of Craig Fairfax had started to lick through her veins.

"My sister was a certified midwife in another life. Before we moved to Kansas City. You'd be surprised what she can get her hands on."

"Roberta's a midwife?" What happened to social worker?

"My sister and I have been a lot of things over the years, Mrs. Payne. Or should I say McCallister?" Craig Fairfax rested the barrel of his gun against Dwight's heart, warning him to be still as he reached beneath Dwight's tie and unbuttoned his shirt. "I don't believe we've had the pleasure, sir."

"Dwight Payne," he insisted.

"Uh-huh. And I'm the fairy godmother." His eyes darted briefly to Maddie, then back to the task of tearing open the front of Dwight's shirt. "To answer your earlier question, no, there *are* no hidden cameras. But microphones are another story. I've been listening to your report from the moment you came in. Fortunately, no one else has."

Dwight never flinched, never looked away from the older man as he reached inside and pulled out the listening wires. He plucked the tape from Dwight's skin, ripped the microphone from inside his collar and ground the whole rig on the tile floor beneath his shoe.

"I've been at this for too many years to let a plant get inside one of my clinics and record anything." Fairfax patted around Dwight's waist and legs while the big man held them at gunpoint. He pulled Dwight's wallet from his back pocket. "No weapon. You're not a cop. You must be the boyfriend Roberta said cleaned the floor with Rinaldi before she shot him. Man, that pissed me off. She could have shot the baby."

"Roberta killed Joe?" The curious question popped out of Maddie's mouth before she could stop it. She replayed those last, chatty conversations with Roberta at the courthouse. "Wait. She talked about Joe in the past tense. Before it was in the papers. She knew he was dead."

Fairfax laughed at her amateur detective work. "My dear sister grew a conscience the day Fitz and Morales here broke Rinaldi out of prison. She said the man was too dangerous to be around any child, that you and your boyfriend here made as good a set of parents as anyone we've ever sold a child to." Fairfax leaned in and stood nose to chin with Dwight. Feeling the tension radiating through Dwight's back, Maddie wondered which man was in greater danger at that moment.

"You're the wild card in all this. Katie never mentioned Aunt Maddie having a boyfriend. All I wanted was for Rinaldi to convince Katie to tell me what she'd done with her baby. And if that didn't work, he'd scare the information out of her by threatening her beloved aunt." He clicked his tongue against his teeth, tsk-tsking the demise of his plan. "But there you were, going all bodyguard on us. I just never counted on there being a boyfriend."

"I'm more than a boyfriend, Fairfax." Dwight's threat startled Maddie. What did that mean?

"Why, yes, so I see." He was reading Dwight's license now. "Dwight Powers of the district attorney's office." He tossed aside the wallet. "I see a little conflict of interest here, Mr. Powers. How do you intend to prosecute me?"

"If you harm this woman or her family, I intend to kill you."

"Dwight." But both men were ignoring her now.

"Oh, I'm counting on that. You see, I *am* a clever little man," Fairfax insisted. "I think I'll use your attachment to Ms. McCallister to my advantage."

"What attach—" Maddie gasped as Fairfax snatched her by the collar of her jacket and jerked her forward.

Dwight spun and reached for her, but she never felt the grasp of his hand. Instead, she shivered at how cold and deadly the tip of the gun felt when Fairfax pressed it to the middle of her forehead. "Back off, Mr. ADA."

It was threat enough for Dwight to raise his hands in surrender and keep his place behind her.

"It's okay, Dwight," she insisted, less worried about herself than the two guns, the mysterious syringe and Dwight's fierce penchant for rescuing her.

"Now *you're* the protector, hmm?" That fact seemed to amuse Fairfax. "It's been a very entertaining conversation, but we're the only ones hearing it. You passed through a dampening field about two miles back. If any of your friends were following you, your signal was scattered. They'll have a pretty wide search grid of woods and farmland to look through before they find you."

Maddie cringed as Fairfax untucked her blouse and reached underneath to pull the wire off her. She felt Dwight's breath stirring the hair at her nape, the rhythm of his lungs quickening as his need to defend her ratcheted up a notch.

Fairfax lingered a little too long at her breasts, enjoyed the sting of tape ripping off skin a little too much for her to remain afraid. She inhaled a deep breath and gave him her best Dwight Powers glare. "Get your hands off me."

She looked down at those very hands and noticed that, in contrast to his tailored suit and tie, Craig Fairfax had the hands of a construction worker. She glanced toward the open panel where Morales and his buddy had entered. "Let me guess. You remodeled this place with secret doors and passageways?"

"Kind of fun, isn't it?" And then Fairfax's smile flatlined. "I'm done chatting. Where's Tyler?"

"You could have killed him two days ago in that parking garage."

He glanced at Morales. "That moron was supposed to take out Roberta, not endanger the child."

"Hey, I'm in the room."

Fairfax ignored his hired help. "She wasn't supposed to be there with you and Tyler."

"Roberta knew you were after her. She was trying to protect us from you."

Fairfax scoffed. "That's loyalty, isn't it? For years, I gave her what she wanted. A chance to put kids in the homes of parents who really want them."

"At the cost of innocent lives?"

"It's good business."

Maddie shook her head. "You're a bastard."

"Yeah, but I'm a rich one. Now where's Tyler?"

"I don't know."

"Don't give me that crap. I get enough of it from your niece."

Hope spiked. "Katie's still alive?"

"She won't be for long if you don't start talking. I have a client waiting for a baby boy to be delivered or his hundred-fifty grand to be refunded. I've already spent his money."

"My heart's breaking." Sarcasm leaked through Maddie's teeth. "I won't tell you where he is."

He ground the gun barrel against her scalp. "Tell me!"

"Threats don't work on the McCallister women," Dwight said from behind her, his voice as deadly and deep as she'd ever heard it. "They fight back."

Take this guy? Fight back?

Dwight's message finally rang through, loud and clear.

Maddie's breath lodged deep in her chest. Oh, God. Three against two? Unarmed against guns? She wasn't a fighter.

"Go get the girl," Fairfax ordered, tapping the gun against Maddie's temple. "I bet if we put a gun to Katie's head, this one'll talk."

Not a fighter?

The hell she wasn't.

"No!" With a primal, maternal scream from deep in her lungs, Maddie smacked the gun out of her face and punched Fairfax square in the nose. Something popped. Blood streamed from his devilish face. Maddie shook her throbbing hand as pain spiked through her knuckles and her fingers went numb. "How the hell do you—"

"Move, Red!" Dwight shoved her to the floor and rammed his shoulder into Fairfax's startled body.

The gun exploded as the two men flew through the air, landed on a coffee table and crushed it. "Dwight!"

Maddie pushed herself to her feet, ducking as chips of plaster and wood rained down from the wall where the bullet struck.

"Get him off me!" Fairfax yelled in a stuffy, nasally whine. Even with a gun, he was no match for Dwight's meaty fists and raging strength.

But the charging hulk and wiry Morales were another story. When they charged Dwight, Maddie leaped onto Morales's back, winding her arms around his neck, clawing her nails into his face.

"Get off me, bitch!"

The big man kicked Dwight in the side. Dwight grunted and rolled. A gun skittered away beneath Fairfax's desk. Maddie scratched for Morales's eyes.

"I said…" Morales stumbled. He dropped the box and syringe and clamped down on Maddie's wrists. "Get… off!"

He slammed backward into a wall, knocking the wind from Maddie's lungs. Twisting her wrists at a painful angle, he pried her off him and threw her to the floor. When she tried to rise, he smacked her across the face.

"Stay down!"

The room was spinning, crashing around her. She tasted blood and tried to crawl someplace safe. Karen must have felt like this—helpless, hurt. But she wasn't Karen. This wasn't any man she loved who'd betrayed her. She was a fighter. She'd learned how to stand up for herself. She fought back.

Dwight took a blow that knocked him to the floor. Fairfax scrambled for his gun. The big man had his hands around Dwight's neck. She had to help him.

The instant Maddie moved, Morales grabbed her by the hair and jerked her head back. Pain tore across her scalp and tears stung her eyes. Her fingers scrambled for something to defend herself with. He stuck his stinky breath right in her face. "I said stay down!" There. Her fingers closed around the long, plastic cylinder. "Or I will do to you what I did to all those other—"

Maddie jabbed the syringe into Morales's ankle and squeezed the plunger, driving the contents deep into his leg.

Morales screamed as he released her. Maddie collapsed as he stumbled back. "What have you done to me?" His breathing became shallow and static. He tripped on an overturned chair and fell to the floor, his stunned eyes damning her. "You've killed me."

If Maddie could catch her own breath, she'd have demanded to know if he'd killed Whitney Chiles, if he'd given this same drug to Katie. She'd want to know how many other lives he'd ruined with his greed and temper and killer combo of drugs.

But Morales was dead before she could speak.

A shot rang out and a man grunted in pain.

"Dwight?" Maddie's voice squeaked from her raw lungs and aching jaw.

The big man was rolling on the floor, holding his gut, bleeding from the wound in his belly. A gun dangled in Dwight's left hand as he pushed himself to his feet. Summoning a leviathan's strength from his battered body, he stood straight and tall. Maddie crouched low as he whirled the gun around the room.

"He's gone," Dwight announced.

For a moment, she didn't understand. She was too overwhelmed with relief to see him standing after that fight. With one eye swelling shut and blood oozing from a scrape along his jaw, he looked like a prizefighter who'd gone ten rounds with an opponent and come up short. And right now, he was the damn handsomest sight she'd ever seen. She started to smile.

But then she understood. She knew.

"Fairfax." Maddie clung to the wall and pulled herself up. "We can't let him get away."

"He won't." Dwight tucked the gun into the back of his waist and kicked aside broken furniture to get to her and help her stand. As soon as he touched her, he pulled her into his arms and wrapped her up in a fierce hug. "Are you all right? How bad are you hurt?"

She clung to him just as tightly. "Nothing serious. Are you okay?"

"I'll mend." He pulled back just enough to look down into her face. His stormy eyes took in every bump, bruise and freckle that might be out of place. He pressed his thumb to her lips and gently wiped the blood from the corner of her mouth. "I thought I was going to lose you."

"You haven't yet." She reached up and framed his beloved, beaten face in her hands. "And you won't. But until we stop Fairfax and find Katie, I don't have time to try to convince you of that."

He pressed a quick, desperate kiss to her lips. They both groaned in a mixture of pain and passion. But then he was pushing away. He crossed to the phone on Fairfax's desk and handed it to her. "Call 911. Get a couple of ambulances out here. Tell them to put you through to A.J. Give him a description of the gravel roads, the iron fence, the building—anything to get them out here ASAP. Then you can tear this place from top to bottom to find Katie."

He pushed the phone into her hand and hurried toward the open passageway in the wall where Fairfax had disappeared. "What are you going to do?" she asked, already punching in the number.

"I'm going to track down the son of a bitch who put a gun to the head of the woman I love."

Love?

Dwight loved her?

Were there any other women he knew who'd been held at gunpoint recently? Maddie shook her head. "Stupid. Stupid debate."

It would be a cruel lie. But Dwight hadn't lied to her

yet. He'd promised to always tell her the truth, even when it was something she didn't want to hear.

Could she trust that it was the truth if they were words she *did* want to hear?

The hoping and second-guessing and worrying that Dwight would find Fairfax before Fairfax's gun found him was plenty enough to keep Maddie from finding what she was looking for. Her room-to-room search had turned up one baby girl, the girl's sedated mother—a blond teenager whose steady pulse had reassured her that it was all right to leave and keep searching—and no one else.

Panic began to seep into the fringes of her already-shot nerves. These were the longest ten minutes of her life. The cops weren't coming. Dwight hadn't returned. She was all alone. Maddie stood in front of the nursery window and looked up and down the abandoned hallway. "Katie, where are you?"

She couldn't lose her.

Saving Katie was as close as she could come to saving her sister. She understood now about Dwight's obsession with keeping her safe, with protecting her at all costs. She wasn't strong enough to lose anyone else she cared about, either.

"Katie!" Maddie's shout echoed through the empty corridors. Flat white walls. Even strips of paneling. One office, one nursery and six patient rooms. She'd searched every one from top to bottom. From door to door. From wall to wall.

Wall to wall. Maddie tipped her head back and shook her fists. "Idiot."

Hidden walls. Secret passageways. Katie could still be here. Craig Fairfax liked his secrets. He liked building things. A physical irony for a man who liked tearing people and families apart.

"Katie?" Maddie kept calling her niece's name as she ran her fingers along every inch of paneling, looking for a hidden room. When that search didn't pan out, she found herself staring at the one door she hadn't opened. The janitor's closet. "Why not?"

She might have detected the blare of sirens in the distance, or maybe that was wishful thinking as she opened the door. Crinkling her nose at the pungent smell of ammonia, she reached overhead to turn on the light. But something else caught her eye instead. A thin, dim line of light across the floor.

A frisson of possibility skipped across her nerves, rekindling her hope. "Katie?" She knelt down to trace the tiny gap with her fingers and found a perpendicular line where the gap turned to form a doorway. "Katie?" Maddie pounded the back wall with the flat of her hand. "Katie?" She found the hinges of the hidden door and threw herself against the smooth panel until a spring gave way and the door popped open. "Katie!"

Maddie dashed through the opening, hearing the soft beep of a medical monitor before her eyes adjusted to the dim light and she spotted the steel-framed hospital bed. There was a lump in the middle of the bed, someone tucked in beneath the sheets. "Katie?"

She darted to the bed, stroked the dark hair resting on the pillow. "Katie, sweetheart." Maddie felt the cool cheek with gentle fingers, waited for warm breath to brush across her hand. "Katie?"

Fumbling in the darkness, Maddie worked her way past wires and switches and machines until she found a string and pulled it. She squeezed her eyes shut as a circle of light pooled around the bed.

But the pain was nothing compared to the joy of seeing

her niece's wan face, scooping her into her arms and hugging her tight. "Katie! It's me! Wake up! I found you. We're going home."

"Or not."

Craig Fairfax's stuffy, broken face materialized from a dark corner of the room.

Maddie cradled Katie's groggy weight against her, turning her shoulder to protect the child who'd just been returned to her arms from the gun Fairfax pointed their way.

"What is it with you McCallister women?" Fairfax shook his fist as he advanced. "This one charges to the rescue to save a friend. You charge in to save her. She takes away the baby I paid for. You take away the business that has paid me so well for so long." He uncurled his fist and pointed a finger at Maddie. "I like a good, submissive woman who does what she's told, who doesn't give me any grief. I had my sister trained. I had my girls trained. And then you two…"

Maddie clutched Katie tighter, watching the gun barrel creep closer and closer. She felt Katie stirring against her. Felt her own heart pounding against her ribs and throbbing through every aching bone in her body.

"You know, even if the police capture me—" cold steel touched her temple "—I will have the satisfaction of shutting you two bitches up." He pointed the gun at Katie and Maddie flinched. "I just can't decide which one of you to shoot first."

"Dwight won't let you get away with this." The fight hadn't died in her yet. Love wouldn't let it die. "He's not a man you want to mess with."

"You just can't keep quiet, can you?" He pointed the gun to Maddie's head. "Thanks for making the decision for me."

A black shadow, large and ominous, filled the room behind Fairfax.

Maddie smiled.

Dwight brought his gun down across the back of Fairfax's head. The man crumpled at Maddie's feet, unconscious.

Dwight retrieved Fairfax's gun, stuck both weapons in his belt, heaved a sigh through that mighty chest and reached for Maddie. "That—" his arms folded around her and Katie both "—was getting old."

Maddie looped an arm around his neck and hugged him tight. She clutched him even tighter when he lifted her onto her toes and buried his face in her hair. She felt the tremors racking his body. Tears spilled down her own cheeks when she felt his first tears burning against her skin.

"I'm okay, Dwight. We're okay." She pressed kisses to his neck, his shoulder, his collar. "You saved us. You saved us."

They stood together for countless minutes, until the flood of emotions had worked their way through him and he could lift his head and speak. But the words she'd hoped to hear again weren't there. This was the old Dwight, back to business. He kissed her forehead and urged her to step aside as he leaned over the bed and picked up Katie in his arms.

Cradling the precious cargo gently against his chest, he led them out of the hidden room and into the bright light of the hallway. "The police are here," Dwight informed Maddie, striding down the hallway toward the front exit. "I pulled some wires from the vehicles outside so Fairfax couldn't escape. An ambulance is on its way for Katie."

"There's another girl here, too. And a baby."

"A.J.'s on his way. He'll do his job. He'll take care of them."

"Mr. Powers?" Katie's slurred voice was muffled against Dwight's chest.

Maddie tugged at his arm to stop him. She circled around and stroked her niece's hair. "Katie? Sweetie? I love you. You're going to be okay now. We'll get you to a real hospital, then take you home. You'll be okay."

Katie nodded, though her eyes never opened. "Is Tyler safe, Mr. Powers? Did Whit get him to you?"

"Yeah, Katie." His deep voice rumbled in his chest. "Tyler's safe. We're all safe."

Tyler. Not *the kid.*

Maddie lifted her startled gaze to Dwight, whose one good gray-green eye was looking intently down at her.

"You said *Tyler.*"

Maybe he was ready to love a new family again.

Dwight leaned over Katie and touched his lips to Maddie's. Hers were swollen and sore, but she didn't care. Dwight's kiss was gentle and hot and very, very thorough.

"Aunt Maddie? Is zat you?" Katie pushed against Dwight's and Maddie's chins with a weak fist.

Maddie pulled back, linking her fingers with Katie's. "Yes, sweetie. What is it?"

"When did you get a boyfriend?"

Epilogue

Dwight unlocked the front door and stepped into the organized chaos that filled his big home. He set his briefcase and keys on the table in the foyer and paused a moment to straighten a framed photograph that adorned the wall.

"Hey, Uncle Dwight." Katie bounced around the corner in blue jeans and a jacket, with a tall, strapping football player in tow.

"Hey, sweetie." Dwight bent down for the kiss she pressed to his cheek before returning the favor. "Trent."

"Mr. Powers." He liked the confident way the young man shook his hand. "Hey, I got a lead on a sweet '63 Mercedes on the Internet. I'd be happy to show you sometime. I know how much you're into the classics."

Classics. Meaning old, no doubt, to the teenager's way of thinking. "That'd be fine. I'll take you up on that sometime."

"Cool." Trent slipped past him to the front door, which he opened for Katie. "See you later, Mr. P."

"Bye, Dwight."

"Mr. P.?" Dwight frowned as the door closed behind

them. He loosened his tie and unbuttoned his collar as he headed into the living room.

A blur of blue-and-white zipped by him across the floor. "Whoa." Dwight smiled as he hurried after Tyler and scooped him up into his arms. "Where are you headin' off to, big guy?"

Dwight smoothed his soft, brown hair as he carried him to the playpen and set him inside. He knelt down beside the eight-month-old and got a good look at the Kansas City Royals shirt he was wearing. "Baseball?" He made a face and Tyler buzzed his lips in delight. "Has Cooper been telling you stories about spring training again? Yeah, yeah, I know that look." He tapped Tyler's tummy with three playful jabs of his fist. "Hya. Hya. Hya." Tyler giggled and Dwight grinned right along with him as if he understood every sound the little boy made. "That's right. Heavyweight title bout this weekend. You and me in front of the TV. Yeah."

The spicy scent of his wife entering the room behind him made Dwight smile even more. "Heavyweight title bout? You're not going to teach him how to box, are you, Dwight?"

Dwight turned as he stood and pulled Maddie into his arms for a kiss. "I taught you, didn't I? Broke Fairfax's nose in one punch. Don't think I've ever been prouder of you. Well, except for that day you testified against him and Roberta Hays in court. Or maybe the day you let me give you a real wedding ring."

Maddie thumped him in the shoulder. "I told you you weren't any good at sweet talk."

He stroked her cheek and let his fingers settle into the copper silk of her hair. "You said you wanted me to always tell you the truth. Never sugarcoat it." He glanced over her shoulder toward the door. "Speaking of truths, is Katie dating that guy?"

"That *guy?* It's Trent Dixon. You like him."

Irrelevant. He knew what he liked to do with Maddie when *they* got a chance to go out on a date. "It's a school night. Should they be going out?"

She smoothed her hand along his tie. "Calm down, Mr. Worrywart. They have play practice for the spring musical. They'll be home by ten-thirty." She stepped back and took his hand. "Besides, you and I need a few minutes alone by ourselves."

Dwight liked that idea. He followed her into the privacy of the kitchen. "Only a few minutes?"

Eight months ago, he couldn't have imagined having a family. Having a life that meant something. Having love. Maddie McCallister Powers had brought a lightness into his world with her smiles and backbone and loving heart.

When she turned to speak, he snuck the opportunity to kiss her neck, her cheek, to claim her lips. He backed her into a counter and aligned her more fully with his body, letting his hands travel from her hair to her hips and back as they shared a kiss that made him forget the length of his day and the forty-fourth birthday coming up next month.

But Maddie wedged her fingers between their lips and pushed him back with a tender smile. "To talk, Dwight. We need to talk."

"Oy." He held up his hands and stepped away, reining in his desires. "I've been talking all day." He occupied himself by sneaking a look at the spaghetti she was fixing for dinner. "So how was school?"

She batted his hand away from the loaf of bread she'd been cutting. "Fine. Finished *Beowulf* with my ninth-graders today. We get to hit grammar next."

"Sounds like fun." He moved on to the salad.

"How was court?"

"The preliminary hearing on the Baby Jane Doe suspect hit a snag. The judge called a recess while the defense lines up a couple more witnesses." The salad got boring and he dipped his head to steal another kiss. "Are we done talking yet?"

Her steeling sigh as she stared at the center of his chest put his libido on hold. "Maddie?"

She raised her gaze to his before pushing him toward a kitchen chair. "I think you'd better sit down for this one."

Dwight was suddenly as serious and worried as he'd ever been. He pulled her into his lap. "What's wrong?"

"Nothing. But something very weird is about to happen."

"What? C'mon, Red. You can tell me anything."

"I know." She caressed his face and offered a smile that didn't quite reassure him. "I think that's one of the first ways I knew you were someone special. I could talk to you—and argue—and not get all tongue-tied with shyness."

"You're stalling."

Her hand settled atop his shoulders. Damn. Those pretty blue eyes were sober enough to scare him. "When our child is born, he's going to be younger than Tyler, who's practically like a grandson to us. That'll be a little awkward, don't you think?"

"We talked about this. Our family isn't traditional. But it's *my* family and I love you guys, no matter what."

"And we love you. *I* love you."

"So if we have a child, he'll be younger than Tyler. It'll give them something cool to talk about at show-and-tell."

"Don't be so dense, counselor. I said *when*, not *if*." She touched her hand to her abdomen and Dwight's stomach turned inside out. "Our nontraditional family is about to get a little bigger."

"You're…? We're…?"

Her face bloomed with color and her beautiful smile told him everything he needed to know.

"Yeah!" He picked her up and spun her around. He set her down and looked in amazement at the gift of love she'd brought back into his life. "I love you, Maddie. I love Tyler and Katie and I'm going to love this baby, too. I'm glad you stood up to me that day at the Fourth Precinct. I'm glad you stayed alive when Joe Rinaldi wanted you dead. I'm glad you—"

"Dwight." She brushed her fingers across his lips.

"What?"

"Shut up." She turned and backed him into the counter. She looped her arms around his neck and gave him the smile of all smiles. "Just shut up and kiss me."

* * * * *

*Look for BASIC TRAINING from Harlequin Blaze
next month!*

INTIMATE MOMENTS™

The MEN of MAYES COUNTY

THERE'S NOTHING LIKE A HOMETOWN HERO...

After a tornado destroys his garage, mechanic Darryl Andrew realizes that more than his livelihood needs rebuilding—his marriage to Faith Meyehauser is crumbling, too. Will the buried secrets stirred up by the storm tear apart their family...or let some fresh air into their relationship?

A HUSBAND'S WATCH

BY KAREN TEMPLETON

Silhouette Intimate Moments #1407

AVAILABLE AT YOUR FAVORITE RETAIL OUTLET.

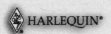

INTRIGUE

Don't miss this first title in Lori L. Harris's
exciting new Harlequin Intrigue series—

THE BLADE BROTHERS
OF COUGAR COUNTY

TARGETED

(Harlequin Intrigue #901)

BY **LORI L. HARRIS**

On sale February 2006

Alec Blade and Katie Carroll think they can start
fresh in Cougar County. Each hopes to bury the
unresolved events of their violent pasts. But they
soon learn just how mistaken they are when a
faceless menace reappears in their lives. Suddenly
it isn't a matter of outrunning the past. Now they
have to survive long enough to have a future.

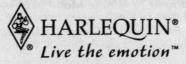

HARLEQUIN®
Live the emotion™